PENGUIN
TWENTY S

Satyajit Ray was born on 2 May 192
from Presidency College, Calcutta
Rabindranath Tagore's university, S.
back in Calcutta and had joined an advertising firm as a visualizer.
He also started designing covers and illustrating books brought out
by the Signet Press. A deep interest in film led to his establishing
the Calcutta Film Society in 1947. During a six-month trip to Europe,
in 1950, Ray became a member of the London Film Club and
managed to see ninety-nine films in only four-and-a-half months.

In 1955, after innumerable difficulties had been overcome, Satyajit
Ray completed his first film, *Pather Panchali*, with financial assis-
tance from the West Bengal Government. The film was an award-
winner at the Cannes Film Festival and established Ray as a director
of international stature. Together with *Aparajito* (The Unvanquished,
1956) and *Apur Sansar* (The World of Apu, 1959), it forms the *Apu*
trilogy—perhaps Ray's finest work to date. Ray's other films include
Jalsaghar (The Music Room, 1958), *Charulata* (1964), *Aranyer Din Ratri*
(Days and Nights in the Forest, 1970), *Shatranj Ke Khilari* (The Chess
Players, 1977), *Ghare Baire* (The Home and the World, 1984),
Ghanashatru (Enemy of the People, 1989), *Shakha Proshakha* (Branches
of a Tree, 1990), and *Agantuk* (The Stranger, 1991). Ray also made
several documentaries, including one on Tagore. In 1987, he made
the documentary *Sukumar Ray*, to commemorate the birth centenary
of his father, perhaps Bengal's most famous writer of nonsense verse
and children's books. Satyajit Ray won numerous awards for his
films. Both the British Federation of Film Societies and the Moscow
Film Festival Committee named him one of the greatest directors of
the second half of the twentieth century. In 1992, he was awarded
the Oscar for Lifetime Achievement by the Academy of Motion Picture
Arts and Science and, in the same year, was also honoured with the
Bharat Ratna.

Apart from being a film-maker, Satyajit Ray was a writer of repute.
In 1961, he revived the children's magazine, *Sandesh*, which his
grandfather, Upendrakishore Ray, had started and to which his
father used to contribute frequently. Satyajit Ray contributed
numerous poems, stories and essays to *Sandesh*, and also published
several novels in Bengali, most of which became best sellers. In 1978,
Oxford University awarded him its D.Litt degree.

Satyajit Ray died in Calcutta in April 1992.

*

Gopa Majumdar was born in Delhi in 1956 and graduated in English Literature from Delhi University. Her translations of Bengali short stories first appeared in the *Namaste* magazine and two of her translations were included in the *Namaste Book of Indian Short Stories*. She lives, at present, in Britain.

SATYAJIT RAY

Twenty Stories

Translated from the Bengali by
Gopa Majumdar

HERTFORDSHIRE
LIBRARY SERVICE

No.

Class

Supplier | Price | Date

PENGUIN BOOKS

Penguin Books India (P) Ltd., B4/246, Safdarjung Enclave,
New Delhi 110 029, India
Penguin Books Ltd., Harmondsworth, Middlesex, England
Penguin Books USA Inc., 375 Hudson Street, New York,
N.Y.10014 USA
Penguin Books Australia Ltd., Ringwood, Victoria, Australia
Penguin Books Canada Ltd., 10 Alcorn Avenue, Suite 300, Toronto,
Ontario M4V 3B2, Canada
Penguin Books (NZ) Ltd., 182-190 Wairau Road, Auckland 10, New Zealand

Copyright © Satyajit Ray 1991, 1992
This translation Copyright © Penguin Books India Pvt Ltd 1991, 1992
Reprinted 1992
All rights reserved

All twenty stories in this selection were first published in Bengali, in book-form, by
Ananda Publishers Pvt Ltd, in the following five books: *Ek Dojon Goppo* (*One Dozen
Stories*), 1971; *Aaro Ek Dojon* (Another Dozen), 1976; *Ebaro Baaro* (Twelve Again),
1984; *Aaro Baaro* (Another Twelve), 1981; and *Eker Pithe Dui* (One Against Two),
1988.

Typeset in Palatino by dTech, New Delhi
Made and printed in India by Ananda Offset Private Ltd., Calcutta

HERTFORDSHIRE
LIBRARY SERVICE

No.
H31 082 2521

Class

Supplier | Price | Date
FARRIES | 5·99 | 21.9.92

This book is sold subject to the condition that it shall not, by way of trade or
otherwise, be lent, resold, hired out, or otherwise circulated without the publisher's
prior written consent in any form of binding or cover other than that in which it is
published and without a similar condition including this condition being imposed
on the subsequent purchaser and without limiting the rights under copyright
reserved above, no part of this publication may be reproduced, stored in or
introduced into a retrieval system, or transmitted in any form or by any means
(electronic, mechanical, photocopying, recording or otherwise), without the prior
written permission of both the copyright owner and the above mentioned publisher
of this book.

Contents

Translator's Note

When Penguin asked me to do this work of translation, I embarked on my task with a mixture of excitement and trepidation. Would I be able to do a good job? Would the author be pleased? After all, the whole world knew to what standards of perfection Satyajit Ray was accustomed.

It was with a trembling heart that I dispatched the first batch of stories for his approval. His reply simply said, 'I am perfectly satisfied with your work. Go ahead with the others.'

Was that all? I stared at his letter in disbelief. He could have, if he had so wished, found fault with every word I had written and made a fuss. Instead, he gave me the encouragement I so badly needed.

If this book can give its readers the same joy that I had felt when reading the stories in the original, the credit must go entirely to the author. Had it not been for his unfailing patience and support, I could not have written a single word.

I would also like to thank David Davidar, editor of Penguin Books in India, who was no less patient with my nervous queries; Nandita M. Aggarwal, senior copy-editor of Penguin for her co-operation in the final editing and corrections; my brother, Jyotirmoy Majumdar, who introduced me to *Sandesh* magazine and the magic of Satyajit Ray's stories, and finally, Monisha Mukundan, editor of *Namaste* magazine, without whose constant reassurances and occasional gentle prodding, I would not have started to work on translations at all.

February 1992   *Gopa Majumdar*

Gagan Chowdhury's Studio

There are some apartments which appear to be quite satisfactory at first and one has to live in them to discover their little inconveniences. Sudheen Sarkar realized this when he moved into a flat in Bhabanipore. This was the only sphere where Lady Luck seemed not to have smiled kindly on him. In everything else she had given him all her support.

Take, for instance, the matter of his promotion. He was now the head of a department in his office. Not many could have made such rapid progress at such an early age. After all, he was only thirty-one. He had already climbed up to the shoulder of the department. The head was Nagendra Kapoor, forty years of age—tall, handsome, efficient. All eyes turned towards him as he entered the office, clad in a light grey safari suit. Who could imagine the same man would succumb to a cardiac arrest on a golf course?

That his death would lead to Sudheen's own promotion was only natural. And it was not just a matter of being lucky. No one could deny that Sudheen deserved it.

Then came the new flat. Sudheen's parents were keen to have him married. Sudheen knew it would be very difficult to live with someone else in the little pigeon-hole he lived in in Park Circus. It being quite a pleasant time of year, he decided to start looking for a bigger flat. Life had become impossible in the old flat, anyway. There was a house nearby that was often let out for weddings. The sound of the *shehnai* on gramophone records played at full blast on loudspeakers, was beginning to drive him mad.

The very first flat the house agent told him about was this one in Bhabanipore.

Situated on the first floor, the three large bedrooms, the two bathrooms, the veranda facing the south, the mosaic floors and the grills on the windows—all bore the stamp of careful planning and good taste.

The rent was eight hundred rupees a month. And the landlord seemed a nice man. Sudheen did not have to look any further.

It was two weeks since he had moved in. He did not notice it at first, but one night he woke to find a bright light streaming through his window and hitting his eyes directly. Where was it coming from at this time of night?

Sudheen went out on the veranda. The whole area was dark except for one room in the second floor of the house opposite. That was where the light was coming from, through an open window, past his veranda and straight on to his bed. Even if he changed his position on the bed, it would still shine in his face.

How annoying! How could anyone sleep in a room that wasn't totally dark? At least Sudheen couldn't. But was this going to trouble him every night?

A week later, Sudheen's suspicions were confirmed. Every night, the light was switched on around midnight and it stayed on until dawn. Sudheen couldn't bear the idea of closing his own window. A south-facing window has a special advantage in Calcutta, especially if there is no building in front to obstruct the breeze. That was really another reason that had prompted Sudheen to take this flat. His veranda overlooked the garden of the opposite house. At least in the near future there was no chance of a new construction coming up here. It was really a rambling old mansion, probably once owned by a *zamindar*, lying now in a state of disrepair. By the look of things, its occupants were few.

But who used that room on the second floor?

Why did its occupant keep the light on all night?

Someshwar Nag lived in the flat downstairs. He had moved in about four months before Sudheen. A man in his mid-fifties, he was a member of the Bengal Club where he liked to spend most evenings. Sudheen happened to run into him near the gate on a Saturday, and could not resist putting a question to him.

'Do you know who lives in that house opposite?'

'Mr Chowdhury. Why? Is anything wrong?'

'No, it's just that it doesn't seem as though too many people live in that house, and yet someone leaves a light on all night in a room on the second floor. Haven't you noticed it?'

'No, I can't say I have.'

'Does that light not get into your room?'

'No, that's not possible. You see, their terrace shields the room from view from the ground floor. In fact, I didn't even know there was such a room!'

'You're lucky. I don't get any sleep because of that light.'

'Very strange. I've been told only a couple of people live in that house. It's owned by one Gagan Chowdhury. He doesn't go out much. At least, I have never seen him, but, apparently, he does exist. Perhaps he's grown quite old. I've heard that he used to paint once. Why don't you go and talk to him? He can at least keep his own window closed. Surely he wouldn't mind showing a little consideration for his neighbour?'

Yes, Sudheen certainly could go and talk to Mr Chowdhury, although there was no guarantee that his request would be granted. But what on earth went on in that room, anyway?

Sudheen realized that in addition to his discomfort over the business of the light coming in through the window, he was also getting quite intrigued by the thought of discovering what went on in that room.

One of his friends, Mahim, often went to the races. He had a large pair of binoculars. Maybe that would help? A pair of binoculars were needed because the room was at some distance. The house Mr Chowdhury lived in was not exactly by the side of the road. There was an extension of the garden beyond the compound wall and a certain portion of the terrace had to be crossed to get to the room on the second floor.

Mahim's binoculars brought the window of the room a lot closer, but nothing could be seen beyond a portion of the wall over the top of a curtain. All he could make out was that a couple of oil paintings hung on the wall. Was this the studio of Mr Chowdhury? But did no one work in it now?

Yes, someone did. A shadow moved behind the curtain, passing from the right to the left. But it was impossible to see who it was.

After about fifteen minutes of looking through the binoculars, Sudheen began to feel tired. How silly to waste time like this and spoil whatever chances there were of getting some sleep!

Sudheen put the binoculars down on the table and went to bed. He had made up his mind about what to do.

He would go straight to Gagan Chowdhury and ask him to keep that particular window closed. If he agreed, well and good. If he didn't, Sudheen would have to learn to live with the situation. What kind of a man was Gagan Chowdhury? Sudheen wished he knew. It would be difficult to put up with fractious behaviour from a neighbour, no matter how old he was. But, in this case, that risk would have to be taken.

The gate was open and there was no *chowkidar*. This surprised Sudheen, though he was secretly quite pleased to have crossed the first hurdle so easily. He had decided to call on Mr Chowdhury at night simply so that he could actually show him how the light from the open window disturbed him.

It was around 11 p.m. The neighbourhood had fallen totally silent already. Last night there had been a full moon. Everything in the overgrown garden of the Chowdhurys was clearly visible in the moonlight. Sudheen passed a marble statue of a nymph and went across towards the dark, dank walls of the porch. The light on the second floor had not yet been switched on. With some luck, he would find Gagan Chowdhury downstairs.

Within seconds of his knocking on the front door, a middle-aged man opened it. He appeared to be a servant.

'Who would you like to see?' he asked.

'Mr Chowdhury—Gagan Chowdhury—has he gone to bed?'

'No.'

'Is it possible to meet him? My name is Sudheen Sarkar. I live in that house opposite. I've come on some urgent business.'

The man went inside and reappeared a few minutes later. 'Please come in.'

Everything was going smoothly. It was rather strange.

Sudheen crossed a landing and entered the living-room.

'Please sit down.'

A strip of moonlight had come in through a window and fallen on a sofa. Sudheen found his way to it and sat down. Why didn't the man switch on the lights? Surely there was no power cut?

He began to look around the room and, suddenly, his heart skipped a beat. Had he arrived amongst a room full of people? Who were all these people staring down at him?

But as his eyes grew used to the semi-darkness, Sudheen realized the eyes fixed on him were not men but masks. Every mask seemed to have turned its eyes on him. It was easy to tell that these masks had come from abroad. Most were from Africa, some may have been from South America. Sudheen himself had once been interested in painting. In fact, if his father hadn't put his foot down, he might have become a professional painter. He was still interested in art and handicrafts.

Sudheen could not help being impressed by his own courage. Anyone else would have had a heart attack sitting in a dark room, in this eerie atmosphere, surrounded by a gallery of fearsome masks.

He did not see anyone enter the room. The deep, sombre voice startled him.

He swivelled round and saw a man seated on the adjacent sofa.

'What brought you here so late?'

Sudheen raised his hands mechanically in a *namaskar* but failed to find words to answer the man.

There was no doubt that this man came from an aristocratic family. The expensive shawl he was wearing bore evidence of that. But Sudheen had never seen anyone so deathly pale and with such a piercing look. The first sight of a man like this would render anyone speechless.

The man continued to stare at him. It took Sudheen about a whole minute to pull himself together. Then, finally, he found his tongue.

'I. . . well, I have come to make a complaint. Please don't mind. You are Mr Gagan Chowdhury, I presume?'

The man nodded. His pepper-and-salt hair hung like the mane of a lion around his broad forehead. He must be about sixty-five, Sudheen thought.

'My name is Sudheen Sarkar,' he continued, 'I live in the first floor flat in the house opposite yours. The fact is. . . you see, the light in that room on your second floor disturbs me very much. It shines directly into my eyes. May I request you to keep your window closed? I can't sleep at all because of that light. You will appreciate how annoying that can be after a hard day's work. . . .'

The man had not stopped gazing at him. Did this room not have even a single light?

Sudheen felt obliged to open his mouth once more. Perhaps he should take the matter a bit further.

'I realize,' he said, 'that an easy way of keeping the light out is to shut my own window. But since it faces the south, I am somewhat reluctant. . . .'

'No, you don't have to close your window.'

'What?'

'I shall close mine.'

Sudheen suddenly felt as though a huge load had been taken off his shoulders.

'Oh. It is most kind of you. Thank you so much. I really am very grateful.'

'Are you leaving?'

Sudheen had half-risen from the sofa but, surprised by this question, sat down again.

'It's quite late, isn't it? I'm sure you'd like to go to bed?' he asked.

'I don't sleep at night.'

The eyes of the man were still fixed on Sudheen.

'Do you read a lot?' Sudheen asked. His throat was beginning to feel a little dry. Gagan Chowdhury's company in these weird surroundings was not really something that one might enjoy, he had to admit.

'No.'

'What do you do then?'

'I paint.'

Sudheen recalled having seen a couple of paintings through his binoculars.

Mr Nag, too, had mentioned that Mr Chowdhury used to paint once.

'Does that mean that room is your studio?'

'Yes, that's right.'

'But I don't think too many people in the neighbourhood know about it.'

Gagan Chowdhury gave a twisted smile. 'Do you have a little time to spare?'

'Time? Now? I mean. . . .'

'Allow me to tell you a few things. I have wanted to speak for a long time, but never found the chance to do so.'

Sudheen realized it was quite impossible to ignore the man's request.

'All right,' he said.

'My neighbours don't know about my work because they are not interested. Nobody's even mildly curious about a man who has spent his whole life as an artist. There was a time when I used to have my own exhibitions. A few people saw what I drew, some even uttered words of praise. But when the trend began to change, when abstract art wiped out the old traditions in painting and portraits ceased to be appreciated, I withdrew. I have never been one for newfangled notions. In my heart, I looked upon da Vinci as my guru. I still do.'

'But. . . what kind of things do you paint?'

'People.'

'People?'

'Portraits.'

'From your imagination?'

'No. I never learnt to do that. I cannot paint unless I have a model sitting for me.'

'In the middle of the night?'

'Yes, I do get models. Every night.'

Sudheen did not know what to say. What on earth was the man talking about? Was he, perhaps, slightly mad?

'You find that difficult to believe, don't you?'

There was a hint of a genuine smile on his lips this time. Sudheen remained silent.

'Come with me.'

Sudheen could not disregard the summons. There was something hypnotic in the man's eyes and his words. Besides, his curiosity had been aroused. What kind of portraits had been done? Who came for sittings in the dead of night? How did Mr Chowdhury get hold of them?

'I have retained an electric connection only in my studio,' said Gagan Chowdhury, as they began climbing up the wooden stairs in the hazy, yellow light of a kerosene lamp, 'I've had it disconnected everywhere else in the house.'

Sudheen was surprised to note that there was not a single painting on the landing, or the walls by the stairs or the living-room. Were all his works kept together in his studio?

There was a door just as they turned left upon reaching the second floor. Mr Chowdhury pushed it open, went in with Sudheen, and then closed it again. Then he pressed a switch on the wall and the whole room was flooded with light.

This was obviously the studio. Every material an artist might need was strewn about the room. There was an easel under the lamp and on it a new white canvas. Mr Chowdhury was probably going to start on a new painting.

Apart from the material for painting, the other thing that claimed one's attention was the large number of portraits that hung on the wall. A lot more were piled up on the floor. There were at least a hundred of these. But it was not possible to see them unless one picked them up from the floor one by one. The ones staring at him were those that were placed on the wall. Most of them were portraits of men. Sudheen's experienced eye immediately caught the touch of an expert in the works, all done in the old traditional style. Once again, he felt as though he was surrounded by a lot of people, all of them alive. At least fifty pairs of eyes were looking straight at him.

But who were these people? A few faces did look vaguely familiar, but. . . .

'How do you like these?' asked Gagan Chowdhury.

'The work of a master,' Sudheen had to admit.

'And yet, the whole tradition of oil painting is now extinct. In such a situation, can you imagine how artists like myself must cope?'

'But, judging by what you've got in this room, it doesn't seem as though you lack work.'

'Yes, but I found work only recently. Before that, for fifteen long years, I kept advertising in the papers. Not a single person responded. In the end I had to give up.'

'And then? How did you happen to start again?'

'The circumstances changed, you see.'

Sudheen refrained from saying anything further for his whole attention was now fixed on the paintings. He had managed to recognize three people. One of them had died four months ago. He was the well-known singer, Anantalal Niyogi. Sudheen had been to a live performance and had heard him sing about eight years ago.

The second was Ashimananda Swami. He had once been a freedom fighter, but later became a sanyasi. He, too, had died a year ago. Sudheen could recall having seen his picture in newspapers.

The third man was a Bengali pilot of Air India, Captain Chakravarty. He had been killed three years ago in an air crash, on his way to London, together with two-hundred-and-fifty others. Sudheen had met him once on a flight to Rome, where he was going on official work.

At this point, Sudheen could not help but ask a question: 'Did all these people come here simply to get their portrait done with no thought of owning them?'

For the first time, Sudheen heard Gagan Chowdhury laugh loudly.

'No, Mr Sarkar,' he said, 'none of these people needed a portrait for themselves. These were made only for my personal collection.'

'Do you mean to say someone or the other still comes and sits for you? Every night?'

'Yes, you will soon see what I mean. I am certainly expecting someone tonight.'

Sudheen's head began to reel.

'But. . . but. . . how do you contact all these people?'

'Wait, I shall explain it all to you. My system is a little different.'

Mr Chowdhury brought down a large ledger from a shelf. 'Open it and see what's inside.'

Sudheen took the ledger near the lamp and opened it.

It was really a scrapbook, each page of which was filled with clippings from newspapers. They were all obituaries. Some of them had a picture of the deceased. A few of these had a pencil mark against them.

'That mark means that a portrait has already been made,' said Mr Chowdhury.

'But you still haven't told me how you get in touch. . . .'

Gagan Chowdhury took the scrapbook from Sudheen and put it back on the shelf. Then he turned around and said, 'Not many can do it. But I am an exception. It's not a matter of sending a letter or making a phone call. There is no way of reaching these people through such means. The place where they live has neither a telephone connection nor a postal system. I have to use a totally different way to get in touch.'

Sudheen's blood chilled, his throat parched. But even so, he simply had to ask another question. 'Are you trying to tell me that you made these portraits after all these people died?'

'How could I have learnt about them unless they were dead, Sudheen Babu? I don't know many people in Calcutta. In any case, no one can be totally free before death. Only a man who is no more has endless freedom, boundless time and patience. He does not mind sitting in that chair for hours, quite motionless, until every detail in the portrait is perfect.'

A clock struck somewhere, shattering the stillness of the night. It must be the clock Sudheen had seen by the staircase.

'Midnight,' said Gagan Chowdhury, 'time for him to come.'

'Who?' Sudheen's voice sounded abnormally hoarse. He had started to feel giddy.

'The man who will sit for me tonight. There—can you hear his footsteps?'

Sudheen's ears were still functioning. He could clearly hear the footsteps downstairs.

'Come and have a look!'

Gagan Chowdhury had moved towards an open window. 'If you don't believe me, come and see for yourself,' he said.

Again, Sudheen felt the hypnotic power behind his words. He moved liked a robot and stood beside Gagan Chowdhury. Then he looked down and screamed involuntarily, 'I know this man!'

The man had the same swift stride, the same height and was wearing the same grey safari suit. It was the same man who had, until recently, been Sudheen's boss—Nagendra Kapoor.

A wave of dizziness swept over Sudheen. He clutched the easel to stop himself from falling.

The footsteps were now coming up the stairs. The whole house seemed to echo with the sound of footsteps on the wooden stairs.

Then the sound stopped.

In the silence, Gagan Chowdhury spoke again.

'Were you not talking about establishing contact, Sudheen Babu? It's very simple. They come just as I beckon at them. Like this.'

Before Sudheen's horrified eyes, Gagan Chowdhury took his right arm out of his shawl and stretched it towards him. It was the arm of a skeleton.

'The same hand that beckons also paints!' said Mr Chowdhury.

Just before he finally lost consciousness, Sudheen heard someone knock on the door.

Rap, rap, rap, rap. . . .

Rap, rap, rap, rap. . . .

'Dada Babu! Dada Babu!'

Sudheen woke with a start, squinting in the daylight. God— what a terrible dream that was!

'Open the door, Dada Babu!'

It was the voice of his servant, Adheer.

'Wait a minute.'

Sudheen rose from his bed and unlocked the door. Adheer came in looking deeply worried.

'It's so late. . . .'

'Yes, I know. I overslept.'

'We had such a to-do in front of our house. Didn't you hear anything?'

'To-do?'

'The old Mr Chowdhury passed away last night, Gagan Babu. He was eighty-four. He'd been ailing for quite some time. They left the light on all night in his room. Didn't you notice it?'

'You knew about his illness?'

'Of course! I used to meet his servant—Bhagirath—so often in the market.'

'Well!' said Sudheen, bereft of speech.

Sadhan Babu's Suspicions

Sadhan Babu found a small twig lying on the floor of his room as he returned from work one evening. This made him frown for he was very fussy about cleanliness. Every piece of furniture in his room had to be spotless, as did all his bedclothes and embroidered tablecloths and curtains. It did mean paying rather a lot to the dhobi, but Sadhan Babu did not mind.

'Pocha!' he called out to his servant.

'Were you calling me, sir?' Pocha appeared.

'Why—do you doubt it?'

'No, sir. Why should I?'

'What is this twig doing here on the floor?'

'I don't know. A bird may have dropped it.'

'Why should a bird be allowed to come in and drop things in my room? Didn't you notice it when you swept the floor today? Or didn't you sweep it at all?'

'Oh, but I sweep your room every day, sir. When I did so today this twig wasn't there.'

'Are you sure?'

'Yes, sir.'

'How strange!'

The next day he noticed a sparrow sitting on his window-sill. This might be the bird trying to build a nest in his room and dropping bits and pieces on the floor. But where could it possibly build a nest? In the skylight? Perhaps.

Sadhan Babu then began to ponder another issue. There were seven rooms on the third floor of the building where he lived. Why was the bird trying to get into his? Did the room have something special to attract birds?

It could, of course, be the new ayurvedic hair oil he had started to use. It did have a rather strong smell and the bird may have come into his room because of it. The oil had been recommended by Nilmani Babu who lived in a flat on the second floor. Nilmani Babu dabbled in ayurvedic medicine and, according to him, this oil was the perfect remedy for dandruff. But could it be that he had played a practical joke on Sadhan Babu, trying deliberately to turn his room into a sanctuary for homeless birds?

The fact was that nearly everyone in the house was aware of

Sadhan Babu's suspicious nature and made fun of him behind his back. When he returned in the evening, very often he had to hear remarks like, 'So tell us about the new suspicions you had today!'

Some people pulled his leg in other ways. Nabendu Chatterjee lived on the ground floor. Sadhan Babu went to his house practically every evening to join the group that gathered there to play cards. Only the other day, Nabendu Babu had said to him as soon as he arrived, 'Take a look at this piece of paper. Does it tell you anything? Someone tossed it in through the window.'

It was only a page torn out of Nabendu Babu's daughter's maths exercise book. Sadhan Babu straightened it out, looked at it carefully and said, 'This seems to be a digital code of some kind.'

Nabendu Babu said nothing. Sadhan Babu went on, 'But we must have it decoded. It may be a sort of warning. . . .'

Nobody had it decoded, of course. But they had achieved their goal, which was only to see how far Sadhan Babu's suspicions could be raised by just a piece of paper.

Sadhan Babu strongly believed that the entire city of Calcutta was filled with cheats and frauds and liars. No one here could be trusted. The only thing that could keep one going was one's own ability to question everything.

One day, Sadhan Babu returned from his office to find a large, square parcel lying on his table. His first reaction was to think it had come to him by mistake. Who would send him such a packet?

His belief grew firmer when he discovered the parcel bore no name on it.

'Who brought it here?' he asked his servant.

'Someone came this afternoon and left it with Dhananjay. He said it was for you.'

Dhananjay worked for another tenant on the first floor, Shoroshi Babu.

'Did he say who had sent it? What does it contain?'

'No idea, sir.'

'Well!'

Sadhan Babu sat down on his bed and stared at the packet. It seemed big enough to hold a large-sized football. But it was impossible to guess who had sent it.

He rose from the bed and picked it up. How heavy it was! At least five kilos.

Sadhan Babu tried to remember the last occasion when he had been sent a parcel. Ah yes, about three years ago, an aunt of his had sent him some mango cake. She had died six months later. He had no close relatives left. He never received more than a couple of letters a month. So a parcel was a rarity indeed. If only there was a note with it!

But who knows—perhaps the sender had indeed enclosed a note and Dhananjay had lost it. He must speak to Dhananjay.

Sadhan Babu went downstairs himself. Dhananjay was busy pounding spicy masala when Sadhan Babu found him. He left his work and came to meet Sadhan Babu.

'Er. . . did someone leave a parcel with you today saying it was for me?'

'Yes, sir.'

'Was there a note with it?'

'Why—no!'

'Did he say where he was from?'

'He did mention a name—Madan, I think he said.'

'Madan?'

'Yes, that's what he said.'

There was no one called Madan among Sadhan Babu's acquaintances. Heaven knows what the man had actually said. Dhananjay was undoubtedly an idiot.

'Was there no letter or any other paper with the parcel?'

'Yes, there was a receipt. My Babu signed it.'

'You mean Shoroshi Babu?'

'Yes, sir.'

But Shoroshi Babu could not help either. He had indeed signed the receipt for Sadhan Babu, but did not notice the name of the place the parcel came from.

Sadhan Babu returned to his own room. It had grown quite cool in the evening. Winter was round the corner. And so was Diwali. Crackers and rockets had started to go off in all directions.

Boom! There went a cracker. And, in that instant, a cold shiver went down his spine.

A time bomb!

Could there be a time bomb inside that packet? God—it could go off any minute and finish him!

There was a lot of talk nowadays about time bombs. They appeared to be the favourite weapon of terrorists.

But why should anyone send him a time bomb?

Why, one of his enemies, of course! His success as a businessman had caused great jealousy among his rivals. He had to keep all clients happy, just like the others. Yet, if a client chose to give him a contract, all the others immediately became his enemies. It happened all the time.

'Pocha?'

His voice sounded hoarse. His throat had started to dry.

Pocha arrived.

'Did you call me, sir?'

'Yes. . . er. . . .'

He stopped. Would it be a wise thing to do? He had wanted to ask Pocha to put his ear to the packet to see if it was ticking. Didn't all time bombs have a device attached that ticked? And didn't this ticking finally result in a huge explosion?

What if it exploded just as Pocha laid his ear against it?

Sadhan Babu could not bear to think any more. But Pocha was still waiting for instructions. In the end, Sadhan Babu had to admit he had called him quite unnecessarily.

The night that followed left an indelible mark on Sadhan Babu's memory. He had spent sleepless nights before, especially during periods of illness. But never had he sat up all night feeling so utterly petrified.

His courage and common sense returned in the morning when it became clear that the parcel was not going to burst and go up in flames. 'I must open it this evening,' thought Sadhan Babu. Even to himself, his suspicions appeared to be crossing the limits of reason.

But something happened in the evening to stop him from unwrapping the parcel.

There are some people who have a passion for reading every word in a newspaper. Sadhan Babu did not fall into this category. He only looked at the headlines every day. This was probably why, that day, he missed the little news item about a murder in north Calcutta. He learnt about it in Nabendu Babu's house in the evening, when he arrived in the middle of a heated discussion.

The name of the deceased was Shibdas Moulik. He lived in Patuatola Lane. The very mention of the name brought back memories of his past that Sadhan Babu had quite forgotten.

He once knew a Moulik fairly well. Was his first name Shibdas? Yes, it was. Sadhan Babu used to live in the same Patuatola Lane in those days. Moulik was his neighbour. A few people went to his house every evening to play rummy. For some strange reason, everyone called Moulik only by his surname. There were two other men who came regularly. One was Sukhen Dutta and the other was Madhusudan Maiti. The latter turned out to be a dangerous crook. Sadhan Babu had often felt that Madhusudan cheated frequently at the game. One day he could not help mention it. Madhusudan's reaction at this was terrifying. No one had known until that day that he carried a knife in his pocket at all times. It had come flying out that evening. Sadhan Babu managed to escape unhurt only because Moulik and Sukhen Dutta stepped in just in time.

When his business began to prosper, Sadhan Babu left his little room in Patuatola Lane and moved into this apartment house in Mirzapur Street. He then lost all contact with Moulik & Co. His fondness for playing cards remained, as did his habit of questioning and suspecting everything. But, apart from these, Sadhan Babu did indeed turn into a different man. The clothes he wore were now more stylish, he smoked cigarettes (having given up beedis) and often went to auctions to buy things like paintings, flower vases and attractive ashtrays for his house. All this had happened over the last six or seven years.

If the Shibdas Moulik who had just been murdered was the same Moulik that Sadhan Babu had once known, then the murderer was undoubtedly Madhu Maiti.

'How did the murder take place?' asked Sadhan Babu.

'Brutal! Oh, but it was really brutal,' said Nabendu Chatterjee, 'there was no way of identifying the body. They found his name from a diary in his pocket.'

'Why? Why was identification not possible?'

'They found the body, but not the head. So how could they identify the person?'

'What? You mean the head. . .?'

'Yes, the head. . . kaput!' Nabendu Babu raised both his hands above his head and then swung them down in a single movement. 'No one knows where the murderer hid the head,' he added.

'Does anyone know who actually committed the murder?'

'I believe a few people used to play rummy in Moulik's house. The police suspect it was one of them.'

As he went up the stairs to his own flat on the third floor, Sadhan Babu began to feel dizzy. He could recall so vividly all that had happened that horrible day, soon after he'd accused Madhu Maiti of cheating. The others did manage to stop Maiti from stabbing him, but he would never forget the look in Maiti's eyes.

'You have escaped today, Sadhan Majumdar,' Maiti had

threatened, 'but you don't know me. One day I will settle scores with you—even if I have to wait for years!'

It was the kind of threat that froze one's blood. Sadhan Babu had thought he had put the whole thing behind him after moving out of Patuatola Lane. But had he?

What if that parcel lying in his room had been sent by Madhu? If Dhananjay had heard the fellow say 'Madan' no doubt Dhananjay was hard of hearing. There was not much difference between 'Madhu' and 'Madan', was there? Obviously it was either Madhu himself or someone sent by him who had left the parcel.

And he had the receipt signed simply to make sure that it did reach Sadhan Babu.

That parcel must contain the hacked head of Shibdas Moulik!

The idea came to him suddenly and took a firm hold on his mind even before he stepped into his room. He could see the packet from the doorway. It was resting on his table, next to a flower vase. Its height and size were now clear indication of its content.

Pocha looked curiously at his master as he saw him hovering near the door. With an enormous effort, Sadhan Babu pulled himself together, came into the room and asked Pocha to make him a cup of tea. 'Ah. . . did anyone come looking for me today?' he asked.

'No, sir.'

'Hmm.'

Sadhan Babu had had this wild vision of the police searching his house. The thought of what they might do to him if they found the head of the murdered man in his room made him break out into a cold sweat once again.

A little later, after a hot cup of tea, some of his courage seeped back. 'Well,' he thought, 'at least it's not a time bomb!'

But if he had to spend another sleepless night just staring at the parcel he knew he would go mad.

The answer, of course, was a sleeping pill. However, there was no escape from nightmares even if the pill did help him sleep.

In one he saw himself playing rummy with a headless Moulik. In another, the bodyless head of Moulik was saying to him, 'Get me out of this box, please—I'm getting suffocated!'

In spite of the pill, Sadhan Babu woke as usual at 5.30 in the morning. And the minute he opened his eyes, his mind hit upon a solution to his problem.

If the hacked head had been passed on to him, why should he

not try to pass it on elsewhere? The main thing was to get rid of it, wasn't it?

Sadhan Babu put the parcel into a large shopping bag and set out, even at that early hour. He had to admit the packing had been done very well for not a drop of blood had oozed out.

It took him twenty-five minutes to reach Kalighat by bus. He walked slowly towards the river and found a relatively quiet spot. And then, taking the parcel out of his bag, he threw it straight into the river.

It fell into the water with a loud splash.

The packet vanished and Sadhan Babu heaved a sigh of relief.

Thirty-five minutes later, he was back home. As he walked in through the front gate, he could hear the wall clock in Shoroshi Babu's house strike seven.

The sound of its chime suddenly shook Sadhan Babu into a new awareness.

For the last few days, there had been this niggling worry at the back of his mind that he was forgetting something he really ought to remember. Some people did, he knew, turn forgetful as they found themselves on the wrong side of fifty.

Upon being told about this, Nilmani Babu had prescribed a special herb.

But now the whole thing had come back to him and there was not a moment to be lost.

Sadhan Babu left home half an hour earlier than usual. He stopped at the auction house called Modern Exchange in Russell Street. Tulsi Babu, its owner, came forward to greet him, a broad smile on his face. 'I hope the table clock is working properly?' he asked.

'Did you send it?'

'Of course I did! Why, didn't it reach you?'

'Yes, yes, I mean. . .er. . . .'

'Look, you gave me an advance of five hundred rupees and I promised to have it delivered to your house, didn't I? You're such an old client of mine. Would I not keep my word?'

'Oh yes. Oh yes. Of course. I mean to say, certainly. . . .'

'That clock will keep excellent time—you mark my words. After all, it was made by such a famous French company! You got it for a song, I tell you. Very lucky.'

Tulsi Babu moved forward to welcome another customer. Sadhan Babu came out of the shop slowly. What he had got for a song now nestled below the rippling waves of the river.

No doubt Madhu Maiti had taken the most perfect revenge. No doubt, too, that what Dhananjay had heard as 'Madan' had, in fact, been 'Modern'!

Mr Brown's Cottage

I had been looking for an opportunity to go to Bangalore ever since I'd found Mr Brown's diary. It happened rather unexpectedly. At the annual re-union of our Ballygunj school, I happened to run into my old classmate, Anikendra Bhowmik. Anik told me he was now working at the Indian Institute of Science in Bangalore. 'Why don't you come and have a holiday where I'm staying?' he asked. 'It's the best place in India! I have a spare room in my house, so you won't have any problem. Will you come?'

Anik and I had been very close friends in school. Then the inevitable happened. He went on to study science and I took up arts. We began walking in opposite directions. After a few years he went to England, and I lost touch with him. This was our re-union after about twelve years.

I said, 'I might. When is the best time to come to Bangalore?'

'Any time. The weather in Bangalore is always pleasant. Why do you think the British were so fond of the place? You can come any time you like. All I need is a week's notice.'

So here was a chance to go and find the house where Mr Brown had lived. But I must first explain about the diary.

I am what is usually described as a bookworm. Old books, especially, fascinate me. I work in a bank and spend at least half my salary on these. Over the last five years I have managed to acquire quite a collection of travel books, shikar tales, autobiographies, diaries and many others. I love their old, faded, brittle, moth-eaten pages. And their smell! The smell of wet earth after the first shower and the smell of old books—I do not think any other smell on earth can match their charm. Not even the scent of attar, kasturi, rose, hasnuhana—or the best perfume in France.

My passion for old books had made me chance upon the diary of Mr Brown. It was not printed, but a genuine diary, many pages of which were filled with entries, handwritten with a quill. Bound in red leather, it had three-hundred-and-fifty ruled pages and measured six by four-and-a-half inches. The cover had a golden border and, in the middle, was embossed in gold letters the owner's name: John Middleton Brown. The first page had his signature and his address just below it—Evergreen Lodge, Fraser Town, Bangalore. This was followed by a date—January 1858, which meant that the diary was a hundred-and-thirteen years old. I found it together with some other books which also bore Mr Brown's name, and it cost me very little. Maqbool, the bookseller, initially asked for twenty rupees. I offered to pay ten and, in the end, I bought it for twelve. Had Mr Brown been someone famous, this diary would have fetched at least twelve thousand rupees.

I did not expect to find anything other than a description of the life led by a British gentleman in those days. In fact, the first hundred pages offered just that. Mr Brown was a schoolmaster. There was a mention of the school he taught in, descriptions of the city of Bangalore, the trees and flowers he saw both in his own garden and elsewhere. He mentioned the Viceroy's wife, Lady Canning's visit to Bangalore. Sometimes he talked of his home in Sussex and all the friends and relatives he had left behind. There was also mention of his wife, Elizabeth, though she had died a few years ago.

But the most interesting thing in his diary was the frequent reference to someone called Simon. Whether he was his son or brother or nephew or friend was impossible to tell. But it was clear that Mr Brown was very deeply attached to him. His diary was full of instances of Simon's intelligence, his courage, his anger, his naughtiness and his occasional waywardness of behaviour. Many of his entries said things like, 'Simon loves to sit in a particular chair,' or 'Simon was not feeling very well today'; 'I feel sad because I have not seen Simon all day'.

Then came the heartbreaking news of Simon's death. On 22nd September, at around 7.30 p.m., Simon was struck by lightning. His body was found the next morning near a charred eucalyptus tree in Mr Brown's garden.

For about a month after Simon's death, he wrote virtually nothing in his diary. Whatever little he did was full of sadness and despair. He thought of going back to Britain, but did not want to leave the place where Simon's soul rested. His health, too, had probably begun to fail. He wrote, 'Today, again I did not go to school,' on at least five different occasions. There was mention of a Dr Lucas, who had examined Mr Brown and suggested a course of remedy.

Then, suddenly—on 2nd November—the diary mentioned a strange incident. And it was the description of this incident that made the diary so special.

Mr Brown wrote about the incident in red ink instead of the blue he usually used. 'The most unexpected and extraordinary thing happened today,' he wrote. 'I had gone to Lal Bagh to see if I could find some peace among the trees and the plants. I returned at around 7.30 p.m. As soon as I stepped into the living-room, I saw Simon sitting by the fireside in his favourite high-backed chair! Simon! Was it really Simon? I felt overjoyed. Simon was looking straight at me with such affection in his eyes. But the room was dark. Thomas, that lazy bearer of mine, had forgotten to light a lamp. So I took out my matchbox to see Simon a little better. But—alas!—he vanished the instant I struck a match. This was truly regrettable; but then, I had never hoped to see Simon again. I should be happy if he appeared occasionally even as a ghost. What a heavenly day it is today! Simon has not forgotten me even after his death. He even remembers his favourite chair! Please, Simon—do come and visit me sometimes. I don't want anything else from you. I can live happily for the rest of my life if I can see you again.'

Not much was written after this date. But the few entries that followed were full of joy, for Simon came and met Mr Brown every day. His ghost did not disappoint him.

The last entry read, 'The knowledge that he who loved me did not lose his love even after death has given me profound peace.'

Here the diary ended. But my curiosity did not. Did this house of Mr Brown—this Evergreen Lodge in Fraser Town—still exist? And did the ghost of Simon still appear every evening? Would it appear before a stranger? If I went and spent an evening there, would I get to see it?

When I arrived in Bangalore, I mentioned nothing about the diary at first. Anik took me sight-seeing all over Bangalore in his Ambassador car. We even went to Fraser Town. Bangalore was really a beautiful place, so the praise and appreciation I expressed as we moved around were quite sincerely felt. After the hustle and bustle of Calcutta, such a quiet and peaceful place seemed like something out of a dream.

The next day was Sunday. I raised the subject of Mr Brown's house in the morning as Anik and I sat under a garden umbrella in his house, sipping tea. Anik listened to the whole story without comment. Then he put his cup down on the cane table and said, 'Look, Ranjan, the house you're talking about may still exist. After all, a hundred years is not a very long time. But if you wish to go there simply to lie in wait for a ghost, I fear I cannot join you. I have always been extra sensitive about certain things. I think life at the moment is just fine—I have no problems. But to go ghost hunting now, I think, would be asking for trouble. You must count me out.'

This clearly showed Anik had not changed. He'd had a reputation of being very timid and something of a coward in school. I remembered one instance when two other boys had covered themselves in a white sheet and pounced upon poor Anik as he was walking alone one evening. He had been so frightened that the next day his father had come and complained to the Headmaster.

Before I could say anything, however, Anik remarked, 'But if you must go, I think I can easily find you company. Hello, Mr Banerjee!'

I turned around and saw a man who had just walked in through the gate and was now coming towards us, smiling a little. He appeared to be around forty-five. Nearly six feet in height, his body seemed both well built and well maintained. He was clad in grey trousers and a dark blue bush-shirt. A black-and-white silk scarf with Batik work on it was casually wound around his neck.

Anik introduced us. 'This is my friend, Ranjan Sengupta—Mr Hrishikesh Banerjee.'

Mr Banerjee, it turned out, worked in the aircraft factory. He had lived in Bangalore for many years.

Anik offered him a cup of tea and went straight to the subject of the house of Mr Brown. Mr Banerjee broke into such a loud guffaw when he heard the tale that the squirrel that was romping around our table dashed up the nearest tree and vanished among the leaves.

'Ghosts? Ghosts? You mean you seriously believe in them? Today? In these times?'

I said hesitantly, 'Well, what's wrong with being interested? It could well be that there is a scientific explanation behind the existence of ghosts that has not yet come to light. But who knows— ten years from now someone might hit upon it!'

Mr Banerjee continued to laugh. His teeth, I noticed, were very white and strong.

Finally, Anik said, 'All right, Mr Banerjee. Ghost or no ghost—all I want to know is whether you'd be prepared to go with Ranjan to such a house if it can be found and spend an evening there. He is my guest and I cannot allow him to go alone. To tell you the truth,

I myself am rather. . . er. . . careful about things. If I went with him, I'd be more of a liability than anything else!'

Mr Banerjee took out a pipe from his pocket and began filling it. 'I wouldn't mind,' he said, 'but I would go only on one condition—both of you must come with me.'

He broke into loud laughter again, causing great panic among the birds that were twittering in the vicinity. Anik went slightly pale, but could not refuse.

'What did you say the place was called?' asked Mr Banerjee.

'Evergreen Lodge.'

'In Fraser Town?'

'That's what the diary said.'

'Hmm.' He began smoking his pipe, 'Fraser Town does have a few old British cottages. Anyway—if we must go, why don't we do so this evening? Say I come back here at about four?'

Mr Banerjee may have been an engineer by profession, but clearly he had a military spirit and a strong sense of punctuality. He arrived in his Morris Minor on the dot.

'What have you taken with you?' he asked, as we got into the car.

Anik gave him the list—a powerful torch, six candles, a first-aid box, some ham sandwiches, a large flask of coffee, a pack of cards, a rug to spread on the floor and a tube of mosquito repellent.

'And arms?'

'Can ghosts be destroyed by arms? Hey, Ranjan—is your ghost a solid one?'

'Never mind,' said Mr Banerjee, 'I have a small revolver. So we needn't worry about whether it's solid or liquid.'

We set off. After a while Mr Banerjee said, 'The place does exist.'

I was surprised, 'You mean you've made enquiries already?'

'I am a very methodical man, Mr Sengupta. Shouldn't one first make sure about the existence of a place before trying to go there? One of my golf mates, Srinivas Deshmukh, lives in that area. I went to his house straight from yours this morning. He told me there is indeed a cottage called Evergreen Lodge in Fraser Town. It has been lying vacant for nearly fifty years. People used to go there for picnics even ten years ago. But no one does so now. Apparently, no one ever lived in that house for very long. However, it is not reputed to be haunted. It had some furniture once—but it was all auctioned a few years ago. Col. Mercer bought some of it. He, too, lives in Fraser Town. As far as I can see, we are going to have no more than a picnic ourselves. I am glad Anikendra has brought the cards.'

Driving through the clean broad roads of Bangalore, it was difficult to imagine the existence of a haunted house. But I could not forget the diary of Mr Brown. Unless one was totally mad, one would not just make up such an extraordinary tale and record it in a diary. Mr Brown did see Simon's ghost—time and again. Would that ghost not appear before us—even once?

I have never been to England, but have seen pictures of English cottages. The sight of Evergreen Lodge made me feel exactly as though I was standing before an old and abandoned house in an English suburb.

There must have been a garden in front of the cottage. Instead of carefully arranged flower beds it now had wild plants and weeds that grew in abundance. There was a small wicket gate through which one had to pass to go into the garden. The name of the place was engraved on the gate. But someone—possibly one of the merry picnickers—had added an N before the word Evergreen which now made it Nevergreen.

We began walking towards the house. There were plenty of trees around it. I saw a few eucalyptus trees but failed to recognize the others. The soil of Bangalore was reported to be so good that plants and trees from anywhere in the world could survive here.

There was a portico with a broken tile roof. Creepers covered its pillars. One side of the front door had come off its hinges. Most of the windows were broken. There was such a thick layer of mould on the walls that it was impossible to guess the original colour of the house.

We walked in through the broken door. There was a long passage that led to a room at the far end. There were more rooms on both sides. The one on our right seemed larger than the others. It must have been the living-room. The floor was wooden, although most of it had rotted away. Every step would have to be taken carefully.

We went into the room. The wooden boards creaked under our feet. It seemed very large indeed, possibly because there was no furniture in it. There were windows on the western and the northern sides. The garden could be seen through these on one side; and the eucalyptus trees on the other. Was it one of these that was struck by lightning? Simon had been standing under it. Instant death. The thought made me shiver.

I looked at the windowless wall on the southern side. The fireplace was on the left. Simon's favourite chair must have been kept by its side. The ceiling of the room was covered with cobwebs. Evergreen Lodge, that must have been a pretty little cottage once, was obviously in bad shape.

Mr Banerjee was humming a western tune. He stopped to light his pipe and asked, 'What do you usually play? Bridge, poker or rummy?'

Anik was about to sit down, having spread the rug and placed on the floor the stuff he was carrying, when we heard a noise. Someone wearing boots was walking about in one of the other rooms.

I looked at Anik. He had gone quite pale.

The footsteps stopped. Mr Banerjee suddenly took the pipe out of his mouth and yelled, 'Is anybody there?' All of us began to move towards the passage. Anik clutched at my sleeve.

We heard the footsteps again as we reached the passage. Then a man came out from one of the rooms on the right. He stopped short as his eyes fell on us. He was an Indian and, despite a heavy stubble on his face and an unkempt air, undoubtedly an educated gentleman.

'Hello!' he said.

None of us knew what to say.

The newcomer himself answered our unspoken question.

'My name is Venkatesh. I am a painter. Are you the owners of this house? Or have you come to buy it?'

Banerjee smiled and replied, 'Neither. We just happened to stroll in.'

'I see. I was wondering if I could have my studio in this house. I don't mind if it's going to pieces—you wouldn't know who the owner is, would you?'

'I am afraid not,' said Banerjee, 'but you might like to ask Col. Mercer. His house isn't far. Straight down the road and then to the left. Shouldn't take you more than five minutes.'

'Thank you,' said Mr Venkatesh and went out.

We heard the gate open and shut. Mr Banerjee broke into yet another guffaw and said, 'Mr Sengupta, that was not your Simon or some other ghost, was it?'

I had to laugh, 'You cannot expect to see the ghost so soon. It's only a quarter-past-five. And even if he was a ghost, he couldn't have been from the nineteenth century. Such a ghost would wear different clothes.'

We returned to the living-room. Anik sat down on the rug and said, 'You make me nervous with your flights of fancy. Come, let's play cards.'

'Light some of the candles first,' said Banerjee, 'dusk falls very quickly here.'

We lit two candles and placed them on the wooden floor after which we took turns drinking coffee from the flask. Then it became impossible for me to keep quiet. There was something I had been wondering about, which showed how obsessed I had become with the idea of a ghost. I said to Banerjee, 'You told us Col. Mercer had bought some of the furniture of this house. If he lives so close, couldn't we go and find out about a particular item?'

'What item?'

'A special kind of high-backed chair.'

Anik grew faintly annoyed at this and said, 'Why? Why should we suddenly start looking for a high-backed chair?'

'Well, you see—Mr Brown mentioned this chair in his diary. He said Simon loved to sit in this chair, even after his death. It used to be kept near that fireplace. So I thought if we could bring it here. . . .'

Anik cut me short, 'How will you bring it? In Mr Banerjee's Morris? Or do you suggest the three of us carry it all the way? Have you gone totally mad?'

Banerjee raised his hand at this point and silenced us both.

'That chair was not among the stuff Col. Mercer bought. I go to his house quite often. I would have seen it. As far as I know, he bought two book-cases, two oil paintings, a few flower vases and little knick-knacks for display—you know, art objects.'

I fell silent. Anik began shuffling the cards. Banerjee said, 'Let's play rummy. It should be more interesting if we played with stakes. Do you mind?'

'Not at all,' I replied, 'but I only have a small job in a bank. I cannot afford to lose much.'

The light outside had faded. We began to play. I have never been lucky at cards. Today was no exception. I would have felt happy to see Anik win for I knew he was feeling uncomfortable and nervous. But nothing of the kind happened. It was Mr Banerjee who appeared to have all the luck. He kept humming that western tune and continued to win every game. We were still busy playing when I heard a cat mew. This disappointed me further. A haunted house should not have even a cat living in it. I said as much to Mr Banerjee who laughed, and said, 'But it was a black cat—saw it going down the passage. Black cats go well with ghosts, don't they?'

We went on playing. Only once did we hear the raucous cry of a bird outside. There was no other noise to spoil our concentration.

It was about 6.30 p.m. Daylight had disappeared almost totally. I had finally been favoured by Lady Luck and had won two games, when we heard a strange noise. Someone was knocking at the door. All of us put our cards down and listened. Tap, tap, tap, tap.

Anik went paler then before. My own heart began trembling. But Mr Banerjee was clearly not one to be frightened easily. He broke the silence by letting out another yell, 'Who is it?'

The knock was repeated. Tap, tap, tap.

Banerjee leapt up to go and investigate. I caught the edge of his trousers and pulled him back. 'Don't go alone!' I whispered.

The three of us went out together. We went into the passage and looked towards our left. There was a male figure standing just outside the door, wearing a suit and carrying a stick. It was impossible to distinguish his features in the dark. Anik clutched at my sleeve even more tightly. I looked at him, and, somehow, my courage returned. In the meantime, Banerjee had taken a few steps forward. Suddenly we heard him exclaim, 'Oh, hello, Dr Larkin! What are you doing here?'

It was now possible to see the middle-aged European. He screwed up his blue eyes slightly behind the golden frame of his glasses and smiled genially, 'Saw your Morris parked outside. Then I saw candlelight from the windows. So I thought I'd drop in and find out what you're up to.'

Banerjee grinned. 'These two young friends of mine had this weird idea. They dragged me along to play cards here. Just for an adventure!'

'Very good, very good. Youth is the time for doing mad things. Old people like me would only sit at home and reminisce. Well, well. Have a good time!'

Dr Larkin raised his hand in farewell and walked away, tapping his stick on the ground.

Another false alarm. We returned to our game. I had lost about four rupees; now I was beginning to regain some of it. Even if Simon's ghost did not appear, today's outing would be worthwhile if I could manage to win something at cards.

I had been looking at my watch frequently. So I can tell exactly when the real thing happened. Mr Brown had mentioned that that was when Simon had died.

I was dealing the cards, Mr Banerjee was lighting his pipe and Anik had just slipped his hand into the packet of sandwiches when the look on his face changed and his whole body became rigid.

His eyes were looking at something beyond the room, in the passage. Banerjee and I automatically followed his gaze. What I saw made me hold my breath.

A pair of brilliant eyes stared at us from the dark passage. They had the pale green and yellow glow of phosphorus and did not flicker.

Mr Banerjee's right hand went into the vest pocket of his coat. And, in that instant, everything fell into place. My voice came back and I said, 'There's no need to take out your revolver, Mr Banerjee. It's that black cat!'

Anik seemed to relax at my words. Banerjee took his hand out of his pocket and said softly, 'How ridiculous!'

The phosphorescent eyes now came closer. As soon as it crossed the threshold, I knew I was right. It was indeed the black cat.

The cat stepped into the room and turned left. Our eyes were following every movement it made. We, too, turned our gaze to the left.

Then all of us made the same sound quite involuntarily. It was the sound one makes when profoundly startled. The reason for this was simple—while we had been sitting playing rummy, from somewhere had appeared a high-backed chair, covered in red velvet, and it had made its way to the fireplace.

Black as a moonless night, the cat walked silently towards the chair. It stopped for a moment, then jumped on to it neatly and curled up.

At that precise moment, I heard something that froze my blood. An invisible old man was laughing merrily in the room, punctuating his laughter with, 'Simon, Simon, Simon, Simon. . . .' There was also the sound of his clapping happily like a child.

A scream told me that Anik had fainted. And Mr Banerjee? He had gathered Anik in his arms and was sprinting towards the main door.

I followed him quickly. The cards, the candles, the food, the rug—everything was left behind. Beyond the door was the main compound and, further down, the gate. We ran like mad men and reached the Morris Minor parked just outside the gate. Thank goodness Bangalore did not have a lot of traffic. If it did, I shudder to think how many people would have been injured that evening by a speeding maniac.

Anik regained consciousness in the car, but did not utter a single word. Mr Banerjee was the first one to speak as we reached home. He snatched the glass of brandy from Anik's bearer, downed half of it at one go, and said hoarsely, 'So, Simon was a cat!'

I was in no condition to converse either. But I felt in my heart that he was right.

It had to be true. Mr Brown's Simon—that intelligent, whimsical, proud, devoted and affectionate being whom he loved so well— was the black cat we had seen today!

The Guest

Montu had heard his parents discuss, over the last few days, the possibility of a visit by his Dadu. His Chhoto Dadu, that is. He was Mother's Chhoto Mama.

Montu happened to be home when Dadu's letter arrived. Mother read it once, then exclaimed softly, 'Just imagine!' Then she raised her voice and called out to Father.

Father was out on the veranda, watching his shoes being repaired. He said, 'What is it?' without even raising his eyes.

Mother came out with the letter and said, 'Mama wants to come here.'

'Mama?'

'My Chhoto Mama. Don't you remember?'

Father turned his head this time, raising his eyebrows. 'Really? You mean he's still alive?'

'Here's a letter from him. Frankly, I didn't even know he could write!'

Father picked up his glasses from the arm of his chair and said, 'Let's have a look.'

After having read the single sheet of paper, he, too, said, 'Just imagine!'

Mother had sat down on a stool.

Montu could guess there was something wrong somewhere.

Father was the first to voice his doubts. 'Where do you think he got our address from? And who told him his niece had married a Suresh Bose and they lived here in Mahmudpur?'

Mother frowned a little, 'He might have learnt all that from Shetal Mama.'

'Who's Shetal Mama?'

'Oh God—can't you remember anything? He was a neighbour of all my uncles in Neelkanthapur. A very close friend of the family. You've seen him. He once bet someone that he could eat fifty-six *rajbhogs* at our wedding. What a laugh we all had!'

'Oh yes, yes. Now I remember.'

'He was very close to Chhoto Mama. I believe, in the beginning, Chhoto Mama used to write only to him.'

'Hasn't Shetal Babu visited us here?'

'Of course, he has. Why—he came to Ranu's wedding, didn't

he?'

'Yes, of course. But didn't your Chhoto Mama leave home and turn into a sanyasi?'

'Yes, that's what I thought. I can't figure out why he wants to visit us now.'

Father thought for a minute and said, 'There is no one else he could possibly visit, is there? All your other uncles and aunts are no more, and among the two cousins you have one is in Canada and the other in Singapore. So who is left here except you?'

'That's true,' said Mother, 'but how shall I recognize a man I have practically never seen? When he left home, I was only two years old and he must have been about seventeen.'

'Didn't you have a photograph in your old album?'

'What good is that? Mama was fifteen when that photo was taken. He must be at least sixty now.'

'Yes, I can see it's going to be a problem.'

'Well, we do have Binu's empty room which we could spare. But who knows what kind of food he likes to eat. . . .'

'I wouldn't worry about that. Surely he can have the same as we do?'

'No, not necessarily. If he has indeed become a sadhu he may want to eat only vegetarian food. That would mean making five different dishes every day!'

'The language he's used in the letter is quite normal. I mean, one wouldn't expect a sadhu to talk like this. Look, he's written the date in English and used other English words. Here it is—"unnecessarily"!'

'But he hasn't given us his address.'

'Yes, that's true.'

'And he says he's coming next Monday.'

It was obvious to Montu that both his parents were deeply worried.

It was certainly an odd situation. How could anyone accept a total stranger as an uncle?

Montu had heard of this Dadu barely once or twice before. He knew Dadu had left home even before leaving school.

In the beginning, he wrote to a few people occasionally; but after that there was no news of him. It was Montu's mother's belief that he had died. Montu had wondered a few times about this man and wished he would come back. But he knew that kind of thing happened only in stories. In stories, there were usually people who could recognize such a man. In this case, there was no one. Anyone could arrive and say he was his Dadu. There was no way of being sure.

Dadu was not going to stay for more than ten days. Having spent his childhood in a small town in Bangladesh, he now wanted to see a small town once again. There was no point in going to his own house in Neelkanthapur for no one lived there any more. So he wanted to visit Mahmudpur. There was at least a niece living there. Montu's father was a lawyer. Montu had an elder sister and a brother. The sister was married and his brother was in Kanpur, studying at the IIT.

His mother finished making all the arrangements by Sunday. A room on the first floor was made ready. A new sheet was spread on the bed, the pillows got new cases—even new soaps and towels were provided. Dadu was expected to make his own way to their house from the station. After that. . . well, one would simply have to wait and see. Father had said only this morning, 'Whether or not he's your real uncle, I just hope the man is civilized and well mannered. Otherwise the next ten days are going to be difficult indeed.'

'I don't like this at all,' grumbled Mother, 'no one knows the man from Adam, and yet we must put up with him. He didn't even send us his address, or we could have written, making some excuse to put him off!'

But Montu thought otherwise. They had not had a visitor for a long time. He was having his summer holidays now and was home all day. Although there were plenty of friends to play with—Sidhu, Aneesh, Rathin, Chhotka—it was such fun to have someone stay in the house. Who wanted to spend the whole day just with parents? And this whole business of is-he-real-or-not was so intriguing. Just like a mystery story. Suppose he did turn out to be an impostor and only Montu learnt the truth about him—how lovely that would be! He would unmask the man and be a hero.

Montu began loitering near the front door from ten-thirty on Monday morning. At a quarter-past-eleven he saw a cycle rickshaw making its way towards their house. Its passenger had a pot of sweets in his hands and a leather suitcase at his feet. One of his feet was resting on the suitcase.

This man was no sadhu. At least, he was not dressed like one. He was wearing trousers and a shirt. Mother had said he would be around sixty. But he looked younger than that. Most of his hair was still black and, though he did wear glasses, they did not appear to be thick ones.

The man paid the rickshawallah, put his suitcase down and, turning to Montu, said, 'Who are you?'

He was clean shaven, had a sharp nose and his eyes, though small, held a twinkle.

Montu picked up the suitcase and replied, 'My name is Satyaki Bose.'

'Which Satyaki are you? The disciple of Krishna? Or the son of Suresh Bose? Can you manage that heavy suitcase? It's got quite a lot of books.'

'Yes, I can.'

'Let's go in then.'

As they came into the veranda, Mother came forward and touched his feet. He handed the pot of sweets to her and said, 'You must be Suhasini?'

'Yes.'

'Your husband is a lawyer, isn't he? He must have gone out on work.'

'Yes.'

'Perhaps I shouldn't have come like this. . . I did feel hesitant. But then I told myself you wouldn't mind putting up with an old man. After all, it's only a matter of ten days. Besides, Shetal was so full of praise for you. But I do realize your problem. There is no way I can prove I am your real Mama. So I am not going to expect any special treatment. All you have to do is give an old man a roof over his head for ten days.'

Montu noticed his mother was giving the man occasional sidelong glances. Now she said, 'Would you like to have a bath?'

'Only if it's not inconvenient.'

'No, no, it's not inconvenient at all. Montu, do go and show him the bathroom upstairs. And. . . er. . . I didn't quite know what sort of food you like. . . .'

'I eat everything. I should be very happy to have whatever you choose to feed me. I mean it.'

'Do you go to school?' he asked Montu as they began going upstairs.

'Yes. Satyabhama High School. Class VII.'

At this point, Montu could not resist asking a question.

'Are you not a sadhu?'

'Sadhu?'

'Mother said you had become one.'

'Oh, I see. That was a long time ago. I'd gone to Haridwar straight from home. I didn't like being at home, so I left. I did, in fact, spend some time with a sadhu in Rishikesh. Then I began to get a bit restless, so I moved on. After that, I never went to a sadhu.'

At lunch, he ate everything with every appearance of enjoyment. He clearly did not object to non-vegetarian food for he ate both fish and eggs.

Montu could see his mother relax a little. But she did not once call him 'Mama', though Montu wanted very much to say, 'Chhoto Dadu!'

As he finished his meal and picked up the plate of yoghurt, Mother said, probably only to make conversation, 'You must have had to do without Bengali food for many years.'

The man laughed and said, 'I had some in Calcutta in the last two days. But before that. . . you'll find it difficult to believe if I tell you exactly how many years I've had to do without it.'

Mother said nothing more. Montu wanted to ask—'Why was this? Where did you use to live?' but stopped himself. If the man was a fraud, he should not be given the chance to cook up stories. One should wait until he came out with the information himself.

But the man did not say anything, either. If he had indeed spent more than forty years just roaming around, he ought to have had lots to talk about. Why, then, was he so quiet?

Montu was upstairs when he heard the sound of his father's car. Their guest had retired to bed with a book. Just before that, Montu had spent half an hour with him. He had called out when he saw Montu hovering outside his room.

'Why don't you come in, O disciple of Krishna? Let me show you something.'

Montu went in and stood by the bed.

'Do you know what this is?' asked the man.

'A copper coin.'

'Where from?'

Montu could not read what was written on the coin.

'This is called a *lepta*. It's a coin used in Greece. And what's this?'

Montu failed to recognize the second coin as well.

'This is one *kuru* from Turkey. And this is from Romania. It's called a *bani*. This coin here is from Iraq—a *fil*.'

Then he produced coins from at least ten different countries, which Montu had neither seen nor heard of before.

'All these are for you.'

Montu was amazed. What was the man saying? Aneesh's uncle also collected coins and he had explained to Montu that those who did so were called numismatists. But even he did not have so many different coins. Montu was sure of that.

'I knew I would find a grandson where I was going. So I decided to bring these coins for him.'

In great excitement, Montu ran down the stairs to show the coins to his mother. But he stopped short as he heard his father's voice. He was saying something about the man.

'. . .ten days! That's really too much. We must make it very clear to him that we cannot be fooled so easily. There is no need to give him any special treatment. I think he will leave soon enough if we don't go out of our way to be hospitable. And, of course, we must not take any risks. I spoke to Sudheer today and he gave me the same advice. Keep all your almirahs and cupboards locked. Montu can't be expected to guard the man all the time. He has his friends and he'll go out to play with them. I will go to work. That leaves just you and Sadashiv in the house. I know Sadashiv sleeps most of the time. And you, too, like to have a little rest in the afternoon, don't you?'

'There is something I'd like to tell you,' said Montu's mother.

'What?'

'This man does look a bit like my mother.'

'Do you think so?'

'Yes, he has the same nose and the same look in his eyes.'

'OK, OK, so I'm not saying he's not your Mama. But then, we don't know what this Mama is like. He hasn't had much education, he's led the life of a vagabond without any discipline. . . I tell you, I don't like this business at all.'

Montu went into the room as his father stopped speaking. He did not like what Father had been saying. Even in these few hours he had started to get quite fond of the newcomer. Well, perhaps Father would change his mind when he saw the coins.

'Did he really give you all these?'

Montu nodded.

'Did he say he had actually visited all these places?'

'No, he didn't say that.'

'That's something, then. Coins like these can be bought in Calcutta. There are dealers who sell them.'

The man came downstairs at around half-past-four and met Father.

'Your son and I have already made friends,' he said.

'Yes, so he's told me.'

Father shot a few quick glances at him, very much like Montu's mother.

'I can make friends with children quite easily. Perhaps they understand people like me better than adults.'

'Have you roamed around all your life?'

'Yes. I was never one for keeping still in one place.'

'We happen to be different. We can't afford to move about aimlessly. You see, we have a responsibility towards our family, children to look after, a job to keep. You never married, did you?'

'No.'

After a few minutes of silence, the man said, 'Suhasini might not remember this, but one of her great-grandfathers—my grandfather, that is—did a similar thing. He left home at thirteen. I returned at times for a few days. He did not come back at all.'

Montu saw his father turn towards Mother.

'Did you know this?'

'Maybe I did once, but can't remember anything now,' said Mother.

Something rather interesting happened after tea. Most of Montu's friends knew about the arrival of this strange relative, who might not be a real relative at all. Being very curious, all of them dropped in to have a look at Montu's Dadu. Dadu seemed very pleased to meet this group of boys, all about ten years old.

He reached for his walking stick and took them all out for a walk. They stopped under the kadam tree that stood in a field at some distance. Here they sat down on the ground for a chat.

'Do you know who the Tuaregs are?'

Everyone shook their heads.

'In the Sahara desert,' said Dadu, 'lives a nomadic tribe called the Tuaregs. They are a bold lot who don't stop at anything—even robbing and stealing. Let me tell you the story of a clever man who managed to escape from the clutches of these people.'

The boys listened to his story, utterly spellbound. Montu told his mother later, 'He told the story so well—we felt as though we could actually see it all happen.'

His father overheard him and said, 'This man appears to have read a lot. I have this vague feeling of having read a similar story in an English magazine.'

Montu had told his parents that he knew Dadu had brought a

lot of books in his suitcase, but he did not know if they were all story-books.

Three days passed. Nothing was stolen, the guest gave them no trouble, ate whatever he was given happily, made no demands and did not complain of anything. Some of Father's colleagues and friends began visiting, which was something they rarely did. Montu guessed they only came to take a look at this old man who might-be-real-and-might-not. His parents seemed to have accepted Dadu's presence. In fact, Montu heard his father say one day, 'Well, one must admit the man is quite simple in his ways. At least he is not trying to be over-friendly. But I fail to see how someone can survive like this. Obviously he left home only to avoid responsibilities. People like him are just parasites. He must have sponged on others all his life.'

Montu happened to call him 'Chhoto Dadu' once. Dadu only looked at him and smiled a little at this, but did not say anything.

Mother had not called him 'Mama' even once. When Montu mentioned this, she said, 'But he doesn't seem to mind! And what if he turns out to be an impostor? Think how embarrassing that would be!'

On the fourth day, their guest said he would go out. 'Isn't there a bus to Neelkanthapur?' he asked.

Father said, 'Yes, a bus leaves every hour from the main market.'

'Then I think I'll go and have a look at the place where I was born. I won't be back until evening.'

'You'll have lunch here, won't you?' asked Montu's mother.

'No. The sooner I leave the better. I'll have lunch somewhere on the way. Don't worry.'

He left before nine.

In the afternoon Montu could not resist the temptation any longer. Dadu's room was empty. Montu was dying to find out what kind of books his suitcase was filled with. Father was not at home and Mother was resting downstairs. Montu went into Dadu's room.

The suitcase was not locked. Clearly the man was not worried about theft.

Montu lifted the lid of the suitcase.

But there were no books inside. Not proper ones, anyway. They were notebooks, at least thirty different ones. About ten of these were bound in hard cover.

Montu opened one of them. There were things written in Bengali. The writing was neat and clear.

Montu climbed on to the bed with the notebook.

And had to climb down the next instant.

Mother had come upstairs, silently.

'What are you doing here, Montu? Are you messing about with his things?'

Montu put the notebook back into the suitcase like a good boy and came out.

'Go back to your own room. You shouldn't fiddle around with other people's belongings. Go read your own books.'

Their guest returned a little after six in the evening.

The same night, as they sat down to dinner, he made an announcement that took them all by surprise.

'I think I'll go back tomorrow,' he said, 'your hospitality is beyond reproach, but I simply cannot stay in one place for very long.'

Montu knew his parents were not too sorry to hear this. But he began to feel quite sad.

'Will you go to Calcutta from here?' asked Father.

'Yes, but not for long. I'll go somewhere else soon enough. I have always tried not to be a burden on anyone. I've been totally independent ever since I left home.'

Mother intervened at this point, 'Why do you have to call yourself a burden? We haven't been put to any inconvenience at all.'

But Montu knew that was not quite true for he had heard Father remark one day on how expensive things were and that it cost a good deal to provide for even one extra person.

This time both Montu and his father went to the station in their car to see their guest off.

Montu could feel the faint uneasiness that still lurked in his father's mind. He knew Father was still wondering, even when the train had actually gone, about whether the man who had stayed with them for these few days was indeed the relative he had claimed to be.

A week later, another old man arrived at their house—Montu's mother's Shetal Mama. Montu had seen him only once before, at his sister's wedding.

'Why, it's you, Shetal Mama! What brings you here?'

'The call of duty. Two duties, in fact, not just one. Why else do you think a man of my age would come travelling in a passenger train? I'm going to have lunch here with you—and that's a warning.'

'Of course you must lunch with us. What would you like to have? We get practically everything here—it's not like Calcutta.'

'Wait, wait. Let me finish doing what I came to do.' He took out a book from his shoulder bag. 'You haven't heard of this book, have you?'

Mother took the book, looked at it and said, 'Why, no!'

'I knew Pulin hadn't told you.'

'Pulin?'

'Your Chhoto Mama! The same man who spent five days here. You didn't even bother to find out his name, did you? Pulin wrote this book.'

'Did he?'

'But don't you read the papers? His name appeared only the other day. How many autobiographies of this kind are there in our literature, tell me?'

'But, but. . . this is a different name. . . .'

'Yes, it's a pseudonym. He's travelled all over the world, yet has stayed so humble.'

'The whole world?'

'I do believe our country has never seen a globe-trotter like Pulin Ray. And he did it all with his own money. He worked as a ship-mate, a coolie, a labourer in the timber trade, sold newspapers, ran a small shop, drove lorries—no work was too small for him. His experiences are stranger than fiction. He's been attacked by a tiger, bitten by a snake, escaped from a violent nomadic tribe in the Sahara, swum to the shore of Madagascar after a shipwreck. He left India in 1939 and made his way through Afghanistan. He says if you can come out of the confines of your house, then the whole world becomes your home. There is no difference then, between whites and blacks and great and small or the civilized and the barbaric.'

'But. . . why didn't he tell us all this?'

'Would you have believed him, insular and parochial as you are? You couldn't even decide whether he was genuine or fake, not once did you call him "Mama" and you expect him to have talked to you about himself?'

'Oh dear, dear. How awful! Could we not ask him to come back?'

'No. The bird has flown away. He said he hadn't yet been to Bali, so that is where he'll now try to go. He gave you this book. Or rather, he left it for your son. He said, "That boy is still a child. My book may make an impression on his young mind."

'But I haven't yet told you just how crazily he behaved. I told him so many times to stay for a few more days for I knew this book was bound to win an academy award. They pay ten thousand rupees these days. But he refused to listen to me. Do you know what he said? He said to me, "If some money does come my way, please give it to my niece in Mahmudpur. She looked after me very well." And then he actually put this down in writing. Here's the money—take it.'

Mother took the envelope from Shetal Mama and then, wiping away her tears, she said in a choked voice, 'Just imagine!'

The Tale of Shibu and the Monster

'Hey—Shibu! Come here!'

Shibu is often hailed thus by Phatik-da on his way to school.

Phatik-da alias the Loony Phatik.

He lives in a small house with a tin roof, just off the main crossing, where an old, rusted steamroller has been lying for the last ten years. Phatik-da tinkers with God knows how many different things all through the day. All Shibu knows is that he is very poor and that people say he went mad because he worked far too hard when he was a student. However, judging by some of the remarks Phatik-da makes, it seems to Shibu that few people have his intelligence.

But it is indeed true that most of what he says sounds perfectly crazy.

'I say—did you notice the moon last night? The left side seemed sort of extended, as though it had grown a horn!' Or, 'All the crows seem to have caught a cold. Haven't you heard the odd way they're cawing?'

Shibu is amused most of the times he hears Phatik-da talk like this but at times he does get annoyed. Getting involved in a totally meaningless and irrelevant conversation is a waste of time. So he does not always stop for a chat. 'Not today, Phatik-da, I shall come tomorrow,' he says and skips along to school.

He did not really want to stop today, but Phatik-da seemed more insistent than usual.

'You may come to harm if you do not listen to what I have to say.'

Shibu has heard that insane people sometimes make true predictions which a normal person would find impossible to do.

He certainly did not want to come to harm. So, a little nervous, he began walking towards Phatik-da's house.

Phatik was pouring coconut water into a hookah. 'Have you noticed Janardan Babu?' he said.

Janardan Babu was the new maths teacher in Shibu's school. He had arrived about ten days ago.

'I see him every day,' said Shibu, 'Why—I have maths today in the very first period!'

Phatik-da clicked his tongue in annoyance, 'Tch, tch. Seeing and observing are two different things, do you understand? Look, can you tell me how many little holes your belt has got? And how many buttons there are on your shirt? Try telling me without looking!'

Shibu failed to produce correct answers.

Phatik-da said, 'See what I mean? You've obviously never noticed these things although the shirt and the belt you're wearing are your own. Similarly, you have never noticed Janardan Babu.'

'What should have I noticed? Anything in particular?'

Phatik began smoking his hookah. 'Yes, say, his teeth. Have you noticed them?'

'Teeth?'

'Yes, teeth.'

'How could I have noticed them? He doesn't ever smile!'

This was true. Janardan Babu was not exactly cantankerous, but no other teacher was grave and sombre like him.

Phatik said, 'All right. Do try to notice his teeth if he does smile. And then come and tell me what you've seen.'

A strange thing happened. Janardan Babu laughed in Shibu's class the same day. It happened when, referring to some geometrical designs, Janardan Babu asked what had four arms. 'Gods, sir,' Shankar cried, 'the gods in heaven have four arms!' At this, Janardan Babu began chuckling noisily. Shibu's eyes went straight to his teeth.

Phatik was crushing some object with a heavy stone crusher when Shibu reached his house in the evening. He looked at Shibu and said, 'If this medicine I'm making has the desired effect, I'll be able to change colours like a chameleon.'

Shibu said, 'Phatik-da, I've seen them.'

'What?'

'Teeth.'

'Oh. What did they look like?'

'They were all right, except that they were stained with paan and two of them were longer than the others.'

'Which two?'

'By the side. About here.' Shibu pointed to the side of his mouth.

'I see. Do you know what those teeth are called?'

'What?'

'Canine teeth. Like dogs.'

'Oh.'

'Have you ever seen any other man with such large canine teeth?'

'Perhaps not.'

'Who has such teeth?'

'Dogs?'

'Idiot! Why just dogs? All carnivorous animals have large canine teeth. They use them to tear through the flesh and bones of their prey. Especially the wild animals.'

'I see.'

'And who else has them?'

Shibu began racking his brain. Who else? Who had teeth, anyway, except man and animals?

Phatik dropped a walnut and a pinch of pepper into the mixture he was making and said, 'You don't know, do you? Why, monsters have these teeth!'

Monsters? What had monsters to do with Janardan Babu? And why talk of monsters today? They were present only in fairy tales. They had large, strong teeth and their backs were bent. . . .

Shibu started.

Janardan Babu's back was definitely not straight. He stooped. Someone had mentioned it was because he had lumbago.

Large teeth, bent backs. . . what else did monsters have?

Red eyes.

Shibu had not had the chance to notice Janardan Babu's eyes for he always wore glasses that seemed to be tinted. It was impossible to tell whether the eyes behind those were red or purple or green.

Shibu was good at maths. LCM, HCF, Algebra, Arithmetic—he sailed through them all. At least, he did until a few days ago. During the time of his old maths teacher, Pearicharan Babu, Shibu had often got full marks. But he now began having problems, although he did try to pull himself together by constantly telling himself, 'It just cannot be. A man cannot be a monster. Not in these modern times. Janardan Babu is not a monster. He is a man.'

He was repeating these words silently in class when a disastrous thing happened.

Janardan Babu was writing something on the blackboard. Suddenly he turned around, took off his glasses and began polishing them absent-mindedly with one end of the cotton shawl he was wearing. He raised his eyes after a while and they looked straight into Shibu's. Shibu went cold with fear. The whites of Janardan Babu's eyes were not white at all. Both eyes were red. As red as a tomato. After this, Shibu got as many as three sums wrong.

Shibu seldom went home straight after school. He would first go to the grounds the Mitters owned and play with the mimosa plants. After gently tapping each one to sleep, he would go to Saraldeeghi: the large, deep pond. There he would try playing ducks and drakes with broken pieces of earthenware. If he could make a piece skip on the water more than seven times, he would break the record Haren had set. On the other side of Saraldeeghi was a brick kiln. Hundreds of bricks stood in huge piles. Shibu usually spent about ten minutes here, doing gymnastics, and then went diagonally across the field to reach his house.

Today, the mimosa plants seemed lifeless. Why? Had someone come walking here and stepped on them? But who could it be? Not many people came here.

Shibu did not feel like staying there any longer. There was something strange in the air. A kind of foreboding. It seemed to be getting dark already. And did the crows always make such a racket—or had something frightened them today?

Shibu took himself to Saraldeeghi. But, as soon as he had put his books down by the side of the pond, he changed his mind about staying. Today was not the day for playing ducks and drakes. In fact, today was not the day for staying out at all. He must get back home quickly. Or else. . . something awful might happen.

A huge fish raised its head from the water and then disappeared again with a loud splash.

Shibu picked up his books. It was very dark under the peepul tree that stood at a distance. He could see the bats hanging from it. It would soon be time for them to start flying. Phatik-da had offered to explain to him one day why bats' brains did not haemorrhage despite their hanging upside down.

Shibu began walking towards his house.

He saw Janardan Babu near the brick kiln.

There was a mulberry tree about twenty yards from where the bricks lay.

A couple of lambs were playing near it and Janardan Babu was watching them intently. He carried a book and an umbrella in his hand.

Shibu held his breath and quickly hid behind a pile of bricks. He removed the top two in the pile and peered through the gap.

He noticed Janardan Babu raise his right hand and wipe his mouth with the back of it.

Clearly, the sight of the lambs had made his mouth water, or he would not have made such a gesture.

Then, suddenly, Janardan Babu dropped the book and the umbrella and, crouching low, picked up one of the lambs. Shibu could hear the lamb bleat loudly. He also heard Janardan Babu laugh. That was enough.

Shibu wanted to see no more. He slipped away but, in his haste to climb over the next pile of bricks, tripped and fell flat on the ground.

'Who's there?'

Shibu was going to pick himself up somehow when he found Janardan Babu coming towards him, having put the lamb back on the grass.

'Who is it? Shibram? Are you hurt? What are you doing here?'

Shibu could not speak. His mouth had gone dry. But he certainly wanted to ask Janardan Babu what *he* was doing there. Why did he carry a lamb in his arms? Why was his mouth watering?

Janardan Babu stretched out a hand. 'Here, I'll help you up.'

But Shibu managed to get to his feet without help.

'You live nearby, don't you?'

'Yes, sir.'

'Is that red house yours?'

'Yes, sir.'

'I see.'

'Let me go, sir.'

'Goodness—is that blood?'

Shibu looked at his legs. His knee was slightly grazed and a few drops of blood oozed from the wound. Janardan Babu was staring at the blood, his glasses glistening.

'Let me go, sir.'

Shibu picked up his books.

'Listen, Shibram.'

Janardan Babu laid a hand on Shibu's back. Shibu could hear his heart beat loudly—like a drum.

'I am glad I found you alone. There is something I wanted to ask you. Are you finding it difficult to follow the maths lessons? Why did you get all those simple sums wrong? If you have any problem, you can come to my house after school. I will give you special coaching. It's so easy to get full marks in maths. Will you come?'

Shibu had to step back to shake off Janardan Babu's hand from his back. 'No, sir,' he gulped, 'I'll manage on my own. I'll be all right tomorrow.'

'OK. But do tell me if there's a problem. And don't be frightened of me. What is there to be frightened of, anyway? Do you think I'm a monster that I'll eat you alive? Ha, ha, ha, ha. . . .'

Shibu ran all the way to his house. He found Uncle Hiren in the living-room. Uncle Hiren lived in Calcutta. He was terribly fond of fishing. Very often he came over on weekends and went fishing at Saraldeeghi with Shibu's father.

They would probably go again this time for he saw certain preparations had been made. But Uncle Hiren had also brought a gun. There was some talk of shooting ducks. Shibu's father could handle guns, although his aim was not as good as Uncle Hiren's.

Shibu went straight to bed after dinner. He had no doubt now that Janardan Babu was a monster. Thank God Phatik-da had already warned him. If he hadn't, who knows what might have happened at the brick kiln? Shibu shivered and stared out of the window.

Everything shone in the moonlight. He had gone to bed early because he had to rise early the next morning to study for his exams. Normally, he could not sleep with the light on. But today, if the moonlight was not so good, he would have left it on. He felt too frightened today to sleep alone in the dark. The others had not yet finished having dinner.

Shibu was still looking out of the window, half asleep, when the sight of a man made him sit up in terror.

The man was heading straight for his window. He stooped slightly and wore glasses. The glasses gleamed in the moonlight.

Janardan Babu!

Shibu's throat felt parched once more.

Janardan Babu tiptoed his way to the open window, Shibu clutched his pillow tight.

Janardan Babu looked around for a bit and then said somewhat hesitantly, in a strange nasal tone, 'Shibram? Are you there?'

Good God—even his voice sounded different! Did the monster in him come out so openly at night?

He called again, 'Shibram!'

This time Shibu's mother heard him from the veranda and shouted, 'Shibu! There's someone outside calling for you. Have you gone to sleep already?'

Janardan Babu vanished from the window. A minute later, Shibu heard his voice again, 'Shibram had left his geometry book among the bricks. Since it's Sunday tomorrow, I thought I'd come and return it right away. He may need it. . . .'

Then he lowered his voice and Shibu failed to catch what he said. But, after a while, he heard his father say, 'Yes, if you say so. I'll send him over to your house. Yes, from tomorrow.'

Shibu did not utter a word, but he screamed silently, 'No, no, no! I won't go, I won't! You don't know anything! He's a monster! He'll gobble me up if I go to his house!'

The next morning Shibu went straight to Phatik-da's house. There was such a lot to tell.

Phatik-da greeted him warmly, 'Welcome! Isn't there a cactus near your house? Can you bring me a few bits and pieces from that plant? I've thought of a new recipe.'

Shibu whispered, 'Phatik-da!'

'What?'

'Remember you told me Janardan Babu was a monster. . .?'

'Who said that?'

'Why, you did!'

'Of course not. You did not notice my words, either.'

'How?'

'I said try to notice Janardan Babu's teeth. Then you came back and said he had large canine teeth. So I said I had heard monsters had similar teeth. That does not necessarily mean Janardan Babu is a monster.'

'Isn't he?'

'I did not say he was.'

'So what do I do now?'

Phatik-da got up, stretched lazily and yawned. Then he said, 'Saw your uncle yesterday. Has he come fishing again? Once a Scotsman called McCurdy killed a tiger with a fishing rod. Have you heard that story?'

Shibu grew desperate, 'Phatik-da, stop talking nonsense. Janardan Babu is really a monster. I know it. I have seen and heard such a lot!

Then he told Phatik-da everything that had happened over the last two days. Phatik grew grave as he heard the tale. In the end he said, 'Hmm. So what have you decided to do?'

'You tell me what I should do. You know so much.'

Phatik-da bent his head deep in thought.

'We have got a gun in our house,' said Shibu suddenly. This annoyed Phatik.

'Don't be silly. You can't kill a monster with a gun. The bullet would make an about turn and hit the same person who pulled the trigger.'

'Really?'

'Yes, my dear boy.'

'So what do I do?' Shibu said again, 'what's going to happen, Phatik-da? My father wants me to start from today. . . .'

'Oh, shut up. You talk too much.'

After about two minutes of silence Phatik-da suddenly said, 'Have to go.'

'Where?'

'To Janardan Babu's house.'

'What?'

'I must look at his horoscope. I am not sure yet. But his horoscope is bound to tell me something. And I bet he has it hidden somewhere in his house.'

'But. . . .'

'Wait a minute. Listen to the plan first. We will both go in the afternoon. It's Sunday today, so the man will be home. You will go to the back of his house and call him. Tell him you've come for your maths lesson. Then keep him there for a few minutes. Say anything you like, but don't let him go back into the house. I will try to find the horoscope in the meantime. And then you shall run away from one side and I from the other.'

'And then?' asked Shibu. He did not like the plan much, but Phatik-da was his only hope.

'Then you'll come to my house in the evening. By then I will have seen his horoscope. If he is indeed a monster, I know what to do about it. And if he's not, there is no cause for anxiety, is there?'

Shibu turned up again at Phatik's house soon after lunch. Phatik-da came out about five minutes later and said, 'My cat has started to take snuff. There are problems everywhere!'

Shibu noticed Phatik-da was carrying a pair of torn leather gloves and the bell of a bicycle. He handed the bell to Shibu and said, 'Ring this bell if you feel you're in danger. I will come and rescue you.'

Janardan Babu lived at the far end of the town. He lived all alone, without even a servant. It was impossible to tell from outside that a monster lived there.

Shibu and Phatik made their separate ways to the house. As he began to find his way to the back of the house, Shibu's throat started to go dry again. What if, when he was supposed to call out to Janardan Babu, his voice failed him?

There was a high wall behind the house, a door in the middle of the wall, and a guava tree near the door. Several wild plants and weeds grew around the tree.

Shibu went slowly forward. He must hurry or the whole plan would be upset.

He leant against the guava tree for a bit of moral support and was about to call out to Janardan Babu when he was startled by the sound of something shuffling near his feet. Looking down, he saw a chameleon glide across the ground and disappear behind a bush. There were some white objects lying near the bush. He picked up a fallen twig and parted the bush with it to take a closer look. Oh no! The white objects were bones! But whose bones were they? Dogs? Cats? Or lambs?

'What are you looking at, Shibram?'

The same nasal voice.

A cold shiver went down Shibu's spine. He turned around quickly and saw Janardan Babu standing at his back door, watching him with a queer look in his eyes.

'Have you lost something?'

'No, sir I... I....'

'Were you coming to see me? Why did you come to the back door? Well, do come in.'

Shibu tried retracing his steps, but discovered one of his feet was caught in a creeper.

'I have got a cold, I'm afraid,' said Janardan Babu, 'I've had it since yesterday. I went to your house. You were sleeping.'

Shibu knew he must not run away so soon. Phatik-da could not have finished his job. He might even get caught. Should he ring the bell?

No, he was not really in danger, was he? Phatik-da might get annoyed if he rang it unnecessarily.

'What were you looking at so keenly?'

Shibu could not think of a suitable answer. Janardan Babu came forward.

'This place is very dirty. It's better not to come from this side.

My dog brings bones from somewhere and leaves them here. I have often thought of scolding him, but I can't. You see, I'm very fond of animals. . . .'

Again, he wiped his mouth with the back of his hand.

'Come on in, Shibram. We must do something about your maths.

Shibu could not wait any longer. 'Not today, sir. I'll come back tomorrow,' he said and ran away.

He did not stop running until he came to the old and abandoned house of the Shahas, quite a long way away. Goodness—he would never forget what had happened today. He didn't know he had such a lot of courage!

But what had Phatik-da learnt from the horoscope? Shibu went to his house again in the evening. Phatik-da shook his head as soon as he saw Shibu.

'Problems,' he said, 'great problems.'

'Why, Phatik-da? Didn't you find the horoscope?'

'Yes, I did. Your maths teacher is undoubtedly a monster. And a Pirindi monster, at that. These were full fledged monsters three hundred and fifty generations ago. But their genes were so strong that even now it's possible to find a half-monster among them. No civilized country, of course, has full monsters nowadays. You can find some in the wild parts of Africa, Brazil and Borneo. But half-monsters are in existence elsewhere in very small numbers. Janardan Babu is one of them.'

'Then where is the problem?' Shibu's voice trembled a little. If Phatik-da could not help, who could?

'Didn't you tell me this morning you knew what to do?'

'There is nothing that I do not know.'

'Well, then?'

Phatik-da grew a little grave. Then, suddenly, he asked, 'What's inside a fish?'

Oh no, he had started talking nonsense again. Shibu nearly started weeping, 'Phatik-da, we were talking about monsters. What's that got to do with fish?'

'Tell me!' Phatik yelled.

'Intestines?' Phatik's yell had frightened Shibu.

'No, no, you ass. With such retarded knowledge, you couldn't even put a buckle on a buck ! Listen. I heard this rhyme when I was only two-and-a-half. I still remember it:

Man or animal whichever thou art
Thy life beats in thy own heart
A monster's life lies in the stomach of a fish
Cannot kill him easily, even if you wish.'

Of course! Shibu, too, had read about this in so many fairy tales.

A monster's life always lay hidden inside a fish. He should have known.

'When you met him this afternoon, how did he seem?' asked Phatik.

'He said he had a cold and a slight fever.'

'Yes, it all fits in,' Phatik's eyes began to sparkle with enthusiasm, 'It has to. His life's in danger, you see. As soon as the fish is out of water, he gets fever. Good!'

Then he came forward and clutched Shibu by the collar. 'Perhaps it's not too late. I saw your uncle go back to your house with a huge fish. I thought Janardan Monster's life might be in it. Now that you've told me about his illness I'm beginning to feel more sure. We must cut open that fish.'

'But how can we do that?'

'We can, with your help. It won't be easy, but you've got to do it. If you don't, I dread to think what might happen to you!'

About an hour later Shibu arrived at Phatik's house dragging the huge fish by the cord he had tied around it.

'Hope no one saw you?'

'No,' Shibu panted, 'Father was having a bath. Uncle was having a massage and Mother was inside. It took me some time to find a cord. God—is it heavy!'

'Never mind, you'll grow muscles!'

Phatik-da took the fish inside. Shibu sat marvelling at Phatik's knowledge of things. If anyone could rescue him from the danger he was in, it could only be Phatik-da. Dear God—do let him find what he was looking for.

Ten minutes later, Phatik came out and stretched a hand towards Shibu, 'Here. Take this. Keep it with you all the time. Put it under your pillow at night. When you go to school, keep it in your left pocket. If you hold it in your hand, the monster is totally powerless and if you crush it into a powder he'll be dead. In my view, you need not crush it because some Pirindi monsters have been known to turn into normal men at the age of fifty-four. The age of your Janardan Monster is fifty-three years, eleven months and twenty- six days.'

Shibu finally found the courage to look down at what he was holding. A small, slightly damp, white stone lay on his palm, winking in the light of the moon that had just risen.

Shibu put it in his pocket and turned to go. Phatik called him back, 'Your hands smell fishy, wash them carefully. And pretend not to know anything about anything!'

The next day, Janardan Babu sneezed once just before entering the class and, almost immediately, knocked his foot against the threshold and damaged his shoe. Shibu's left hand, at that precise moment, was resting in his left pocket.

After a long time, Shibu got full marks in maths that day.

The Citation

For about a minute, no one among those present at the meeting of the Shatadal Club could utter a word when their secretary, Pranabesh Datta, dropped the bomb.

It was an emergency meeting, being held just five days before the Bengali New Year. Pranabesh did not tell anyone why he wanted them there. All his note said was there was a crisis and a meeting of the members was essential.

Jayanta Sarkar was the first to speak.

'Are you absolutely sure?' he asked.

'Look at this letter if you don't believe me,' said Pranabesh. 'Here it is—Samar Kumar himself signed the letter. What better surety could you want?'

The letter made its rounds among the members and returned to Pranabesh.

No, there was no doubt. The signature was indeed Samar Kumar's. Thanks to the film magazines, there were very few people who had not seen that famous signature before.

'Did he give a reason?' asked Naren Guin.

'Shooting,' said Pranabesh, 'outdoor shooting in Kalimpong. Came up most unexpectedly. So he's very sorry, but. . . .'

'Strange!' exclaimed Shantanu Rakshit. 'How could the man simply turn his "yes" into a "no"?'

Naren Guin remarked, 'I told you in the beginning not to get involved with film-stars. They never keep their word.'

'What a catastrophe!' said Jayanta. He liked being dramatic.

'Could you not think of an alternative arrangement?' asked Chunilal Sanyal, who taught Bengali at the local Vivekananda Institute.

'What alternative arrangement do you expect us to make, Chuni-da, at this last minute?' asked Pranabesh. 'Besides, I have already tried everything. I spoke twice to Nimu in Calcutta. Told him to get hold of someone else—it didn't matter if it was a singer or dancer or painter or sportsman. We've done all the publicity possible for our felicitation, we've got the citation written. We've held such felicitations regularly for the last ten years, it has become our tradition and we cannot do without it. But Nimu said, no chance. Seven felicitations have been arranged in Calcutta alone.

There isn't much of a choice in the matter of candidates, is there? All the well known people are already engaged. Paltu Banerjee is being felicitated twice on the same day. But he can manage it because both are in Calcutta. Shyamal Shome, Rajat Manna, Harabilash Gupta, Debraj Saha—everyone's been booked by some club or the other.'

'The citation you just mentioned,' said Indranath Ray, who happened to be the oldest among those present, 'well—how can you use a citation meant for Samar Kumar for someone else?'

'You haven't seen the citation, have you, Indra-da?'

'No.'

'That explains it. You see, it doesn't talk about films or film-stars. It begins with Dear Artist. So it could be anyone.'

'May I see it now?'

Pranabesh took out a rolled parchment from a drawer.

'It took Monotosh a whole week to write it by hand. The language used was Chuni-da's.'

Chunilal coughed softly, a polite reminder of his presence.

'"We look at you, and our wonder knows no bounds". . . why, I seem to have heard this one before!'

Indranath had unrolled the paper. His brows were puckered in a frown, his eyes fixed on Chunilal.

'So you have,' said Chunilal. 'Sir Jagadish Bose had once read an address at a reception given in honour of Tagore. This was the opening sentence. The speech had been written by Sarat Chandra.'

'And you just lifted it?'

'It's only a quotation, Indra-da. Surely no one can object to that? It's a famous line—every educated Bengali would recognize it. Besides, it makes such a good introduction.'

'How many other quotations have you got in this citation?'

'That's the only one. The rest is totally original.'

Indranath dropped the roll on the table, yawned and said, 'Well, then—you must decide on the next course of action.'

Akshay Bagchi was a rather grave and sombre man of about fifty. He now lit a cigarette and said, 'If you can give up the idea of having someone very well known, I can suggest a name. Since you must felicitate someone, you may wish to think about it.'

'Yes, it's obvious we can't get anyone all that well known,' said Pranabesh, 'but, at the same time, we can't get hold of any Tom, Dick or Harry, can we? The person you have in mind ought to have made some kind of fruitful contribution.'

'Yes,' said Akshay Bagchi, 'he has indeed.'

'Who are you talking about?' Pranabesh grew slightly impatient.

'Haralal Chakravarty.'

Silence fell. Clearly, nobody had heard the name before. Indranath Ray was the only person who frowned a little and then said, 'Haralal Chakravarty? You mean the illustrator?'

'Yes, that's right,' Akshay Bagchi nodded, 'we used to see his illustrations quite often in story-books when we were small. Most of these were mythological in nature. He was once very popular. He even used to do illustrations for magazines. I think felicitating him is a better idea than doing something for people who are already quite successful.'

'Not a bad idea at all,' Indranath sat up, 'I quite agree with Akshay. Now I can recall those illustrations clearly. The edition of the *Mahabharat* we had at home had pictures drawn by Chakravarty.'

'Were they really good?' asked Jayanta Sarkar. 'I mean, this man in whose honour we'll arrange a reception—does he deserve it?'

This time Naren Guin said, 'Yes, I remember now. We had a copy of *Hatemtai*, and the illustrations were signed H. Chakravarty.'

'Any good?' Jayanta wanted to know.

'Yes, certainly stronger than the average kitsch,' said Naren and went out of the room. It was time for a smoke, but not where so many older people were present.

'Whether the pictures he drew were of a high standard or not is not really important,' said Indranath, 'what matters is that he worked continuously over a long period of time. He could not have done so if there was no demand for his work. So he must have known a certain amount of popularity. But, as Akshay just said, true recognition never came his way. Our Shatadal Club can now give him that.'

'And the most important thing,' said Akshay Bagchi, 'also, if you like, the most convenient thing, is that he lives in this town. You don't have to run around Calcutta to get him.'

'Good heavens!' said Pranabesh, 'we didn't know that!'

The whole idea was so new that everyone started talking at once.

'But where does he live?' Pranabesh looked at Akshay Bagchi enquiringly.

'I know the place,' said Bagchi. 'If you go to the crossing at the end of Kumorpara and turn left, you will soon come to

Dr Manmatha's house. He told me once that Haralal Chakravarty was his neighbour.'

'Do you know Haralal?'

'Well, I saw him once at the Mukherjees' about five years ago; and that too, only for a few seconds. I think he was painting something for their family.'

'But. . . .' Pranabesh still sounded a little doubtful.

'But what?'

'No, I mean, we shall have to announce his name if he accepts our proposal.'

'So what?'

'If no one has heard his name, then. . . .'

'Then they'll wonder who on earth he is. Is that what you're worried about?'

'Exactly.'

'Don't worry. Just add "Distinguished Doyen of Illustrators" before his name. Those who haven't heard his name will get to know of it this way. Isn't that one of the aims of our club?'

'Yes, rescuing men from oblivion,' said Jayanta. 'A very good idea.'

Everyone agreed. The idea revived their waning enthusiasm and they had to admit that, if anything, such a step would only enhance the prestige of the club. What they were going to arrange was not just an ordinary reception, it was their commitment to society. This could well become their policy in the future: to bring into the limelight once more, all those gifted sons of Bengal who were languishing in the darkness.

It was decided that Akshay Bagchi would call on Haralal Chakravarty, together with Pranabesh and some other members of the club. They would have to go the very next day for there was no time left. If Mr Chakravarty agreed, the name of Samar Kumar would have to be replaced on all the posters.

And, of course, one must not forget to add the words, 'Distinguished Doyen of Illustrators' before his name.

The pink house by the side of the road had a name plate proclaiming 'Haralal Chakravarty, Artist'. This made their job a lot simpler. Akshay Bagchi was right. Dr Manmatha lived only two houses away. Akshay Bagchi and Pranabesh were accompanied by Chunilal Sanyal.

They opened the gate and went in.

There were a few flower beds in front of the house and an amra tree.

The surroundings were clean, but showed no sign of affluence. Obviously, Haralal Chakravarty had missed out not just on recognition, but also on earning a comfortable living.

There was no need to knock. Their arrival had probably been seen from a window. An elderly gentleman, wearing glasses and sporting a pair of grey moustaches, opened the door. He was clad in a dhoti draped like a lungi, and a vest with sleeves.

Akshay Bagchi greeted him with a *namaskar* and went forward.

'You may not remember, but we met briefly about five years ago in Dharani Mukherjee's house.'

'I see. . . .'

'We. . .er. . . wanted to talk to you about something,' said Pranabesh, 'could we come in?'

'Yes, of course.'

The living-room was to the left. There were a few framed paintings on the wall. At the bottom of each one, clearly visible, was the painter's signature: H. Chakravarty. Except for these, the room was devoid of any trimmings. The visitors sat on wooden chairs and a wooden bench.

'We have come from the Shatadal Club,' began Pranabesh.

'Shatadal Club?'

'Yes. It's a rather well-known club in this area. Barada Babu— you know, Barada Majumdar, M.L.A—is our President.'

'I see.'

'We have a function every year to celebrate the first of *Baisakh*. There's usually music, a one-act play and a reception given in honour of someone who has made a significant contribution to our art and culture. This time we thought of you. I mean—you live in the same town, and yet not many people know about you, so. . . .'

'Hmm. The first of *Baisakh*, did you say?'

'Yes.'

'But that's only four days away.'

'Yes. Yes, I realize it's late. There were,' Pranabesh coughed, 'a few difficulties.'

'I see. But what does this reception really entail?'

'Oh, nothing much. We'll come and collect you at around six in the evening. Your reception will be the last item in our function. A citation will be presented, Mr Bagchi here will say a few words about you and, in the end, if you yourself could give a short speech, we'd all be very pleased. The whole thing would be over by 9 p.m.'

'Hmm.'

'Your family—I mean, your wife. . . .'

'She suffers from arthritis.'

'Oh. But if there's someone else you'd like to invite. . . .'

'Let me think about it.'

At this point, Akshay Bagchi raised a different issue.

'We would like an introduction about yourself.'

'All right. I shall write a few facts down. Please have it collected.'

'I shall come and collect it myself,' said Pranabesh.

The three members of the Shatadal Club rose to take their leave.

Haralal Chakravarty appeared to have finally grasped the significance of their proposal. His eyes seemed moist.

The Shatadal Club lived up to its reputation of being supremely efficient in organizing the New Year celebrations. The reception for Haralal Chakravarty was a resounding success. Those who had indeed asked, 'Who on earth is this man?' before the reception, ceased to raise queries afterwards.

Everyone learnt about how, after graduating from the Government Art School, Haralal had had to struggle to establish himself as a professional artist. Fifty-six books had been published in a mythological series that contained his illustrations, in addition to a large number of children's magazines that also published his pictures. Rai Bahadur L.K. Gupta had given him a silver medal. Finally, at the age of sixty-two, arthritis affected his right thumb, forcing him to retire.

When it was his turn to speak, Haralal expressed his appreciation for the efforts made by the Shatadal Club and said just one thing about himself: 'I do not deserve such praise.' His humility made a deep impression on the audience.

As he climbed into the car of Nihar Chowdhury, the Vice President of the club, carrying a garland and the citation, duly framed, it was difficult to tell who was more moved by the whole experience—Haralal himself or the members of the club.

Indranath had the last word.

'My dear Pranabesh,' he said, 'I suggest you give a reception for Bagchi next year. After all, wasn't it he who saved the prestige of the club this time?'

The next day, someone left a packet in the club office. It was addressed to Pranabesh. He opened it and found, to his utter surprise, the framed citation given to Haralal the day before.

It was accompanied by a note that said:

To the Secretary,
Shatadal Club.
Dear Sir,
I could see when you called on me the other day that you were indeed in a difficult situation and had decided to give a reception for Haralal Chakravarty simply because there was no other alternative. I am thrilled to have been able to play the role of your saviour. But I feel obliged to return the citation for two reasons. First, I can see that it may be used quite easily next year for a different person. All you need to do is change the name and the date. And, secondly, it is true that I do not really deserve it. The artist Haralal Chakravarty died three years ago in this town. He was my elder brother. I work as a clerk in the post office in Kanthi. I happened to be here on a week's holiday.
Yours truly,
Rasiklal Chakravarty.

Anukul

'He's got a name, hasn't he?' Nikunja Babu asked.

'Oh yes, he has.'

'What is it?'

'Anukul.'

A robot supplying agency had opened in Chowringhee about six months ago. Nikunja Babu had always wanted a mechanical servant. His business had lately been doing rather well, so he could now afford to fulfil his little desire.

Nikunja Babu looked at the robot. It was an android, which meant that it looked exactly like an ordinary human being although it was really a machine. It was reasonably good looking—appeared to be a young man of about twenty-two.

'What kind of work will this robot do?' Nikunja Babu asked.

The man behind the counter lit a cigarette and replied, 'He'll do more or less everything an ordinary servant does. The only thing he doesn't know is how to cook. Apart from that, he can do the washing and cleaning, make the beds, make tea, open doors and windows—just about everything. But don't send him out. He can manage everything in the house, but he couldn't go and do your shopping. And. . .er. . .you must talk to him politely. He expects one to say "please" and "thank you".'

'He's not ill tempered, I hope?'

'No, no. You'll find him troublesome only if you raise your hand. Our robots cannot stand physical assault.'

'There is no likelihood of that. But suppose someone gives him a slap. What will he do?'

'He will take revenge.'

'How?'

'He might use the middle finger of his right hand. He can give a high voltage electric shock with that finger.'

'Can that result in death?'

'Certainly. And the law cannot do anything about this for a robot cannot be punished like a normal human being. But I must say there has never been a case like this so far.'

'Does he sleep at night?'

'No. Robots don't sleep.'

'What does he do then all night?'

'He just sits quietly in the corner. Robots don't lack patience.'

'Does he have a mind?'

'Robots can, at times, feel and understand things that a human being can't. But then, not all robots are so sensitive. It's a matter of luck, really. Only time can tell how gifted a robot is.'

Nikunja Babu turned towards the robot and said, 'Anukul, you have no objection to working for me, have you?'

'Why should I object?' said Anukul in a perfectly normal voice.

He was wearing a blue striped shirt and black shorts. His neatly brushed hair had a side parting, his complexion was fair, his teeth bright and clean and his mouth parted in a half smile. His whole appearance inspired confidence.

'Come along then.'

Nikunja Babu's Maruti van was waiting outside. He paid for Anukul by cheque and came out with him. Anukul's movements were no different from those of an ordinary man.

Nikunja Babu lived in Salt Lake. He was not married. A few of his friends often dropped in to play cards in the evening. They had already been told about the arrival of a mechanical servant. Nikunja Babu had, in fact, done a bit of research before acquiring Anukul. Quite a number of people in the upper classes of Calcutta had already got robots to work for them. Mr Mansukhani, Girija Bose, Pankaj Datta Roy, Mr Chhabria—everyone said they were very satisfied and that their servant gave them no trouble at all.

'Our Jeevanlal does everything immediately, just as he's told,' said Mr Mansukhani, 'I'm convinced he's not just a machine—he must have a real brain and a heart!'

Nikunja Babu formed a similar opinion within seven days. Anukul's way of working was just perfect. He seemed to have grasped fully the logical link between one task and another. If asked whether the water for his bath was ready, he would not only bring the water immediately but would also provide a soap and a towel for his master. He would then get his master's clothes and shoes and everything else that might be needed. And he did everything so willingly that there was no question of being impolite to him.

Nikunja Babu's friends took a little time to get used to Anukul, especially Vinay Pakrashi. He often spoke rather rudely to his own servants and, on one occasion, he happened to address Anukul a little harshly. Anukul did not lose his calm. 'If you are rude to me, old boy,' he said quietly, 'I am going to be rude to you!'

Vinay Babu did not make the same mistake again.

Nikunja Babu formed a very good relationship with Anukul. Anukul began to do things for him without being told. His master found this surprising, but recalled that the man in the robot supplying agency had indeed told him that certain robots had something akin to a brain and could think. Anukul must belong to that category.

But what was most difficult to believe was that Anukul did not sleep at all. He was so much like a real human being, surely he slept a little at night? Nikunja Babu decided to check this out one night. Just as he peeped into Anukul's room, he heard Anukul say, 'Do you want anything, sir?'

Embarrassed, Nikunja Babu said, 'No,' and retraced his steps.

It was possible to converse with Anukul on a wide range of subjects. He appeared to know a lot about sports, cinema, theatre, literature. . . practically everything one could think of. Nikunja Babu marvelled at the extent of his knowledge and the skill of the robot makers.

But all good things come to an end.

Nikunja Babu happened to make a few wrong moves in his business and, within a year of Anukul's arrival, his earnings grew considerably less. He continued to pay the hire charges for Anukul, which was two thousand rupees a month. But if his financial situation did not improve, who knew when he would have to stop? The robot supplying agency had told him Anukul would be taken away if the monthly payment was not made. Clearly, Nikunja Babu would have to be very careful with his money.

But something happened at this time to upset all his plans.

One fine day, Nikunja Babu's uncle turned up. 'I was getting rather bored in Chandan Nagar all by myself—so I thought I'd come and spend a few days with you,' he said.

This uncle of Nikunja Babu—called Nibaran Banerjee—came occasionally to stay with his nephew. Nikunja Babu had lost his father many years ago and Nibaran was the only uncle left among the three he had had. An irascible old man, he was reported to have made a lot of money as a lawyer, although that was impossible to tell from the way he lived. The truth was that the man was extremely stingy.

'You're very welcome to spend a few days here, Uncle,' said Nikunja Babu, 'but I must tell you something right away. I have now got a mechanical servant. You must have heard of the companies that are making robots in Calcutta.'

'Yes, I've seen the advertisements. But where is your servant from? You know I'm a little fussy in this matter. Is this new servant doing the cooking?'

'No, no, no,' reassured Nikunja Babu, 'I've still got the old cook. So you needn't worry. The new one is called Anukul and. . . er. . . you must speak to him politely. He doesn't like being shouted at.'

'Doesn't like it, eh?'

'No, he doesn't.'

'Do I have to act according to *his* likes and dislikes?'

'That applies to everyone, not just you. But you won't find fault with his work.'

'Why did you have to get into this mess?'

'I've told you already—he is a very good worker.'

'Well, then call him. Let's see what he's like.'

'Anukul!' Nikunja Babu called out. Anukul arrived immediately.

'Meet my uncle,' said Nikunja Babu, 'he's going to stay here for some time.'

'Very good, sir.'

'My goodness—he speaks just like a man,' exclaimed Nibaran Banerjee. 'All right then, could you please give me some hot water? I'd like to have a bath. It's turned a little chilly after the rains—but I am so accustomed to having a bath twice a day.'

'Yes, sir.'

Anukul left to carry out the instructions.

Nibaran Babu's arrival did not result in any improvement in his nephew's financial status. All that happened was that Nikunja Babu's friends stopped coming in the evening. It was not seemly to play rummy or poker in front of an uncle; besides, Nikunja Babu could no longer afford to gamble.

It was difficult to tell how long his uncle would stay. He usually came and went just as he liked. This time it seemed as though he was going to stay for a while—and the reason was Anukul. Anukul appeared to be attracting and repulsing him equally. He could not deny that Anukul's efficiency as a worker was irreproachable. At the same time, however, he could not quite accept the fact that one was expected to be careful in one's behaviour when dealing with a mere servant.

He said to his nephew one day, 'Nikunja, this servant of yours is giving me a lot of trouble at times.'

'Why, what happened?' Nikunja Babu asked, worried.

'I was reciting a few lines from the *Gita* the other day and that damned servant had the cheek to correct what I was saying. Even if the words I'd spoken were wrong, it's not for him to correct me, is it? Isn't that a bit too much? I felt like giving him a tight slap. But, in the end I managed to control myself.'

'No, no, Uncle, you must never raise your hand—it can have a disastrous effect. The suppliers told me so. The best thing would be not to speak at all when he's around.'

Nibaran Babu went away muttering to himself.

As the days went by, Nikunja Babu's earnings grew less and less. He began to find it very difficult to make the monthly payment for Anukul. He could not help mentioning this to Anukul one day.

'Anukul, my business isn't doing very well.'

'I know.'

'Yes, perhaps you do. But what I don't know is how long I shall be able to keep you. I don't wish to part with you, and yet. . . . '

'Let me think about it.'

'Think about what?'

'If there's a solution to the problem.'

'How is your thinking going to help? Running a business is not your line, is it?'

'No, but do let me try.'

'All right. But it may not be possible for me to keep you for very long—I just wanted to warn you.'

'Yes, sir.'

Two months passed. It was a Sunday. Nikunja Babu's careful calculations showed that he could, at the very most, afford to keep Anukul for another two months. After that, he would have to look for a human servant. In fact, he had already started looking for one. The whole thing depressed him no end. And, to make matters worse, it was pouring cats and dogs outside.

Nikunja Babu pushed the newspaper aside and was about to call Anukul to ask for a cup of tea when Anukul appeared.

'What is it, Anukul?'

'There's been an accident, sir.'

'Accident? What happened?'

'Your uncle was standing near the window and singing a Tagore song about the rain. He got some of the words wrong, so I felt obliged to correct him. He got so angry at this that he gave me a slap. So I had to pay him back.'

'Pay him back?'

'Yes. I had to give him a high voltage shock.'

'Does that mean. . .?'

'He is dead. But there was a clap of thunder just as I gave him the shock.'

'Yes, I heard it.'

'So you needn't tell people what the real reason for his death was.'

'But. . . .'

'Don't worry, sir. This will do you a lot of good.'

And so it did. Two days after his uncle's death, Nikunja Babu got a call from his uncle's lawyer, Bhaskar Bose. Nibaran Babu had left all his property to his nephew. Its total value was a little more than a million rupees.

Bhuto

Naveen came back disappointed a second time. He had failed to get Akrur Babu's support.

It was at a function in Uttarpara that Naveen had first learnt about Akrur Babu's amazing talent—ventriloquism. Naveen did not even know the word. Dwijapada had told him. Diju's father was a professor and had a library of his own. Diju had even taught him the right spelling of the word.

Akrur Chowdhury was the only person present on the stage but he was conversing with someone invisible, hidden somewhere near the ceiling in the middle of the hall. Akrur Babu would throw a question at him. He would answer it from above the audience's heads.

'Haranath, how are you?'

'I am fine, thank you, sir.'

'Heard you have become interested in music. Is that true?'

'Yes, sir.'

'Classical music?'

'Yes, sir, classical music.'

'Do you sing yourself?'

'No, sir.'

'Do you play an instrument?'

'That's right, sir.'

'What kind of instrument? The sitar?'

'No, sir.'

'Sarod?'

'No, sir.'

'What do you play, then?'

'A gramophone, sir.'

The hall boomed with laughter and applause. Akrur Babu looked at the ceiling to ask a question and then bent his head slightly to catch the reply. But it was impossible to tell that he was answering his own questions.

His lips did not move at all.

Naveen was astounded. He had to learn this art. Life would not be worth living if he did not. Could Akrur Chowdhury not be persuaded to teach him? Naveen was not much interested in studies. He had finished school, but had been sitting at home for the last three years. He simply did not feel like going in for further studies.

Having lost his father in childhood, he had been brought up by an uncle. His uncle wanted him to join him in his plywood business. But Naveen was interested in something quite different. His passion lay in learning magic. He had already mastered a few tricks at home. But after having seen a performance by Akrur Chowdhury, all that seemed totally insignificant.

Naveen learnt from the organizers of the show that Akrur Babu lived in Amherst Street in Calcutta. He took a train to Calcutta the very next day and made his way to the house of the man who, in his mind, had already become his guru. But the guru rejected his proposal outright.

'What do you do?' was the first question the ventriloquist asked him. The sight of the man at close quarters was making Naveen's heart beat faster. About forty-five years old, he sported a pair of deep black bushy moustaches and his jet black hair, parted in the middle, rippled down to his shoulders. His eyes were droopy, though Naveen had seen them sparkle on the stage under the spotlights.

Naveen decided to be honest. 'I've always been interested in magic,' he said, 'but your performance the other day got me passionately interested in ventriloquism.'

Akrur Babu shook his head, 'This kind of art is not for all and sundry. You have to be extremely diligent. No one taught me this art. Go and try to learn it by yourself, if you can.'

Naveen left. But, only a week later, he was back again, ready to fall at Akrur Babu's feet. He had dreamt of nothing but ventriloquism over the last seven days.

But this time things got worse. Akrur Babu practically threw him out of his house. 'You should have realized the first time I was not prepared to teach you at all,' he said, 'this clearly shows your lack of perception and intelligence. No one can learn magic without these basic qualities—and certainly not my kind of magic.'

The first time Naveen had returned feeling depressed. This time he got angry. Let Akrur Chowdhury go to hell. He would learn it all by himself.

He bought a book on ventriloquism in College Street and began to practise. Everyone—including he himself—was surprised at his patience and perseverance.

The basic rule was simple. There were only a few letters in the alphabet like 'b', 'f', 'm' and 'p' that required one to close and open one's lips. If these letters could be pronounced slightly differently, there was no need to move the lips at all. But there was one other thing. When answering one's own questions, the voice had to be changed. This required a lot of practice, but Naveen finally made it. When his uncle and some close friends openly praised him after a performance at home, he realized he had more or less mastered the art.

But this was only the beginning.

The days of the invisible audience were over. Modern ventriloquists used a puppet specially designed so that it was possible to slip a hand under it and make its head turn and its lips move. When asked a question, it was the puppet who answered.

Pleased with the progress he had made, his uncle offered to pay for such a puppet for Naveen. Naveen spent about a couple of weeks trying to think what his puppet should look like. Then he hit upon the most marvellous idea.

His puppet would look exactly like Akrur Chowdhury. In other words, Akrur Babu would become a mere puppet in his hands! What a wonderful way to get his own back!

Naveen had kept a photograph of Akrur Babu that he had once found on a hand-bill.

He now showed it to Adinath, the puppet maker.

'It must have moustaches like these, a middle parting, droopy eyes and round cheeks.'

What fun it would be to have a puppet like that! Naveen hoped fervently that Akrur Babu would come to his shows.

The puppet was ready in a week. Its clothes were also the same as Akrur Chowdhury's: a black high-necked coat and a white dhoti under it, tucked in at the waist.

Naveen happened to know Sasadhar Bose of the Netaji Club. It was not difficult to get himself included in one of their functions.

He was an instant hit. His puppet had been given a name—Bhutnath, Bhuto for short. The audience thoroughly enjoyed their conversation. Bhuto, Naveen told them, was a supporter of the East Bengal Football Club; and he himself supported their opponents, Mohun Bagan. The verbal exchange was so chirpy that no one noticed Bhuto say 'East Gengal' and 'Ohan Agan'.

Naveen became famous practically overnight. Invitations from other clubs began pouring in. He even started to appear on television. There was now no need to worry about his future. He had found a way to earn his living.

At last, one day, Akrur Babu came to meet him.

Naveen had, in the meantime, left Uttarpara and moved into a flat in Mirzapur Street in Calcutta. His landlord, Suresh Mutsuddi, was a nice man. He knew of Naveen's success and treated him with due respect. Naveen had performed recently in Mahajati Sadan and received a lot of acclaim. The organizers of various functions were now vying with one another to get Naveen to perform for them. Naveen himself had changed over the last few months. Success had given him a new confidence and self-assurance.

Akrur Babu had probably got his address from the organizers of his show in Mahajati Sadan. Bhuto and he had talked about the underground railway that evening.

'You know about *pataal* rail in Calcutta, don't you, Bhuto?'

'No, I don't!'

'That is strange. Everyone in Calcutta knows about it.'

Bhuto shook his head.

'No. I haven't heard of that one. But I do know of hospital rail.'

'Hospital rail?'

'Of course. It's a huge operation, I hear, the whole city's being cut open under intensive care. What else would you call it but hospital rail?'

Today, Naveen was writing a new script on load shedding. He had realized that what the audience liked best were subjects that they could relate to—load shedding, crowded buses, rising prices. His script was coming along quite well when, suddenly, someone knocked on the door. Naveen got up to open it and was completely taken aback to find Akrur Babu standing outside.

'May I come in?'

'Of course.'

Naveen offered him his chair.

Akrur Babu did not sit down immediately. His eyes were fixed on Bhuto.

Bhuto was lying on the table, totally inert.

Akrur Babu went forward, picked him up and began examining his face closely.

There was nothing that Naveen could do. He had started to feel faintly uneasy, but the memory of his humiliation at Akrur Babu's house had not faded from his mind.

'So you have turned me into a puppet in your hands!'

Akrur Babu finally sat down.

'Why did you do this?'

Naveen said, 'That should not be too difficult to understand. I had gone to you with great hope. You crushed it totally. But I must say this—this puppet, this image of yours, has brought me all my success. I am able to live decently only because of it.'

Akrur Babu was still staring at Bhuto. He said, 'I don't know if you've heard this one already. I had a show in Barasat the other day. The minute I arrived on the stage, the cat-calls began—"Bhuto! Bhuto!" Surely you realize this was not a very pleasant experience for me? I may be responsible, in a way, for your success, but you are beginning to threaten my livelihood. Did you think I would accept a situation like this so easily?'

It was dark outside. There was no electricity. Two candles flickered in Naveen's room. Akrur Babu's eyes glowed in their light just as Naveen had seen them glow on the stage. The little man cast a huge shadow on the wall. Bhutnath lay on the table, as droopy-eyed as ever, silent and immobile.

'You may not be aware of this,' said Akrur Babu, 'but my knowledge of magic isn't limited only to ventriloquism. From the age of eighteen to thirty-eight I stayed with an unknown but amazingly gifted magician, learning his art. No, not here in Calcutta. He lived in a most remote corner, in the foothills of the Himalayas.'

'Have you ever shown on stage any of those other items you learnt?'

'No, I haven't because those are not meant for the stage. I had promised my guru never to use that knowledge simply to earn a living. I have kept my word.'

'But what are you now trying to tell me? I don't understand.'

'I have come only to warn you, although I must admit I have been impressed by your dedication. No one actually taught me the art of ventriloquism. I had to teach myself, just as you have done. Professional magicians do not teach anyone else the real tricks of the trade—they have never done so. But I am not prepared to tolerate the impertinence you have shown in designing your puppet. That is all I came to tell you.'

Akrur Babu rose from his chair. Then he glanced at Bhutnath and said, 'My hair and my moustaches have only recently started to grey. I can see that you have, in anticipation, already planted a few grey strands in your puppet's hair. All right, then. I'll now take my leave.'

Akrur Babu left.

Naveen closed the door and stood before Bhutnath. Grey hair? Yes, one or two were certainly visible. He had not noticed these before, which was surprising since he held the puppet in his hand and spoke to it so often. How could he have been so unobservant?

Anyway, there was no point in wasting any more time thinking about it. Anyone could make a mistake. He had obviously concentrated only on Bhutnath's face and not looked at his hair closely enough.

But it was impossible to rid himself of a snealing suspicion.

The next day, he stuffed Bhuto into the leather case he'd had made specially for him and went straight to Adinath Pal. There he brought Bhuto out of the case, laid him flat on the ground and said, 'Look at these few strands of grey hair. Did you put these in?'

Adinath Pal seemed quite taken aback. 'Why, no! Why should I? You did not ask for a mixture of black and grey hair, did you?'

'Could you not have made a mistake?'

'Yes, of course. Those few strands might have been pasted purely by mistake. But would you not have noticed it immediately when you came to collect the puppet? You know what I think? I do believe someone has planted these deliberately without your knowledge.'

Perhaps he was right. The whole thing had happened without his knowledge.

A strange thing happened at the function organized by the Friends Club in Chetla.

A clear evidence of Bhuto's popularity was that the organizers had saved his item till the last. In the midst of a rather interesting dialogue on the subject of load shedding, Naveen noticed that Bhuto was uttering words that had not been written in the script. These included difficult words in English which Naveen himself never used—at the very most, he knew what they meant.

This was a totally new experience for Naveen, although it made no difference to the show for the words were being used quite appropriately and drawing frequent applause from the crowd. Thank goodness none of them knew Naveen had not ever been to college.

But this unexpected behaviour of his puppet upset Naveen. He kept feeling some unseen force had assumed control, pushing him into the background.

Upon reaching home after the show, he closed the door of his room and placed Bhuto under a table lamp.

Did Bhuto have that little mole on his forehead before? No, he most certainly did not. Naveen had noticed a similar mole on Akrur Babu's forehead only the other day. It was really quite small, not easily noticeable unless one looked carefully. But now it had appeared on Bhuto's face.

And that was not all. There was something else.

At least ten more strands of grey hair.

And deep dark rings under the eyes.

These were definitely not there before.

Naveen began pacing up and down impatiently. He was beginning to feel decidedly uneasy. He believed in magic—but his kind of magic was something in which man was in full command. Anything to do with the supernatural, for Naveen, was not just unacceptable, it was evil. He could see signs of evil in the changes in Bhuto.

At the same time, however, it was impossible to think of Bhuto as anything other than an inert, lifeless object, a mere puppet in his hands despite his droopy eyes and the slight smile on his lips. And yet, his whole appearance was undergoing a change.

It was Naveen's belief that the same changes were taking place in Akrur Babu.

He, too, must have started to go grey; his eyes, too, must have got dark circles under them.

Naveen had the habit of talking to Bhuto every now and then, simply to practise his technique. Their conversation went like this:

'It's rather hot today, isn't it, Bhuto?'

'Yes, it's very stuwy.'

'But you have an advantage, don't you? You don't sweat and perspire.'

'How can a -u-et sweat and ers-ire? Ha, ha, ha, ha. . . .'

Today, Naveen asked him quite involuntarily, 'What on earth is going on, Bhuto? Why is all this happening?'

Bhuto's reply startled him.

'Karwa, karwa!' he said.

Karma!

The word slipped out through Naveen's lips, just as it would have done on the stage. But he knew he had not said it consciously.

Someone had made him utter that word; and he had a very good idea who that someone might be.

That night, he refused his dinner despite repeated requests from his cook.

Normally, he slept quite well. But tonight he took a pill to help him sleep. At around one in the morning, the pill began to work. Naveen put down the magazine he was reading, switched off the light and fell asleep.

Only a little while later, however, he opened his eyes.

Who had been coughing in the room?

Was it himself? But he did not have a cough. And yet, it seemed as though someone at close quarters was coughing very softly.

He switched on the lamp.

Bhutnath was still sitting in the same spot, motionless. But he now appeared to be slouching a little and his right arm was flung across his chest.

Naveen looked at the clock. It was a half-past-three. The *chowkidar* outside was doing his rounds, beating his stick on the ground. A dog barked in the distance. An owl flew past his house, hooting raucously. Someone next door had obviously got a cough. And a gust of wind must have made Bhuto bend forward slightly. There was no earthly reason to feel scared today, in the twentieth century, living in a busy street of a large city like Calcutta.

Naveen switched off the light and fell asleep once more.

The next day, for the first time in his career, he experienced failure.

The Finlay Recreation Club had invited him to their annual function. A large audience was packed into an enormous hall. As always, his item was the last. Songs, recitations, a Kathak recital and then ventriloquism by Naveen Munshi.

Before setting off from home, he had done all that he always did to take care of his voice. He knew how important it was for a ventriloquist to have a clear throat.

His voice sounded perfectly normal before he went on to the stage. In fact, he noticed nothing wrong when he asked Bhuto the first question. Disaster struck when it was Bhuto's turn to speak.

His voice sounded hoarse, like that of a man suffering from an acute attack of cough and cold. Naveen knew the audience could not hear a word Bhuto was saying. Strangely enough, it was only Bhuto's voice that seemed to be affected. His own still sounded normal.

'Louder, please!' yelled a few people from the back. Those sitting in the front rows were too polite to yell, but it was obvious that they could not hear anything, either.

Naveen tried for another five minutes and then had to withdraw, defeated. Never had he felt so embarrassed.

He declined the organizers' offer to pay him his fee. He could not accept any money under the circumstances. But surely this horrible situation could not last for ever? In spite of his embarrassment, Naveen still believed that, soon, things would return to normal.

It was a very hot and sultry night, added to which was this new and unpleasant experience. When Naveen returned home at about eleven-thirty, he was feeling positively sick. For the first time, he began to feel a little annoyed with Bhuto, although he knew Bhuto could not really be blamed for anything. His failure was Naveen's own fault.

He placed Bhuto on the table and opened one of the windows. There was not much hope of getting a cool breeze, but whatever came in was a welcome relief for there was a power cut again. Today being Saturday, Naveen knew the power supply would not be resumed before midnight.

He lit a candle and set it down on the table. Its light fell on Bhuto and Naveen went cold with fear.

There were beads of perspiration on Bhuto's forehead.

But was that all? No. His face had lost its freshness. The cheeks looked sunken. His eyes were red.

Even in a situation like this, Naveen could not help but take a few steps forward towards his puppet. It was as though he had to find out what further shocks and horrors were still in store.

But something made him stop almost immediately.

There was a movement on Bhuto's chest, under the high-necked jacket. His chest rose and fell.

Bhuto was breathing!

Could his breathing be heard?

Yes, it could. In the totally silent night, two people breathed in Naveen's room instead of one.

It was perhaps both his fear and amazement that made Naveen exclaim softly, 'Bhuto!'

And, immediately, another voice spoke, the sound of which made Naveen reel back on his bed.

'This is not Bhuto. I am Akrur Chowdhury!'

Naveen knew he had not spoken the words. The voice was the

puppet's own. Heaven knows through what magical powers Akrur Chowdhury could make it speak.

Naveen had wanted to turn Akrur Babu into a puppet in his hands. But never did he expect anything like this. It was impossible for him to stay in the same room with a puppet that had come to life. He must.

But what was that?

Was the sound of Bhuto's breathing growing faint?

Yes, so it was.

Bhuto had stopped breathing. The beads of perspiration on his forehead had gone. His eyes were no longer red and the dark rings had vanished.

Naveen rose from his bed and picked him up.

Something queer had happened in this short time.

It was no longer possible to move Bhuto's head or open his lips. The mechanical parts had jammed. Perhaps a little more force would help.

Naveen tried to twist the head forcibly. It came apart and fell on the table with a clatter.

In the morning, Naveen ran into his landlord, Suresh Mutsuddi, on the staircase.

'Why, Mr Munshi, you never showed me your magic with the puppet,' he complained, 'ventricollosium or whatever it is called!'

'I've given that up,' said Naveen, 'I'll try something new now. But why do you ask?'

'One of your fellow performers died yesterday. Saw it in the papers this morning. Akrur Chowdhury.'

'Really?'—Naveen had not yet looked at the newspaper—'what happened to him?'

'Heart attack,' said Suresh Babu, 'nearly seventy per cent of people seem to die of a heart attack nowadays.'

Naveen knew that if anyone bothered to enquire about the time of his death, they would discover that the man had died exactly ten minutes after midnight.

The Maths Teacher,
Mr Pink and Tipu

Tipu closed his geography book and looked at the clock. He had studied non-stop for exactly forty-seven minutes. It was now thirteen minutes past three. There was no harm in going out for a little while, was there? That strange creature had appeared the other day at about the same time. Didn't he say he would come back again if ever Tipu had reason to feel sad? There was a reason now. A very strong one at that. Should he pop out for a minute?

Oh no. Mother had come out on to the veranda. He heard her shoo a crow away. Then the cane chair creaked. That meant she had sat down to sun herself. Tipu would have to wait.

He could remember the creature so well. He had never seen anyone like him. So very small in size, no sign of a beard or a moustache—yet he was not a child. No child ever spoke with such a deep voice. But then, the creature was not old, either. At least, Tipu had been unable to figure out if he was. His skin was smooth, his complexion like sandalwood tinged with pink. In fact, Tipu thought of him as Mr Pink. He did not know what he was actually called. He did ask, but the creature replied, 'It's no use telling you my name. It would twist your tongue to pronounce it.'

Tipu felt affronted by this. 'Why should I start stuttering? I can say things like gobbledygook and flabbergasted. I can even manage floccinaucinihilipilification. So why should your name be a tongue-twister?'

'You couldn't possibly manage with just one tongue.'

'You mean you have more than one?'

'You need only one to talk in your language.'

The man was standing under the tall, bare shimul tree just behind the house. Not many people came here. There was a large open space behind the tree, followed by rice fields. And behind these, in the far distance, stood the hills. Tipu had seen a mongoose disappear behind a bush only a few days ago. Today, he had brought a few pieces of bread with the intention of scattering them on the ground. The mongoose might be tempted to reappear.

His eyes suddenly fell on the man standing under the tree.

'Hello!' said the man, smiling.

Was he a westerner? Tipu knew he could not converse for very long if the man spoke only in English. So he just stared at him. The man walked across to him and said, 'Do you have reason to be sad?'

'Sad?'

'Yes.'

Tipu was taken aback. No one had ever asked him such a question. He said, 'Why, no, I don't think so.'

'Are you sure?'

'Of course.'

'But you're supposed to be sad. That's what the calculations showed.'

'What kind of sadness? I thought I might see the mongoose. But I didn't. Is that what you meant?'

'No, no. The kind of sadness I meant would make the back of your ears go blue. Your palms would feel dry.'

'You mean a very deep sadness.'

'Yes.'

'Sorry, I don't happen to be feeling so very sad.'

Now the man began to look rather sad himself. He shook his head and said, 'That means I cannot be released yet.'

'Released?'

'Yes, released. I cannot be free.'

'I know what release means,' said Tipu, 'would you be set free if I felt unhappy?'

The man looked straight at Tipu, 'Are you ten-and-a-half years old?'

'Yes.'

'And your name is Master Tarpan Chowdhury?'

'Yes.'

'Then there is no mistake.'

Tipu had no idea how the man knew such a lot about him. He asked, 'Does it have to be me? If someone else felt sad, wouldn't that do?'

'No. And it's not enough simply to feel sad. The cause of sadness must be removed.'

'But so many people are unhappy. A beggar called Nikunja comes to our house so often. He says he has no one in the world. He must be very unhappy indeed.'

'No, that won't do,' the man shook his head again. 'Tarpan Chowdhury, ten years old—is there someone else near here of the same name and age?'

'No, I don't think so.'

'Then it must be you.'

Tipu could not resist the next question.

'What release are you talking about? You appear to be walking about quite freely!'

'This is not my land. I have been exiled here.'

'Why?'

'You ask too many questions.'

'I'm interested, that's all. Look, I've met you for the first time. So naturally I'd like to know who you are, what you do, where you live, who else knows you—things like that. What's wrong with being interested?'

'You'll get jinjiria if you try to learn so much.'

The man did not actually say 'jinjiria'. What he did say sounded so completely unpronounceable that Tipu decided to settle for jinjiria. God knows what kind of ailment it was.

But who did the man remind him of? Rumpelstiltskin? Or was he one of Snow White's seven dwarfs?

Tipu was passionately fond of fairy tales. His grandfather brought him three or four books of fairy tales every year from Calcutta. Tipu read them all avidly, his flights of fancy taking him far beyond the seven seas and thirteen rivers and thirty-six hills. In his mind, he became a prince, a pearl-studded turban on his head, a sword slung from his waist, flashing diamonds. He set forth to look for priceless jewels or to fight a dragon.

'Goodbye!' said the man.

Was he leaving already?

'You didn't tell me where you live!'

The man paid no attention. All he said was, 'We shall meet again when you feel sad.'

'But how will you know?'

There was no answer for, by then, the man had jumped over a mulberry tree and vanished from sight having broken all possible world records in the high jump.

This had happened about six weeks ago. Tipu did not see the man again. But he needed him now for he was desperately unhappy.

The reason for this was the new maths teacher in his school, Narahari Babu.

Tipu did not like him from the very beginning. When he first came to class he spent the first two minutes just staring at the boys. How hard he'd stared! As though he wanted to kill everyone with that look before he began teaching. Tipu had never seen anyone with such a huge moustache. And his voice! What a deep, loud voice it was! Why did he have to speak so loudly? No one in the class was deaf, after all.

The disaster occurred two days later. It was a Thursday. The sky was overcast and it was cold outside. Tipu did not feel like going out in the lunch break. So he sat in his class, reading the story of Dalimkumar. Who was to know his maths teacher would walk past his classroom and come in upon seeing him?

'What book is that, Tarpan?'

One had to admit the new teacher had a remarkable memory for he had already learnt the name of each boy.

Tipu felt slightly nervous but took courage from the thought that no one could object to his reading a story-book in the lunch break. '*Tales from Grandma*, sir!' he said.

'Let's have a look.'

Tipu handed the book to his teacher. The latter thumbed its pages for a minute. Then he exploded, 'Kings, queens, princes and demons—birds of pearls on a tree of diamonds, abracadabra—what on earth are you reading? What a pack of nonsense this is! How do you suppose you'll ever learn mathematics if you keep reading this idiotic stuff?'

'But these are only stories, sir!' Tipu stammered.

'Stories? Shouldn't all stories make sense? Or is it enough simply to write what comes into one's head?'

Tipu was not going to give in so easily.

'Why, sir,' he said, 'even the *Ramayana* talks of Hanuman and Jambuvan. The *Mahabharata*, too, is full of tales of demons and monsters.'

'Don't argue,' snarled Narahari Babu, 'those tales were written by sages more than two thousand years ago. Ganesh with the head of an elephant and the body of a man, and the goddess Durga with ten arms are not the same as the kind of nonsense you're reading. You should read about great men, about explorers, about scientific inventions, about the evolution of man—things to do with the real world. You belong to the twentieth century, don't you? Foolish, ignorant people in villages might once have enjoyed such absurd stories. Why should you? If you do, you ought to go back to a village school and try learning maths with the help of rhymed couplets. Can you do that?'

Tipu fell silent. He had not realized a small remark from him would trigger off such a tirade.

'Who else in your class reads such books?' his teacher asked.

To tell the truth, no one did. Sheetal had once borrowed *Folk Tales of Hindustan* from Tipu and returned it the very next day, saying, 'Bosh! Phantom comics are a lot better than this!'

'No one, sir,' Tipu replied.

'Hmm. . . what's your father's name?'

'Taranath Chowdhury.'

'Where do you live?'

'Station Road. At number five.'

'Hmm.' His teacher dropped the book back on Tipu's desk with a thud and left.

Tipu did not go back to his house straight after school. He wandered off beyond the mango grove near the school and found himself in front of Bishnuram Das' house. A white horse was tethered outside it. Tipu leant against a jamrool tree and stared at the horse absent-mindedly. Bishnuram Babu owned a beedi factory. He rode to his factory every day. He was still fit enough to do so, although he had crossed fifty.

Tipu came here often to look at the horse; but today his mind was elsewhere. Deep down in his heart he knew the new maths teacher would try to put a stop to his reading story-books. How would he survive without his books? He read them every day—and he liked reading best the ones his teacher had described as stuff and nonsense. Why, his reading such stories had never stopped him from doing well in maths, had it? He had got forty-four out of fifty the last time. His old maths teacher, Bhudeb Babu, never once ticked him off for reading story-books!

The days being short in winter, Tipu knew he had to return home soon, and was about to leave when he saw something that made him quickly hide behind the tree.

His maths teacher, Narahari Babu, was coming towards him, a book and an umbrella under his arm.

Did that mean he lived somewhere close by? There were five other houses next to the one where Bishnuram Babu lived. Beyond these houses was a large, open space known as Hamlatuni's Field. A long time ago, there used to be a silk factory on the eastern side of the field. Its manager, Mr Hamilton, was reputed to be a hard taskmaster. He worked as manager for thirty-two years and then died in his bungalow, not far from the factory. His name got somewhat distorted, but the whole area came to be known as Hamlatuni's Field.

In the gathering dusk of the winter evening, Tipu watched Narahari Babu from behind the jamrool tree. He was surprised at his behaviour. Narahari Babu was standing beside the horse, gently patting its back and making a strange chirrupping noise through his lips.

At that very moment, the front door of the house opened and, holding a cheroot in his hand, Bishnuram Babu himself came out.

'Namaskar.'

Narahari Babu took his hand off the horse's back and turned.

Bishnuram Babu returned his greeting and asked, 'How about a game?'

'That's precisely why I've come!' said Tipu's teacher. This meant he played chess because Tipu knew Bishnuram Babu did.

'Nice horse,' said Narahari Babu, 'where did you get it?'

'Calcutta. I bought it from Dwarik Mitter of Shobhabazar. It used to be a race horse called Pegasus.'

Pegasus? The name seemed vaguely familiar but Tipu could not recall where he had heard it.

'Pegasus,' said the maths teacher, 'what a strange name!'

'Yes, race horses usually have funny names. Happy Birthday, Shobhan Allah, Forget-me-not. . . .'

'Do you ride this horse?'

'Of course. A very sturdy beast. Hasn't given me a day's trouble.'

Narahari Babu kept staring at the horse.

'I used to ride once.'

'Really?'

'We lived in Sherpur in those days. My father was a doctor. He used a horse for making house calls. I was in school then. I used to ride whenever I could. Oh, that was a long time ago!'

'Would you like to ride this one?'

'May I?'

'Go ahead!'

Tipu stared in amazement as his teacher dropped his book and his umbrella on the veranda and untied the horse. Then he climbed on to its back in one swift movement and pressed its flanks with his heels. The horse began to trot.

'Don't go far,' said Bishnuram Babu.

'Get the chessmen out,' said Narahari Babu, 'I'll be back in no time!'

Tipu did not wait any longer. What a day it had been!

But there was more in store.

It was around seven in the evening. Tipu had just finished his homework and was contemplating reading a few stories when his father called him from downstairs.

Tipu walked into their living-room to find Narahari Babu sitting there with his father. His blood froze.

'Your teacher would like to see the books your grandfather has given you,' said Father. 'Go bring them.'

There were twenty-seven books. Tipu had to make three trips to get them all together.

His maths teacher took ten minutes to go through the lot, shaking his head occasionally and saying, 'Pooh!' Finally, he pushed the books aside and said, 'Look, Mr Chowdhury, what I am going to tell you is based on years of thinking and research. Fairy tales or folklore, call it what you will, can mean only one thing—sowing the seed of superstition in a young mind. A child will accept whatever it's told. Do you realize what an enormous responsibility we adults have got? Should we be telling our children the life of a man lies inside a fish and things like that, when the truth is that one's life beats in one's own heart? It cannot possibly exist anywhere else!'

Tipu could not figure out if Father agreed with all that the teacher said, but he did know that he believed in obeying a teacher's instructions.

'A child must learn to obey, Tipu,' he had told him so many times, 'especially what his elders tell him. You can do whatever you like after a certain age, when you have finished your studies and are standing on your own feet. You would then have the right to voice your own opinion. But not now.'

'Do you not have any other books for children?' asked Narahari Babu.

'Oh yes,' said Father, 'they're all here on my bookshelf. I won them as prizes in school. Haven't you seen them, Tipu?'

'I have read them all, Father,' said Tipu.

'Each one?'

'Each one. The biographies of Vidyasagar and Suresh Biswas, Captain Scott's expedition to the South Pole, Mungo Park's adventures in Africa, the story of steel and spaceships. . . you didn't win that many prizes, Father.'

'All right,' said Father, 'I'll buy you some more.'

'If you tell the Tirthankar Book Stall here, they can get you some books from Calcutta,' said Narahari Babu, 'you will read only those from now, Tarpan. Not these.'

Not these! Two little words—but they were enough to make Tipu's world come to an end. Not these!

Father took the books from Narahari Babu and locked them away in his cupboard.

Now they were quite out of reach.

Mother, however, appeared to be on Tipu's side. He could hear her grumble and, while having dinner, she went to the extent of saying, 'A man who can say such a thing does not deserve to be a teacher at all!'

Father disagreed, 'Can't you see what he has suggested is for Tipu's good?'

'Nonsense,' said Mother. Then she ruffled Tipu's hair affectionately and said, 'Don't worry. I will tell you stories. Your grandmother used to tell me lots of stories. I haven't forgotten them all.'

Tipu did not say anything. He had already heard a number of stories from his mother and did not think she knew any more. Even if she did, hearing a story from someone was not the same as reading it. With an open book in front of him, he could lose himself in a totally different world. But how could he make his mother see that?

Two days later, Tipu realized he was really feeling sad. It was decidedly the kind of sadness Mr Pink had mentioned. Now he was Tipu's only hope.

Today was Sunday. Father was having a nap. Mother had left the veranda and was now at her sewing machine. It was three-thirty. Should he try to slip out of the back door? If only the man had told him where he lived! Tipu would have gone to him straightaway.

Tipu tiptoed down the stairs and went out through the backdoor.

Despite a bright sun, there was quite a nip in the air. In the distance, the rice fields looked golden in the sunlight, stretching right up to the hills. A dove was cooing somewhere and the occasional rustle that came from the shirish tree meant that there was a squirrel hidden in the leaves.

'Hello!'

Oh, what a surprise! When did he arrive? Tipu had not seen him come.

'The back of your ears are blue, your palms seem dry. I can tell you have reason to feel sad.'

'You can say that again,' said Tipu.

The man came walking towards him. He was wearing the same clothes.

The wind blew his hair in tufts.

'I need to know what has happened, or else I'm gobbledygasted.'

Tipu wanted to laugh, but made no attempt to correct what the man had said. Instead, he briefly related his tale of woe. Tears pricked at his eyes as he spoke, but Tipu managed to control himself.

'Hmm,' said the man and began nodding. His head went up and down sixteen times. Tipu began to feel a little nervous. Would he never stop? Or was it that he could find no solution to the problem? He felt like crying once more, but the man gave a final nod, stopped and said, 'Hmm' again. Tipu went limp with relief.

'Do you think you can do something?' he asked timidly.

'I shall have to think carefully. Must exercise the intestines.'

'Intestines? You mean you wouldn't exercise your brain?'

The man did not reply. He said instead, 'Didn't I see Narahari Babu ride a horse yesterday in that field?'

'Which field? Oh, you mean Hamlatuni's Field?'

'The one that has a broken building in it.'

'Yes, yes. Is that where you stay?'

'My tridingipidi is lying just behind that building.'

Tipu could not have heard him right. But even if he had, he would probably have been totally unable to pronounce the word.

The man had started nodding again. This time he stopped after the thirty-first nod and said, 'There will be a full moon tonight. If you wish to see what happens then come to that field just as the moon reaches the top of the date tree. But make sure no one sees you.'

Suddenly a rather alarming thought occurred to Tipu.

'You will not try to kill my maths teacher, will you?'

For the first time he saw the man throw back his head and laugh.

He also saw there were two tongues in his mouth and no teeth.

'Kill him?' The man stopped laughing, 'No, no. We don't believe in killing. In fact, I was banished from my land because I had thought of pinching someone. The first set of calculations gave us the name, 'Earth' where I had to be sent. Then we got the name of this place; and then came your own name. I will be set free as soon as I can snuff out the cause of your sadness.'

'All right then. See you. . . .'

But the man had already taken another giant leap over the mulberry tree and disappeared.

The faint tingle that had set in Tipu's body stayed all evening. By an amazing stroke of luck his parents were going out to dinner that night. Tipu, too, had been invited, but his mother felt he should stay at home and study. His exams were just round the corner.

They left at 7.30. Tipu waited for about five minutes after they had gone. Then he set off. The eastern sky had started to turn yellow.

It took him almost ten minutes to reach the house of Bishnuram Babu through the short cut behind his school. The horse was no longer there. It must be in its stable behind the house, Tipu thought. Light streamed through the open window of the living-room. The room was full of smoke from cheroots.

'Check.'

It was the voice of his maths teacher. He was obviously having a game of chess with Bishnuram Babu. Was he not going to ride tonight? How could he tell? But the man had asked Tipu to go to Hamlatuni's Field. He must go there, although he had no idea what might happen.

The moon had risen. It looked golden now, but would turn silver later. It would take another ten minutes to reach the top of the date tree. The moonlight was not yet very bright, but things were fairly easily visible. There were plenty of plants and bushes. The derelict old factory stood at a distance. The man was supposed to be staying behind it. But where?

Tipu hid behind a bush, and prepared to wait. In his pocket was some jaggery wrapped in a piece of newspaper. He bit off a small portion of it and began chewing. He could hear jackals calling from the jungle far away. That black object that flew past must be an owl.

Tipu was wearing a brown shawl over his coat. It helped him both merge into the darkness and to keep warm.

A clock struck eight somewhere, probably in Bishnuram Babu's house.

And, soon afterwards, Tipu heard another noise: Clip-clop, clip-clop, clip-clop.

Was it the horse?

Tipu peeped from behind the bush and stared at the lane.

Yes, it was indeed the same horse with Narahari Babu on its back.

Disaster struck at this precise moment. A mosquito had been buzzing around Tipu's ears. He tried to wave it away, but it suddenly went straight into one nostril!

Tipu knew it was possible to stop a sneeze by pressing the nose hard. But if he did that now, the mosquito might never come out. So he allowed himself to sneeze, shattering the stillness of the night.

The horse stopped.

Someone flashed a powerful torch on Tipu.

'Tarpan?'

Tipu began to go numb with fear. Why, why, why did this have to happen? He had gone and ruined whatever plans that man must have made. What on earth would he think of Tipu?

The horse began to trot up towards him with his maths teacher on its back. But suddenly it raised its forelegs high in the air, neighed loudly, and veered off from the lane. Then it jumped into the field.

What followed took Tipu's breath away. The horse took off from the ground, flapping two large wings which had grown from its sides! Tipu's teacher flung his arms around the horse's neck and hung on as best as he could. The torch had fallen from his hand.

The moon had reached the top of the date tree. In the bright moonlight, Tipu saw the horse rise higher and higher in the sky until it disappeared among the stars.

Pegasus!

It came back to Tipu in a flash. It was a Greek tale. Medusa, the ogress—every strand of whose hair was a venomous snake, the very sight of whom made men turn into stone. The valiant Perseus chopped off her head with his sword and from her blood was born Pegasus, the winged horse.

'Go home, Tarpan!'

That strange man was standing beside Tipu, his golden hair gleaming in the moonlight.

'Everything is all right.'

Narahari Babu had to go to a hospital. He stayed there three days, although there was no sign of any physical injury. He talked to no one. Upon being asked what the matter was, he only shivered and looked away.

On the fourth day he was discharged. He came straight to Tipu's house. What transpired between him and Father, Tipu could not make out. But, as soon as he had gone, Father called Tipu and said, 'Er. . . you may take your books from my cupboard. Narahari Babu said he didn't mind your reading fairy tales any more.'

Tipu never saw the strange man again. He went looking for him behind the old factory and passed Bishnuram Babu's house on the way. The horse was still tethered to the same post. But there was absolutely nothing behind the factory, except a chameleon—pink from head to tail.

Hopeless

The word 'hopeless' is often used for people. Take our servant, Nobokeshto, for instance. I have heard my mother say many times to him, 'Nobo, you are totally hopeless.' But Nobo actually did his work quite well. His only fault was that he was wont to sleep rather a lot. His afternoon siesta frequently dragged beyond a reasonable hour. As a result, tea in the evening would get delayed and Mother, in sheer annoyance, would call him 'hopeless'.

But I have never known the word to be more aptly used than for Shejokaka. His real name was Khetromohan, Khetu for short. My father had four brothers. He was the eldest, followed by Mejo, Shejo, Shona and Chhoto. With the exception of Shejo, everyone was successful in life. Father was a well known lawyer. Mejo was a professor, an MA in both Sanskrit and History, a much respected man. Shona was a wealthy businessman, the owner of three houses in Calcutta, and Chhoto, the youngest, was a talented singer, mainly interested in classical vocal music. He had won thirty-six gold and silver medals and much acclaim from well known *ustaads* for his singing.

And Shejokaka?

Wait. This whole story is about him.

There had, apparently, been an earthquake when Shejokaka was born. Many thought this had damaged his brain. All children have measles and chicken pox. Shejokaka had both and, in addition, at some time or the other during his childhood, suffered from whooping cough, diphtheria, dengue, mumps, eczema and small pox. As a child, on seven different occasions, he had had attacks of hiccups that did not stop until he went blue in the face and fainted. He began to stammer at the age of seven. At nine-and-a-half, he fell down from a guava tree which cured the stammer. However, it also caused a fractured ankle, which Dr Biswas could not quite fix. This gave him a life-long limp. He could not, therefore, shine in sports; nor play carrom or cards since the former required a good aim and the latter a certain amount of intelligence.

Shejokaka did go to a school. But when he failed in the school leaving exam for the third time, his father (my grandfather, that is) told him not to bother any more. 'Khetu,' he told his son, 'you are so completely hopeless, I am not going to spend my money on your education any more. But, of course, you must learn not to be a burden on anyone. I suggest you start going with Bhombol to the market every day and learn to buy vegetables and fish and things like that. Then you can handle the shopping yourself.' Bhombolkaka was a distant relative. He had lived with us for a long time.

Shejokaka began going to the market with Bhombolkaka. A few days later, one day—when some guests were expected to dinner—my grandfather stuffed two ten-rupee notes in Shejokaka's pocket and said, 'All right, you do the shopping alone today. Let's see what you've learnt.'

But Shejokaka could not do any shopping at all, for his pocket was torn and the money slipped through it and was lost even before he reached the market. Who could ever trust him after that?

One of my earliest memories of Shejokaka is when he was thirty-three and I only three. It was the night of Diwali. Shejokaka was crawling on the front veranda, carrying me on his back, pretending to be my horse. Suddenly, a sparkling rocket came flying from the house next door and landed on the veranda. 'Oh my God!' cried Shejokaka in horror and stood up. I slipped from his back, fell with a thud on the concrete floor and lay there in a pool of blood. Nearly everyone in the house got cross with him that evening. But I felt sorry for him every time I thought about the incident afterwards. Poor man! No one loved him, no one had any time for him. In fact, no one appeared to treat him like a normal human being.

As I grew up, I began to feel an odd sympathy for this man.

He was of medium height, his complexion neither dark nor fair, and the expression on his face was always a mixture of joy and sadness. So what if he lacked brains, I thought. Surely everyone in the world did not have to be bright and brainy?

I used to go and talk to Shejokaka as often as I could in his little room on the ground floor. I learnt soon enough that it was no use asking him to tell me a story because he could never get to the end of one:

'After that? Hmm, after that. . .now, wait a minute. . .after that. . . .' And his voice would trail off slowly. He would then start to hum tunelessly and gradually fall totally silent and nod off. I would then tiptoe out of the room, knowing Shejokaka would not call me back.

When I was about twelve years old, I found him reading a big fat book one day. 'It is a book on ayurveda,' he told me.

'Why are you reading it?'

Shejokaka thought for a minute and said, 'This is a kind of ailment, isn't it?'

'What is?'

'This business of my not being able to think, or understand or remember anything—it must be some sort of an illness.'

What could I say? 'Yes, you may be right,' I said eventually.

'Why then should I not get myself treated?'

'Are you going to treat yourself?'

I knew no one had ever thought of consulting a doctor about Shejokaka. Strangely enough, after all those illnesses in his childhood, he had never been seriously ill and his general health was quite good.

'I found this book in the Chowk bazaar. It cost me less than a rupee. I think I will find in it a remedy for myself,' said Shejokaka.

Two days later, I found him getting ready to go out in the evening. Stout walking shoes on his feet, a cotton scarf around his neck, an umbrella in his hand. 'I have learnt of a plant that I may find among the wild shrubs behind the old Shiv temple. All I need is its roots. And then—have no fear—I shall be all right.'

Shejokaka went out. The sky was overcast. If it started to rain, all his plans would go *phut*.

I returned to my room upstairs. Luckily, it did not rain.

Much later, just as it was about to get dark, I saw Shejokaka coming back to the house. I ran down the stairs and met him at the front door.

'Did you find it?'

'No. I made the mistake of not taking a torch with me. The place was quite dark.'

'But what is that?'

I had noticed it even as he was speaking. There was a red patch on his chest.

'Good heavens—what is it? Hadn't noticed it at all!' he said.

He took off his kurta. A leech fell out. Just as in the *Mahabharata* Bheem had drunk the blood of Duhshasan, the leech had feasted on Shejokaka's chest.

But there were more. We found as many as fourteen leeches eventually, stuck to Shejokaka's shoulder, elbow, waist, calf, knees and ankle. He must have lost at least six ounces of blood. Needless to say, this incident put an end to his ayurvedic quest.

I was always a good student. I stood third in the University. When I finished college I went to Calcutta for further studies in Physics; I spent the next two years in a hostel doing my M Sc and went to America thereafter. I became quite well known over a period of time for my research work. In addition to this, I began to teach at Chicago University.

My staying abroad had resulted in a loss of contact with Shejokaka. Once—I had just started teaching then—my mother gave me a strange piece of news in one of her letters. Shejokaka had apparently started working in a film! It was, of course, true that his face did resemble that of Swami Vivekananda. Shejokaka heard of a film being made on Sri Paramahansa which had the role of Vivekananda. He went straight to the producer and offered his services. The producer took one look at his face and signed him.

But I learnt only a week later that he had been dropped from the film. The reason was simple. Despite his best efforts, Shejokaka would forget the right dialogues. He had learnt his lines well, but would speak the lines meant for the third scene when the first was being shot. In short, he proved once again how hopeless he was, even as a film actor.

When I turned forty-eight, my brother wrote saying Shejokaka had found a guru and had gone to Coimbatore with him.

I returned to Calcutta to attend the wedding of my Chhotokaka's daughter, Kakoli. There had been no news of Shejokaka for a long time. So when I learnt that he was not only alive and well but also in town, I naturally wanted to meet him. I was then sixty. Shejokaka, therefore, was ninety years old.

I heard that he was staying on Fern Road with Ramesh Gupta, his nephew and my cousin. I also learnt that religion had not suited him. In all these years he had not been able to get used to the food in south India. He had apparently lost about thirty kilos. But, upon being told that I was in Calcutta, he had said to his nephew, 'Please tell Jhontu to come and meet me.'

I went to the house on Fern Road one evening. The whole area was plunged in darkness, the result of load shedding. A candle flickered in Shejokaka's room. He sat propped up in bed, wrapped in a cotton shawl and a green muffler.

It was not difficult to recognize him. He looked pretty well maintained for his age. All his hair had gone white, but at least he still had some left. When he smiled at me, I could see that some of his original teeth were also intact and when he spoke, his voice—although weak—sounded confident. I had never heard him sound so sure of himself. Perhaps it was the thought that he was now the oldest member of the family and did not have to bow to the wishes of those older than him that gave him so much self- assurance.

'Hello, Jhontu,' he said, 'so what have you been up to in the States?'

I told him about my work as modestly as I could. But Ramesh's mother, my seventy-seven-year-old aunt, told him about the acclaim I had won, yelling at the top of her voice, tearing my modesty to pieces.

'Really?' asked Shejokaka, 'have you won the Nobel prize yet?'

I laughed lightly and shook my head.

'Why—you have nothing to boast about in that case. Tch, tch, tch—you're quite hopeless!'

Even before I could surface from such an attack, Shejokaka discharged a few more salvoes, 'At least you managed to escape abroad. I thought I might come back to Calcutta and spend my last few days with my near and dear ones. But what do I find? A dead city, its skeleton being pecked at by vultures. Power cuts for ten hours every day. The pollution is so bad it is impossible to breathe freely. And the inflation! I can't even eat the things I want to. Shame on everyone—they are all so totally hopeless!'

I realized the old fondness I had once felt for him was still very much in evidence, for his remarks made me happy. It did seem to me that we had all misjudged him completely. It was he who was normal and balanced. The rest of the world was hopelessly crazy.

But Shejokaka himself proved me wrong a few days later.

One morning, word come from my aunt's house that Shejokaka had left for his heavenly abode. He could not have chosen a more crucial time to make his departure for, the same evening, my cousin was supposed to get married!

Fritz

After having stared at Jayant for about a whole minute, I could not help asking him, 'Are you well? You appear a little dispirited today.'

Jayant quickly lost his slightly preoccupied air, gave me a boyish smile and said, 'No. On the contrary, I am feeling a lot better. This place is truly wonderful.'

'You've been here before. Didn't you know good it was?'

'I had nearly forgotten,' Jayant sighed. 'Now some of my memories are slowly coming back. The bungalow certainly appears unchanged. I can even recognize some of the old furniture, such as these cane tables and chairs.'

The bearer came in with tea and biscuits on a tray. I poured.

'When did you come here last?'

'Thirty-one years ago. I was six then.'

We were sitting in the garden of the circuit house in Bundi. We had arrived only that morning. Jayant and I were old friends. We went to the same school and college. He now worked in the editorial division of a newspaper and I taught in a school. Although we had different jobs, it had not made any difference to our friendship. We had been planning a visit to Rajasthan for a long time. The main difficulty lay in both of us being able to get away together. That had, at last, been made possible.

Most people go to Jaipur, Udaipur, Chittor in Rajasthan; but Jayant kept talking about going to Bundi. I had no objection for, having read Tagore's poem 'The Fort of Bundi', I was certainly familiar with the name of the place and felt a pleasurable excitement at the prospect of actually seeing the fort. Not many people came to Bundi. But that did not mean that there was not much to see there. It could be that, from the point of view of a historian, Udaipur, Jodhpur and Chittor had a lot more to offer; but simply as a beautiful place, Bundi was perfect.

However, Jayant's insistence on Bundi did puzzle me somewhat. I learnt the reason on the train when we were coming down. Jayant had, apparently, visited Bundi as a child and had always wanted to return after growing up, just to see how far the modern Bundi matched his memories. Jayant's father, Animesh Das Gupta, had worked in the Archaeological Department. His work sometimes took him to historical places, which is how Jayant had had the chance to come to Bundi.

The circuit house was really rather splendid. Built during the time of the British, it must have been at least a hundred years old. It was a single-storeyed building with a sloping tiled roof. The rooms had high ceilings and the skylights had long, dangling ropes which could be pulled to open and shut them. The veranda faced the east. Right opposite it was a huge garden with a large number of roses in full bloom. Behind these were a lot of trees which obviously housed a vast section of local birds. Parrots could be seen everywhere; and peacocks could be heard, but only outside the compound.

We had already been on a sightseeing tour of the town. The famous fort of Bundi was placed amidst the hills. We saw it from a distance that day but decided to go back to take a closer look. The only things about that were reminders of modern times were the electric poles. Otherwise it seemed as though we were back in old Rajputana.

The streets were cobbled, the houses had balconies hanging from the first floor. The carvings done on these and the wooden doors bore evidence of the work of master craftsmen. It was difficult to believe we were living in the age of machines.

I noticed Jayant had turned rather quiet after arriving in Bundi. Perhaps some of his memories had returned. It is easy enough to feel a little depressed when visiting a place one may have seen as a child. Besides, Jayant was certainly more emotional than most people. Everyone knew that.

He put his cup down on the table and said, 'You know, Shankar, it is really quite strange. The first time I came here I used to sit cross-legged on these chairs. It seemed as though I was sitting on a throne. Now the chairs seem both small in size and very ordinary. The drawing-room here used to seem absolutely enormous. If I hadn't returned, those memories would have remained stuck in my mind for ever.'

I said, 'Yes, that's perfectly natural. As a child, one is small in size, so everything else seems large. One grows bigger with age, but the size of all the other things remains the same, doesn't it?'

We went for a stroll in the garden after tea. Jayant suddenly stopped walking and said, 'Deodar.'

I stared at him.

'A deodar tree. It ought to be here somewhere,' he said and

began striding towards the far end of the compound. Why did he suddenly think of a deodar tree?

A few seconds later I heard his voice exclaiming jubilantly, 'Yes, it's here! Exactly where it was before!'

'Of course it's where it was before,' I said. 'Would a tree go roaming about?'

Jayant shook his head impatiently. 'No, that is not what I meant. All I meant was that the tree is where I thought it might be.'

'But why did you suddenly think of a tree?'

Jayant stared at the trunk of the tree, frowning. Then he shook his head slowly and said, 'I can't remember that now. Something had brought me near the tree. I had done something here. A European . . . .'

'European?'

'No, I can't recall anything at all. Memory is a strange business. . . .'

They had a good cook in the circuit house. Later in the evening, while we sat having dinner at the oval dining table, Jayant said, 'The cook they had in those days was called Dilawar. He had a scar on his left cheek and his eyes were always red. But he was an excellent cook.'

Jayant's memories began returning one by one soon after dinner when went back to the drawing-room. He could recall where his father used to sit and smoke a cheroot; where his mother used to knit, and what magazines lay on the table.

And, slowly, in bits and pieces, he recalled the whole business about his doll.

It was not the usual kind of doll little girls play with. One of Jayant's uncles had brought for him from Switzerland a twelve-inch long figure of an old man, dressed in the traditional Swiss style. Apparently, it was very life-like. Although it was not mechanized it was possible to bend and twist its limbs. Its face had a smile on it and, on its head, it wore a Swiss cap with a little yellow feather sticking out from it. Its clothes, especially in their little details, were perfect—belt, buttons, pockets, collars, socks. There were even little buckles on the shoes.

His uncle had returned from Europe shortly before Jayant left for Bundi with his parents. The little old man had been bought in a village in Switzerland. The man who sold him had said to Jayant's uncle jokingly, 'He's called Fritz. You must call him by this name.

He won't respond to any other.'

Jayant said, 'I had a lot of toys when I was small. My parents gave me practically everything I wanted, perhaps because I was their only child. But once I had Fritz, I forgot all my other toys. I played only with him. A time came when I began to spend hours just talking to him. Our conversation had to be one-sided, of course, but Fritz had such a funny smile on his lips and a look in his eyes, that it seemed to me as though he could understand every word. Sometimes I wondered if he would actually converse with me if I could speak to him in German. Now it seems like a childish fantasy, but at that time the whole thing was very real to me. My parents did warn me not to overdo things, but I listened to no one. I had not yet been put in a school, so I had all the time in the world for Fritz.'

Jayant fell silent. I looked at my watch and realized it was 9.30 p.m. It was very quiet outside. We were sitting in the drawing-room of the circuit house. An oil lamp burnt in the room.

I asked, 'What happened to the doll?'

Jayant was still deep in thought. His answer to my question came so late that, by that time, I had started to think that he had not heard me at all.

'I had brought it to Bundi. It was destroyed here.'

'Destroyed? How?'

Jayant sighed.

'We were sitting out on the lawn having tea. I had kept the doll by my side on the grass. I was not really old enough to have tea, but I insisted and, in the process, the cup tilted and some of the hot tea fell on my trouser. I ran inside to change and came back to find that Fritz had disappeared. I looked around and found quite soon that a couple of stray dogs were having a nice tug-of-war with Fritz between them. Although he didn't actually come apart, his face was battered beyond recognition and his clothes were torn. In other words, Fritz did not exist for me any more. He was dead.'

'And then?' Jayant's story intrigued me.

'What could possibly happen after that? I arranged his funeral, that's all.'

'Meaning?'

'I buried him under that deodar tree. I had wanted to make a coffin. Fritz was, after all, a European. But I could find nothing, not even a little box. So, in the end, I buried him just like that.'

At last, the mystery of the deodar tree was solved.

We went to bed at around ten. Our room was a large one and our beds had been neatly made. Not being used to doing a lot of walking, I was feeling rather tired after the day's activities. Besides, the bed was very comfortable. I fell asleep barely ten minutes after hitting the pillow.

A slight noise woke me a little later. I turned on my side and found Jayant sitting up on his bed. The table lamp by his bed was on and, in its light, it was easy to see the look of anxiety on his face.

I asked, 'What is it? Are you not feeling well?'

Instead of answering my question, Jayant asked me one himself.

'Do you think this circuit house has got small animals? I mean, things like cats or mice?'

'I shouldn't be surprised if it does. Why?'

'Something walked over my chest. That's what woke me.'

'Rats and mice usually come in through drains. But I've never known them to climb on the bed.'

'This is the second time I've woken up, actually. The first time I heard a shuffling noise near the window.'

'Oh, if it was near the window, it is more likely to be a cat.'

'Yes, but. . . .'

Jayant still sounded doubtful. I said, 'Didn't you see anything after you switched the light on?'

'Nothing. But then, I didn't switch it on immediately after opening my eyes. To tell you the truth, I felt rather scared at first. But when I did switch it on, there was nothing to be seen.'

'That means whatever came in is still in the room.'

'Well . . . since both the doors are bolted from inside. . . .'

I rose quickly and searched under the bed, behind our suitcases and everywhere else in the room. I could not find anything. The door to the bathroom was closed. I opened it and was about to start another search when Jayant called out to me softly, 'Shankar!'

I came back to the room. Jayant was staring hard at the cover of his quilt. Upon seeing me, he pulled a portion of it near the lamp and said, 'Look at this!'

I bent over the cloth and saw tiny, brown circular marks on it.

I said, 'Well, these *could* have been made by a cat.'

Jayant did not say anything. It was obvious that something had deeply disturbed him. But it was 2.30 in the morning. I simply had to get a little more sleep, or I knew I would not stop feeling tired. And we had plans of doing a lot of sightseeing the following day.

So, after murmuring a few soothing words—such as, don't worry, I am here with you and who knows, those marks may have been on your quilt already when you went to bed—I switched off the light once more and lay down. I had no doubt that Jayant had only had a bad dream. All those memories of his childhood had upset him, obviously, and that was what had led to his dreaming of a cat walking on his chest.

I slept soundly for the rest of the night. If there were further disturbances, Jayant did not tell me about them. But I could see in the morning that he had not slept well.

'Tonight I must give him one of the tranquillizers I brought with me,' I thought.

We finished our breakfast by nine, as we had planned, and left for the fort. A car had already been arranged. It was almost nine-thirty by the time we reached it.

Some of Jayant's old forgotten memories began coming back again, though—fortunately—they had nothing to do with his doll. In fact, his youthful exuberance made me think he had forgotten all about it.

'There—there's that elephant on top of the gate!' he exclaimed, 'and the turrets! And here is the bed made of silver and the throne. Look at that picture on the wall—I saw it the last time!'

But within an hour, his enthusiasm began to wane. I was so engrossed myself that I did not notice it at first. But, while walking through a hall and looking at the chandeliers hanging from the ceiling, I suddenly realized Jayant was no longer walking by my side. Where was he?

We had a guide with us. 'Babu has gone out on the terrace,' he told me.

I came out of the hall and found Jayant standing absent-mindedly near a wall on the other side of the terrace. He did not seem to notice my presence even when I went and stood beside him. He started when I called him by his name.

'What on earth is the matter with you?' I asked. 'Why are you standing here looking morose even in a beautiful place like this? I can't stand it.' Jayant simply said, 'Have you finished seeing everything? If so, let's . . . .'

Had I been alone, I would definitely have spent a little more time at the fort. But one look at Jayant made me decide in favour of returning to the circuit house.

A road through the hills took us back to town. Jayant and I were both sitting in the back of the car. I offered him a cigarette, but he refused. I noticed a veiled excitement in the movement of his hands. One moment he placed them near the window, then on his lap and, immediately afterwards, began biting his nails. Jayant was generally quiet by nature. This odd restlessness in him worried me.

After about ten minutes, I could not take it any more.

'It might help if you told me about your problem,' I said. Jayant shook his head.

'It's no use telling you for you're not going to believe me.'

'OK, even if I don't believe you, I can at least discuss the matter with you, can't I?'

'Fritz came into our room last night. Those little marks on my quilt were his footprints.'

There was very little I could do at this except put my hands on his shoulders and shake him. How could I talk sensibly to someone whose mind was obsessed with such an absurd idea?

'You didn't see anything for yourself, did you?' I said finally.

'No. But I could feel distinctly that whatever was walking on my chest had two feet, not four.'

As we came out of the car at the circuit house, I decided Jayant must be given a nerve tonic or some such thing. A tranquillizer might not be good enough. I could not allow a thirty-seven-year-old man to be so upset by a simple memory from his childhood.

I said to Jayant upon reaching our room, 'It's nearly 12 o'clock. Should we not be thinking of having a bath?'

'You go first,' said Jayant and flung himself on the bed.

An idea came to my mind in the bath. Perhaps this was the only way to bring Jayant back to normalcy.

If a doll had been buried somewhere thirty years ago and if one knew the exact spot, it might be possible to dig the ground there. No doubt most of it would have been destroyed, but it was likely that we'd find just a few things, especially if they were made of metal, such as the buckle of a belt or brass buttons on a jacket. If Jayant could actually be shown that that was all that was left of his precious doll, he might be able to rid himself of his weird notions; otherwise, he would have strange dreams every night and talk of Fritz walking on his chest. If this kind of thing was allowed to continue, he might actually go totally mad.

Jayant seemed to like my idea at first. But, after a little while, he said, 'Who will do the digging? Where will you find a spade?'

I laughed, 'Since there is a garden, there is bound to be gardener. And that would mean there's a spade. If we offered him a little tip, I have no doubt that he would have no objection to digging up a bit of the ground near the trunk of a tree at the far end of the lawn.'

Jayant did not accept the idea immediately; nor did I say anything further. He went and had his bath after a little bit of persuasion. At lunch, he ate nothing except a couple of chapatis with meat curry, although I knew he was quite fond of his food.

After lunch we went and sat in the cane chairs on the veranda that overlooked the garden. There appeared to be no one else in the circuit house. There was something eerie about the silence that afternoon. All we could hear was the noise made by a few monkeys that sat on the gulmohar tree across the cobbled path.

Around 3 p.m., we saw a man come into the garden, carrying a watering can. He was an old man. His hair, moustaches and side-burns had all turned white.

'Will you ask him or should I?'

At this question from Jayant, I raised a reassuring hand and went straight to the gardener. After I had spoken to him, he looked at me rather suspiciously. Clearly, no one had ever made such a request. 'Why, Babu?' he asked. I laid a friendly hand on his shoulder and said, 'Don't worry about the reason. I'll give you five rupees. Please do as you're told.'

He relented at this, going so far as to give me a salute accompanied by a broad grin.

I beckoned to Jayant, who was still sitting on the veranda. He rose and began walking towards me. As he came closer, I saw the pallor of his face.

I did hope we would find at least a certain portion of the doll.

The gardener, in the meantime, had fetched a spade. The three of us made our way to the deodar tree.

Jayant pointed at the ground about a yard from the trunk of the tree and said, 'Here.'

'Are you sure?' I asked him.

Jayant nodded silently.

'How much did you dig?'

'At least eight inches.'

The gardener started digging. The man had a sense of humour. As he lifted his spade, he asked if there was hidden treasure under the ground and, if so, whether we would be prepared to share it with him. I had to laugh at this, but Jayant's face did not register even the slightest trace of amusement. It was the month of October and not at all warm in Bundi. Yet, the collar of his shirt was soaked in sweat. He was staring at the ground unblinkingly. The gardener continued to dig. Why was there no sign of the doll?

The raucous cry of a peacock made me turn my head for a moment and, in that instant, Jayant made a strange sound. I quickly looked at him. His eyes were bulging. He raised his right hand and pointed at the hole in the ground with a finger that was trembling visibly.

Then, he asked in a voice turned hoarse with fear, 'What. . . what is that?'

The spade slipped from the gardener's hand. I, too, gaped at the ground, open-mouthed in horror, amazement and disbelief.

There lay at our feet, covered in dust, lying flat on its back, a twelve-inch-long, pure white, perfect little human skeleton.

The Chameleon

Nikunja Saha occupied a chair in the New Mahamaya Cabin, ordered a cup of tea and a plate of potato cutlets, and looked around carefully. Were any of his acquaintances present in the restaurant? Yes, Rasik Babu and Sreedhar were already here. Panchanan would probably turn up in about ten minutes. The more the merrier. The success of his disguise lay in not being recognized by anyone who knew him.

But, then, all his disguises had been remarkably successful so far. Today, half his face was covered by a beard and the shape of his nose had been altered a little with the help of plasticine. But he had changed his gait and style of speech so completely that even Panchanan Gui, who had known him for ten years, could not recognize him when he came to ask for a match from Nikunja. Mustering all his courage, Nikunja had even ventured to speak, 'You may keep the whole box. I have another.' Panchanan had given no sign of recognition even at the sound of his voice. This was the essence of real art.

Nikunja had lost all his other interests. This passion for disguises had now become almost an obsession. He had plenty of time, for he had given up the job he had before. He used to be a salesman in the Orient Book Company on College Street. A childless uncle of his had died recently, leaving Nikunja all the money he had made in the share market. The capital brought an interest of seven hundred and fifty rupees every month. He could, therefore, easily afford to leave his job.

The same uncle often used to tell him, 'Read, Nikunja, read as much as you can. There's nothing that one can't learn from books. You needn't go to a school, you needn't have a teacher—all you need are books. I have even heard that it is possible to learn to fly aeroplanes simply from instructions in a book.' There were two things his uncle himself had learnt quite well from books—palmistry and homoeopathy. Nikunja took his advice and bought books on leatherwork and photography. Very soon, he managed to learn the rudiments of both.

About six months ago, he had seen a fat American book on make-up on a footpath in College Street. Unable to resist the temptation, he had bought it and, since then, this new interest had taken a firm hold on his mind.

The strange thing was that Nikunja was not interested in the one place where make-up was needed every day—in the theatre, although he did toy with the idea of putting to some fruitful use what he had learnt. Who knows, he might even manage to make some extra money, he had thought.

He happened to know Bhulu Ghosh of the Naba Natta Company. Both were members of the East Bengal Club. Nikunja went to Bhulu's house on Amherst Street one day and told him of his wish.

Bhulu, however, was not very encouraging.

'Why,' he asked, 'do you want to mess about in the theatre? We already have Aparesh Datta in our company. He's been our make-up man for thirty-six years. It's not going to be easy to replace him. He has the entire art of make-up on his fingertips. If you went and told him you've been dabbling in it for just over six months, he wouldn't even look at you. Forget about getting a break, Nikunja. You appear to be leading a fairly happy and carefree life. Don't get involved in something you don't know enough about!'

Nikunja dropped the idea of becoming a professional make-up man.

But what was he to do with his knowledge? On whom could he practise his skill? He could not, after all, open a shop like a hair-cutting salon where people would come and pay to have their appearances altered.

Then an idea occurred to him. What about his own self? There were certain natural advantages in his appearance. Everything about him was average. He was of medium height, neither too dark nor very fair, his features neither sharp nor blunt. A straight, long nose could not be hidden. If one was tall, one's height could not be disguised. And the amount of make-up that was required to conceal a dark complexion was very likely to give the show away.

Nikunja studied his own appearance for two days and decided to start experimenting with himself.

But what after that? What could he possibly hope to achieve with his make-up and disguises?

Well, two things, certainly. The first would be to take his art to the very peak of perfection; and the second, to enjoy fooling all his friends.

Nikunja began buying materials for his make-up. He had read

in the book that the best in the market was the pancake make-up produced by Max Factor. But it was not available in India. Nikunja, therefore, had to go to his neighbour, Dr Biraj Chowdhury. Dr Chowdhury had once treated him for jaundice. Nikunja knew that his son, who was studying in America, was supposed to be returning home soon to attend his sister's wedding.

Nikunja did not beat about the bush and came straight to the point.

'Could your son please be asked to bring me something from America? I shall pay him here as soon as he arrives.'

'What is it that you want?'

'Stuff for make-up. I've got the name written down. One can't get it here.'

'All right. If you let me have the details, I shall certainly write to him.'

The Max Factor pancake make-up arrived within three weeks. Nikunja had already bought every other requisite—brushes, spirit gum, eyebrow pencils, black enamel paint to create missing teeth, white powder for grey hair and a number of fine nylon nets to help wear wigs. In addition to all these, he had also bought loose strands of hair which he fixed on some of the nylon nets one by one and made at least twenty different moustaches, twenty types of beards and various wigs: rough, smooth, straight, wavy, curly like Africans—the lot.

But, of course, it was not enough simply to change one's face. One had to have a change of clothes as well. Nikunja took about a week to make a round of New Market, Bara Bazaar and Grant Street to collect clothes of all kinds. Some of these had to be tailor-made since ready-made material was not always available. After sorting out his clothes, he turned his attention to other things he would wear and, eventually, managed to collect seven types of glasses, twelve pairs of sandals, ten different caps—including the cap of a police inspector. He also bought five types of fabric to make *pugris* and five wrist watches. The *kada* of Sikhs, the sacred thread of the Brahmins, the different prayer beads of the Vaishnavas and other religious groups, a wide assortment of medallions and talismans and, finally, paste diamond earrings to go with the attire of an *ustaad*—all were added to his collection.

A large mirror was bought and a strong bulb was fixed over it. In order to be able to work even during a power cut he also had to invest in a Japanese generator and teach his servant, Nitai, how to operate it.

He began practising from 16th November. He noted the date in his diary. At eight in the morning, he began working on his make-up and finished by 4 p.m. He knew it would be best if he dressed as someone from the average middle class. There was no point in dressing as a beggar or a labourer for the real test lay in being able to visit the New Mahamaya Cabin and having a cup of tea amidst his friends and acquaintances.

The very first day brought him success. He was made up as a solicitor: dark, bushy eyebrows and matching moustaches, white trousers, a much-used black gown, an old briefcase, a pair of worn out black shoes and loose white socks.

Panchanan came and sat at his table. The flutter in Nikunja's heart persisted for as long as he sat there, sipping a cup of tea. But he realized that day how totally incurious one could be about a fellow being, especially if one's attention was engaged elsewhere.

Panchanan saw him all right, but took not the slightest notice of him. He kept reading the little race book he was holding in his left hand and with his right, tearing pieces from an omelette with a spoon, and stuffing them into his mouth. He did not glance at Nikunja even when he asked the waiter for his bill. This was an entirely new experience, a new thrill. Nikunja knew that from that day, this would be his only occupation.

Something rather funny happened that evening when he returned home. He really ought to have anticipated it, but the thought had not occurred to him.

Shashi Babu lived in the ground floor flat, right next to the front door. It was possible to see from his living-room all those who came in and went out of the building.

It was about a quarter-past-seven in the evening when Nikunja returned. The light in the passage was on.

'Who is it?' asked Shashi Babu as Nikunja stepped in, still dressed as a solicitor.

Nikunja stopped. Then he walked towards Shashi Babu's room. Now they were facing each other.

'Who are you looking for?' said Shashi Babu.

'Does Nikunja Saha live in this house?'

'Yes. Turn right as you go up the stairs. His is the first room.'

Shashi Babu turned away to go inside. Nikunja removed his eyebrows and moustaches in an instant and said, 'I need some information.'

'Yes?' Shashi Babu turned back and grew round-eyed, 'Why—it's you, Nikunja!'

Nikunja went straight into Shashi Babu's room. Shashi Babu should be told about what he was doing. It might make things easier if someone in the building could be taken into confidence.

'Listen, Shashi-da, you may find me returning like this now and then, dressed differently. I may come as a solicitor or a doctor, or perhaps a Sikh or a Marwari—do you understand? I'll go out in the evening and return at night. I'd like to come straight in here and remove my make-up. But this is just between you and me, all right?'

'How odd! When did you develop such a weird interest? Are you in the theatre?'

Shashi Babu was a true gentleman. He had read a lot and was the librarian of the local Bankim Library. He knew something of human nature. 'All right,' he said, 'as long as you don't do anything wrong, it's fine. Some people do have strange hobbies, I know.'

Nikunja knew he could not go out in disguise more than twice a week since putting on the right make-up was a time-consuming task. So he decided to spend the rest of his time making a study of people. New Market was undoubtedly a gold mine for this purpose. Just one visit was enough to show him the wide variety of people who came there. Apart from New Market, he went to look at people in the stadium, and in the queues for Hindi films. He noted down in his diary details of all who struck him as interesting. On a few occasions, he even found an excuse to speak to them. Questions like, 'Could you tell me the time?' or 'Which bus do you think would take me to Gariahat?' often proved useful. On the days when he happened to be free, he continued to visit the New Mahamaya Cabin, dressed in his own normal clothes, to spend a few hours with his friends, discussing the world's problems. He would then return as usual to his flat in Vrindavan Basak Lane. His young servant, Nitai, knew about his master's disguises and seemed to enjoy the whole experience as much as Nikunja himself. But not much could be said of Nitai's own intelligence.

'Can you recognize me? Can you recognize me as your Babu?'

'But you *are* my Babu. I know it!'

'Does your Babu have moustaches like these? Is he bald? Does he wear such clothes? Such glasses? Does he take a shawl?'

Nitai only smiled at these questions and kept leaning against the door, watching him. Nikunja realized his art was something a fool like Nitai would never learn to appreciate.

But was it enough simply to deceive a few close friends?

This question kept coming back to Nikunja. He discovered that a stronger ambition was rising in his heart. He must find out how his skill at make-up and disguise worked on a larger audience.

He found an opportunity soon enough.

A few inmates of the house were gathered in Shashi Babu's room one day, including Nikunja. Among the others was Bhujanga Babu, who was interested both in religion and yoga. Rumour had it that he had once very nearly become a sanyasi. In fact, even now, he knew a lot of sadhus and had been on a tour of Kedar–Badri, Varanasi and Kamakshya. It was he who happened to mention that a Tantrik sadhu had arrived in Tarapeeth. He was reputed to have more supernatural powers than even the mythological sadhus one had read about.

'What name, did you say?' asked Harabilas, who worked in a bank.

'I didn't,' replied Bhujanga Babu, annoyed. His eyebrows had a habit of rising whenever he was irritated and his glasses would come slipping down his nose.

'Is it Hiccups Baba?' said Harabilas.

The papers had indeed carried a story on Hiccups Baba. It was said that he was given to having severe fits of hiccups while talking to his visitors, as though his end was near, but he recovered each time and resumed his conversation as if nothing had happened. Yet, doctors had confirmed that those hiccups were indeed of the variety that one might have just before dying.

Bhujanga Babu pushed his glasses back with a finger and said that the sadhu in question was called Kalikananda Swamy.

'Will you go and visit him?' asked Tanay Babu, an insurance agent, 'I'll come with you, if I may. A look at a sadhu always gives me a feeling of . . . you know. . . of something. I'm disgusted with this wholesale filth in Calcutta.'

Bhujanga Babu said that he did intend going one day.

Nikunja went back to his room without a word. His heart beat faster. He must check immediately what kind of things he would need to dress as a Tantrik, and how many of those things he had already got.

He cast a quick glance through the description of a Tantrik in Bankimchandra's *Kapalkundala*. Nothing had changed. Sadhus and sanyasis dressed today just as they had done hundreds of years ago. Nikunja had once gone to Varanasi. A look at the Dashashwamedh Ghat had given him a glimpse of ancient India.

He made his plans.

Tarapeeth was in Beerbhum, near Rampurhat. A cousin of his lived in Rampurhat. He would first go to his cousin's house, with his make-up kit. There he would get dressed and then go to Tarapeeth. That was where the real challenge lay. He had to find out if he could mingle easily with the other sadhus. Besides, if Bhujanga Babu and the others were also going to be there, so much the better. It would give him added pleasure if they failed to recognize him.

Nikunja already had most of what was required. All he needed was a large walking stick, a pair of tongs and a copper bowl. He would also need a special wig, but that could be arranged quite easily.

Bhujanga Babu and his family were going to leave for Tarapeeth on Wednesday. Nikunja left the day before. He had already told his cousin, Santosh, of his arrival, although Santosh did not yet know the reason.

Santosh's father had been the owner of Purnima Talkies in Rampurhat. After his death the year before, its ownership went to Santosh who began to show popular Hindi films and earn a fair amount. Possibly as a result of his interest in Hindi films, he grew quite excited at the prospect of an adventure when he learnt of Nikunja's plans. 'Don't worry about a thing, Nikunja-da,' he said, 'I shall take you in my car and drop you near the cremation ground.'

Nikunja had forgotten that the cremation ground in Tarapeeth had a temple and it was in the cremation ground that the sadhus stayed. The famous Tantrik, Bama Khepa, had lived here.

On Wednesday, Nikunja began working on his make-up quite early in the morning. The real Nikunja was wiped out the minute he fixed on a long beard, moustaches and a wig. Long hair rippled down to his shoulders, his forehead was smeared with sandalwood paste with a vermilion mark in the centre; three rows of *rudraksha* beads were wound around his neck. When he finally slipped out of his own clothes and put on a saffron robe, Santosh jumped up and quickly touched his feet.

'Oh, my God, Nikunja-da! This is perfect! No one on earth can recognize you now. I can tell only because I have been standing here throughout. Or I, too, would have been fooled!'

The experience of the last few months had taught Nikunja's hands to move faster. He was ready by half-past-two. The tongs and the copper bowl were brand new; so they, too, had to be made to look as though they had been used for some time. By 4 p.m., Nikunja Saha alias Ghanananda Maharaj was ready to depart. It was necessary to have a new name, but Nikunja had decided to speak as little as possible. Sadhus were different from ordinary folk. If a sadhu did not speak, no one would find it odd. The new name was Santosh's idea. 'When you get down from the car, Nikunja-da,' he said, 'people are bound to ask me who you are. You must have a name.'

Ghanananda had a deep, sombre ring to it. Santosh felt quite pleased.

Normally he drove himself. But, today, he took a driver.

'I shall have to go around with this sadhu baba,' he told the driver, 'you must keep an eye on the car.'

Here, Nikunja felt it was necessary to mention something to Santosh. 'I must be left alone when we reach there. I will try to get as close as possible to Kalikananda. I'm sure there will be groups of other sadhus near him. I will try to join one of these. You go and sit among the visitors.

'All right. Don't worry, Nikunja-da, I'll manage.'

By the time Santosh's car reached the cremation ground in Tarapeeth, there was barely half-an-hour left before sunset. This place was no different from other holy places—a crowd outside the temple, little shops on both sides of the road selling flowers, vermilion, books, calendars, tea, biscuits, *samosas* and fly-ridden *jalebis*.

But Nikunja's experience here turned out to be very different from that in the New Mahamaya Cabin. It was amazing how a saffron-clad figure could arouse respect and admiration. The minute he came out of the car, people—young and old, men, women, boys and girls—started touching his feet. Nikunja's hand rose automatically in a gesture of blessing as he began to move forward. Soon, it became impossible to put his hand down even for a second. Had Santosh not been with him, he would probably have stayed stuck in the same spot all night. 'Please, please, give way,' said Santosh and pushed through the crowd. They finally managed to get inside and reach a relatively quiet corner. There were other sadhus, all dressed in saffron, so there was not much of a chance here for being singled out for attention.

Nikunja glanced around. A small crowd had gathered under a banyan tree at some distance. Not many were wearing saffron, so presumably they were ordinary people who had come to look at a sadhu.

'Wait here for a minute, Nikunja-da,' said Santosh, 'while I go and check if that is where Kalikananda is sitting. I will take you near him and then leave you. But I won't go far. Let me know when you wish to leave.'

Santosh returned a few moments later and confirmed that Kalikananda was indeed sitting under that tree and the crowd was listening to his words of wisdom.

'Go ahead, Nikunja-da. There's nothing to worry about.'

Nikunja made his way to the banyan tree. He was not worried. A feeling of complete satisfaction had enveloped his mind the minute he had set foot here. His make-up was flawless. He was the perfect artist, he felt convinced.

Kalikananda's discourse could be heard from where Nikunja had been standing. His voice grew louder as Nikunja came closer. Then he saw him. A strong personality, no doubt, made stronger by the tiger skin he was sitting on. What he was saying was nothing new, but the man was clearly a gifted speaker. There was something special in the way he spoke. And his eyes! The whites of his eyes were not really white. There was a tinge of pink in them. Could it be a result of smoking *ganja*? Possibly.

About fifty people were gathered around and the number was increasing steadily. There was Bhujanga Babu with his wife! Tanay Babu must also be sitting somewhere in the crowd. Bhujanga Babu must have arrived quite early, for he was sitting right in the front.

On both sides of Kalikananda and behind him, sat other sadhus. All had flowing beards, long hair, *rudraksha* beads round their necks and their bodies were smeared with ash. There was no difference at all between their appearance and Nikunja's.

Nikunja passed the crowd and moved towards this group of sadhus. From somewhere in the distance, came the faint strains of a *bhajan*. Suddenly the song started to sound louder. The reason was simple. Kalikananda had stopped talking.

Nikunja looked at the sadhu. Kalikananda's bloodshot eyes were fixed on him in an unblinking stare.

Nikunja stopped.

Everyone else turned their eyes on him.

This time Kalikananda spoke.

'A disguise, eh? Is a saffron costume all that is required to make a sadhu? And a few beads round one's neck? And ash on one's body? How dare you! What if I pulled at your hair? Do you realize what might happen? Could you still go on pretending?'

Santosh was beside Nikunja in a flash.

'That's enough, Nikunja-da. Back to the car. At once.'

Nikunja's whole body felt numb. He had to lean on Santosh for support as they began walking towards the main gate. His eyes were virtually closed, but he could not shut his ears. Kalikananda's final words boomed in the air: 'Do you know the result of such deception, Nikunja Saha?'

Nikunja had to move into a new flat in Calcutta, far away from where he had lived before. Bhujanga Babu was a witness to the Tarapeeth episode. No doubt he would have gossiped, and then it would have been quite impossible to face all the others who knew him. Luckily, he found a small flat in Bhabanipore. The rent was Rs 250 per month.

Even after his return to Calcutta, Nikunja shivered every time he thought of Kalikananda. Heavens—what acute perception that Tantrik had! Nikunja got rid of all the 'religious' costumes he had. Dresses meant for priests, pandits, *maulvis* and monks were all thrown into the river.

It took him about three weeks to come back to his normal self. He had made a few friends in the meantime. There was another restaurant here, not very far from his house, called Parashar Cabin. The people he met here—Tarak Babu, Nagenda, Shibu—knew nothing of his scandalous past. Shibu, as a matter of fact, worked in a theatre. He took Nikunja with him one day to see his play, *Fiery Sparks*. 'You must see the first class make-up I'm given,' Shibu said before they left.

Nikunja did not know whether to laugh or cry when Shibu's make-up was done. What kind of make-up was this? Had they never seen what really good make-up could be like? If they saw his own, they would be bound to feel ashamed!

The next instant he recalled the incident in Tarapeeth. But, then, Tantriks did often have special supernatural powers. There was nothing surprising in that. Nikunja himself had made a wrong move, that was all.

Yes, that experience had been a frightening one. But surely that was no reason to give up his favourite occupation altogether? No, that could never be. There were so many other different characters he had not tried his hand at. Why, he had not yet tried disguising himself as a criminal, had he? With the only exception of the Tantrik, every other disguise he had donned was harmless and nondescript. No one would give such characters a second glance, anyway. The real challenge lay in disguising oneself as someone everyone would look at and yet fail to recognize the real person behind the make-up.

What should the criminal look like? Crew-cut hair, heavy stubble, a scar under one eye, a broken nose—like a boxer—a tattoo on his hand, a chain round his neck, a buttonless checked shirt and a Burmese lungi.

After his Tarapeeth experience, Nikunja should not have gone anywhere near a disguise. But his passion had developed into a kind of addiction. He forgot the Tantrik and began working with renewed enthusiasm.

Nikunja sat down before his mirror fairly early one morning, soon after a cup of tea. He did not, therefore, get a chance to glance at the newspaper and so missed the news of the double murder in Kidderpore and the photograph of the absconding miscreant, Bagha Mandal. If he did see it, no doubt he would have done his make-up a little differently.

A photograph of Bagha Mandal had been published about six months ago, after a daring robbery. On that occasion, too, Bagha had managed to hoodwink the police. His photo had been published simply to warn the general public. Had Nikunja seen his photo at that time and had it, somehow, remained embedded in his memory? Why else should he start disguising himself exactly as Bagha Mandal?

But even if he had seen the photograph, he had obviously not grasped the significance of the story that had accompanied it. If he had, he would not have felt any surprise at the way people quickly left the Parashar Cabin as soon as he came in and sat at a table.

What was the matter? Why was everyone behaving so strangely? Where did the manager disappear to? Why had the waiter gone so pale?

How was Nikunja to know that the manager had gone to the

chemist next door to telephone the police and that his phone call would bring the police van to Nikunja's neighbourhood?

But, at this critical moment, Nikunja's guardian angel stepped in. While he did not exactly offer a helping hand to get him out of the mess, he certainly offered a little finger. Nikunja's eyes suddenly fell on a newspaper that was lying on a vacant chair. The page it was opened at carried Bagha Mandal's photograph, together with a short, brisk write-up.

This was the face that had gradually come to life this morning in Nikunja's mirror.

Nikunja's limbs began to feel rather heavy. But he could not stop himself from grabbing the paper to read the article. Everything fell into place at once.

He forced himself to get up and walk out of the restaurant as casually as he could. Then he began walking towards his house as fast as his legs could carry him (running would attract attention). It took him ten minutes to reach his house. On his way, he heard the sound of a vehicle and assumed—correctly—that it was the police van, but paid no attention. Let them come. The police would be fooled. By the time they came up the stairs, Nikunja Saha's disguise would have vanished. It did not matter if the police found Nikunja Saha. After all, it was not Nikunja who was the culprit.

He told his servant to make him a cup of tea and bolted the door. Oh no! There was a power cut. It would take him a little while to start the Japanese generator.

Never mind. There were candles. But first he must remove his clothes, and that could be done in the dark.

Nikunja slipped out of the lungi, shirt and the black jacket and threw them on his bed. Then he changed into his pyjamas and took a candle out of the drawer of his table. He lit it and placed it before his mirror.

There was still no sign of the police. They were perhaps searching the whole area to see where Bagha was hiding. Certainly, no one in this building had seen him come in. But people from the neighbouring houses might have done.

Nikunja started to remove his make-up. He must first take off his false moustaches.

False?

If the moustaches were false, why didn't they come off? Anything stuck with spirit gum usually came off at the first pull. Why didn't these?

Nikunja brought the candle closer to his face and peered at the mirror. His blood froze.

The moustaches were real. Each hair had sprung from his own skin. There was no sign of gum on them!

The wig was not a wig, either. It was his own hair. And the stubble, which he had created by pasting each individual hair, also appeared to be perfectly genuine.

And the scar? No artist on earth could have created that scar simply with the help of paint and plasticine. It was the result of the fight fought nineteen years ago with Badru Sheik in Entail. Bagha, then called Radhu Mandal, was still an apprentice in the world of crime and criminals, learning the tricks of the trade from Meghanad Rakshit. . . .

The police had to break the door open. The inspector turned a powerful torch on the figure of Bagha Mandal, lying flat on the ground, unconscious.

'Does this man live in this house?' he asked Nitai.

'Yes, sir. He's my master.'

'What is he known as?'

'Nikunja Babu. Saha Babu.'

'Ha! Pretending to be a gentleman, was he?'

Then he said to his constable, 'Shake him. Shake him well, until he regains consciousness. Then we shall decide what to do with him.'

The inspector raised his revolver and aimed at the inert figure.

The wig came off and fell on the ground with the first shake. Then came the moustaches. And then the scar slipped off, together with the nylon net and the extra bit of plasticine with which the shape of the nose had been altered.

By then, Nikunja was fully conscious.

A stern warning from the police had the effect a Tantrik's threat had failed to produce.

Nikunja is now reading a lot on clay modelling. Since the river is not far away, it is possible for Nitai to bring him all the clay he needs. Nikunja plans to use Nitai as his first model.

The Pterodactyl's Egg

Badan Babu has stopped going to Curzon Park after work. He used to enjoy his daily visits to the park. Every evening he would go straight from his office and spend about an hour, just resting quietly on a bench, next to the statue of Suren Banerjee. Then, when the crowds in the trams grew marginally thinner, he would catch one back to his house in Shibthakur Lane.

Now new tram lines had been laid inside the park. The noise of the traffic had ruined the atmosphere totally. There was no point in trying to catch a few quiet moments here. Yet, it was impossible to go back home straight after office, packed into a bus like a sardine in a tin.

Besides, Badan Babu simply had to find some time every day to try and enjoy the little natural beauty that was left in the city. He might be no more than an ordinary clerk, but God had given him a lively imagination. He had thought up so many different stories sitting on that bench in Curzon Park. But there had never been the time to write them down. Had he, indeed, managed to find the time, no doubt he would have made quite a name for himself.

However, not all his efforts had been wasted.

His seven-year-old son, Biltu, was an invalid. Since he was incapable of moving around, most of his time was spent in listening to stories. Both his parents told him stories of all kinds—fairy tales, folk tales, funny tales and spooky tales, tales they had heard and tales they had read. In the last three years, he had been told at least a thousand stories. Badan Babu had lately been making up stories himself for his son. He usually did this sitting in Curzon Park.

Over the last few weeks, however, Biltu had made it plain that he no longer enjoyed all his stories. One look at Biltu's face was enough to see that he had been disappointed.

This did not surprise Badan Babu very much. It was not possible to think up a good plot during the day, which was spent in doing his work in the office. And now that the peace of Curzon Park had been shattered, his only chance of sitting there in the evening and doing a bit of thinking was lost forever.

He tried going to Lal Deeghi a few times. Even that did not work. The huge, monstrous communications building next to the Deeghi blocked a large portion of the sky. Badan Babu felt suffocated.

Then even the park near Lal Deeghi was invaded by tram lines and Badan Babu was forced to look for a different spot.

Today, he had come to the riverside.

After walking along the iron railings for about a quarter of a mile on the southern side of Outram Ghat, he found an empty bench.

There was Fort William, not far away. In fact, he could see the cannon. The cannonball stood fixed at the end of an iron rod, almost like a giant lollipop.

Badan Babu recalled his school days. The cannon went off every day at 1 p.m., the boys came rushing out for their lunch-break and the headmaster, Harinath Babu, took out his pocket watch religiously and checked the time.

The place was quiet, though not exactly deserted. A number of boats were tied nearby and one could see the boatmen talking among themselves. A grey Japanese ship was anchored in the distance. Further down, towards Kidderpore, the skyline was crowded with the masts of ships and pulleys.

This was a pleasant place.

Badan Babu sat down on the bench.

Through the smoke from the steamers he could see a bright spot in the sky. Could it be Venus?

It seemed to Badan Babu that he had not seen such a wide expanse of sky for a long time. Oh, how huge it was, how colossal! This was just what he needed for his imagination to soar high.

Badan Babu took off his canvas shoes and sat cross-legged on the bench.

He was going to make up for lost time and find new plots for a number of stories today.

He could see Biltu's face—happy and excited!

'Namaskar.'

Oh no! Was he going to be disturbed even here?

Badan Babu turned and found a stranger standing near the bench: a man, exceedingly thin, about fifty years old, wearing brown trousers and a jacket, a jute bag slung from one shoulder. His features were not clear in the twilight, but the look in his eyes seemed to be remarkably sharp.

A contraption hung from his chest. Two rubber tubes attached to it were fixed into the man's ears.

'Hope I'm not disturbing you,' said the newcomer with a slight smile, 'please don't mind. I've never seen you before, so. . . .'

Badan Babu felt considerably put out. Why did the man have to come and force himself on him? Now all his plans were upset. What was he going to tell poor Biltu?

'You've never seen me for the simple reason that I have never come here before,' he said, 'in a big city like this, isn't it natural that the number of people one has never seen should be more than the number of people one has?'

The newcomer ignored the sarcasm and said, 'I have been coming here every day for the last four years.'

'I see.'

'I sit here in this very spot every day. This is where I do my experiments, you know.'

Experiments? What kind of experiments could one do in this open space by the riverside? Was the man slightly mad?

But what if he was something else? He could be a hooligan, couldn't he? Or a pickpocket?

Good God—today had been pay day! Badan Babu's salary—two new, crisp hundred-rupee notes—was tied up in a handkerchief and thrust into his pocket. His wallet had fifty-five rupees and thirty-two paise.

Badan Babu rose. It was better to be safe than sorry.

'Are you leaving? So soon? Are you annoyed with me?'

'No, no.'

'Well, then? You only just came, didn't you? Why do you want to leave so soon?'

Perhaps Badan Babu was being over-cautious. There was no need to feel so very scared. After all, there were all those people in the boats, not far away.

Still Badan Babu hesitated.

'No, I must go. It's getting late.'

'Late? It's only a half-past-five.'

'I have to go quite far.'

'How far?'

'Right up to Bagbazar.'

'Pooh—that's not very far! It's not as though you have to go to a suburb like Serampore or Chuchro or even Dakshineshwar!'

'Even so, it will mean spending at least forty minutes in a tram. And then it takes about ten minutes to get to my house from the tram stop.'

'Yes, there is that, of course.'

The newcomer suddenly grew a little grave. Then he began muttering to himself, 'Forty plus ten. That makes fifty. I am not very used to calculating minutes and hours. My system is different . . . do sit down. Just for a bit. Please.'

Badan Babu sat down again. There was something in the man's eyes and his voice that compelled him to stay back. Was this what was known as hypnotism?

'I don't ask everyone to sit by me for a chat. But you strike me as a man different from others. You like to think. You're not bound only by monetary considerations, like ninety-nine point nine per cent of people. Am I right?'

Badan Babu said hesitantly, 'Well, I don't know. . . I mean. . . .'

'And you're modest! Good. I can't stand people who brag. If it was all just a question of bragging, no one would have the right to do so more than me.'

The newcomer stopped speaking. Then he took out the rubber tubes from his ears and said, 'I get worried sometimes. If I pressed the switch in the dark accidentally, all hell would break loose.'

At this point, Badan Babu could not help asking the question that was trembling on his lips.

'Is that a stethoscope? Or is it something else?'

The man ignored the question completely. How rude, thought Badan Babu. But, before he could say anything further, the other man threw a counter question at him, quite irrelevantly.

'Do you write?'

'Write? You mean—fiction?'

'Fiction or non-fiction, it does not matter. You see, that is something I have never been able to do. And yet, so many adventures, such a lot of experience and research. . . all this should be written and recorded for posterity.'

Experience? Research? What was the man talking about?

'How many kinds of travellers have you seen?'

His questions were really quite meaningless. How many people were lucky enough to have seen even one traveller?

Badan Babu said, 'I didn't even know travellers could be of more than one kind!'

'Why, there are at least three kinds. Anyone could tell you that! Those on water, those on land and those in the sky. Vasco-da-Gama, Captain Scott and Columbus fall into the first category; and in the second are Hiuen Tsang, Mungo Park, Livingstone and even our own globe-trotter, Umesh Bhattacharya.

And in the sky—say, Professor Picquard, who climbed up to fifty thousand feet in a balloon and that youngster, Gagarin. But all of these are ordinary travellers. The kind of traveller I am talking about doesn't move in water or land or even in the sky.'

'Where does he move, then?'

'Time.'

'What?'

'He moves in time. A journey into the past. A sojourn in the future. Roaming around freely in both. I don't worry too much about the present.'

Badan Babu began to see the light. 'You're talking about H.G.Wells, aren't you? The *Time Machine?* Wasn't that a contraption like a cycle with two handles? One would take you to the past and the other to the future? Wasn't a film made on this story?'

The man laughed contemptuously.

'That? That was only a story. I am talking of real life. My own experiences. My own machine. It's a far cry from a fictitious story written by an Englishman.'

Somewhere a steamer blew its horn.

Badan Babu started and pulled his *chadar* closer. In just a few minutes from now, darkness would engulf everything. Only the little lights on those boats would stay visible.

In the quickly gathering dusk Badan Babu looked at the newcomer once more. The last rays of the sun shone in his eyes.

The man raised his face to the sky and, after a few moments of silence, said, 'It's all quite funny, really. Three hundred years ago, right here by this bench, a crocodile happened to be stretched in the sun. There was a crane perched on its head. A Dutch ship with huge sails stood where that small boat is now tied. A sailor came out on the deck and shot at the crocodile from a rifle. One shot was enough to kill it. The crane managed to fly away, but dropped a feather in my lap. Here it is.'

He produced a dazzling white feather from his shoulder bag and gave it to Badan Babu.

'What. . . are these reddish specks?'

Badan Babu's voice sounded hoarse.

'Drops of blood from the injured crocodile fell on the bird.'

Badan Babu returned the feather.

The light in the man's eyes had dimmed. Visibility was getting poorer by the second. There had been loose bunches of grass and leaves floating in the river. Now they were practically invisible.

The water, the earth and the sky had all become hazy and indistinct.

'Can you tell what this is?'

Badan Babu took the little object in his hand—a small triangular piece, pointed at one end.

'Two thousand years ago. Right in the middle of the river—near where that buoy is floating—a ship with a beautifully patterned sail was making its way to the sea. It was probably a commercial vessel, going to Bali or some such place, to look for business. Standing here as the west wind blew, I could hear all its thirty-two oars splashing in the water.'

'You?'

'Yes, who else? I was hiding behind a banyan tree in this same spot.'

'Why were you hiding?'

'I had to. I didn't know the place was so full of unknown dangers. History books don't often tell you these things.'

'You mean wild animals? Tigers?'

'Worse than tigers. Men. There was a barbarian, about that high,' pointing to his waist, 'blunt-nosed, dark as darkness. Earrings hung from his ears, a ring from his nose, his body was covered with tattoo marks. He held a bow and an arrow in his hand. The arrow had a poisonous tip.'

'Really?'

'Yes, every word I utter is the truth.'

'You saw it all yourself?'

'Listen to the rest of the story. It was the month of April. A storm had been brewing for some time. Then it started. Oh, what a storm it was, the likes of which I have never seen again! That beautiful ship disappeared amidst the roaring waves before my eyes.'

'And then?'

'One solitary figure managed to make it to the shore, riding on a broken wooden plank, dodging the hungry sharks and alligators. But as soon as he got off that plank. . .oh, my God!'

'What?'

'You should have seen what that barbarian did to him. . .but then, I didn't stay till the end. An arrow had come and hit the trunk of the banyan tree. I picked it up and pressed the switch to return to the present.'

Badan Babu did not know whether to laugh or cry. How could that little machine have such magical powers? How was it possible?

The newcomer seemed to read his mind.

'This machine here,' he said, 'has these two rubber tubes. All you need to do is put these into your ears. This switch on the right will take you to the future and the one on the left will take you to the past. The little wheel with a needle has dates and years written on it. You can fix the exact date you wish to travel to. Of course, I must admit there *are* time when it misses the mark by about twenty years. But that doesn't make too much difference. It's a cheap model, you see. So it's not all that accurate.'

'Cheap?' This time Badan Babu was truly surprised.

'Yes, cheap in only a financial sense. Five thousand years of scientific knowledge and expertise went into its making. People think science has progressed only in the west. And that nothing has happened in this country. I tell you, a tremendous lot has indeed happened here, but how many know about it? We were never a nation to show off our knowledge, were we? The true artist has always stayed in the background, hasn't he? Look at our history. Does anyone know the names of the painters who drew on the walls of Ajanta? Who carved the temple of Ellora out of ancient hills? Who created the Bhairavi raga? Who wrote the Vedas? The *Mahabharata* is said to have been written by Vyasa and the *Ramayana* by Valmiki. But does anyone know of those hundreds of people who worked on the original texts? Or, for that matter, those that had actually contributed to their creation? The scientists in the west have often made a name for themselves by working on complex mathematical formulae. Do you know the starting point of mathematics?'

'Starting point? What starting point?' Badan Babu did not know.

'Zero,' said the man.

'Zero?'

'Yes, zero.'

Badan Babu was taken aback. The man went on.

'One, two, three, four, five, six, seven, eight, nine, zero. These are the only digits used, aren't they? Zero, by itself, means nothing. But the minute you put it next to one, it becomes ten: one more than nine. Magic! Makes the mind boggle, it does. Yet, we have accepted it as a matter of course. All mathematical formulae are based on these nine digits and zero. Addition, subtraction, multiplication, division, fractions, decimals, algebra, arithmetic—even atoms, rockets, relativity—nothing can work without these ten numbers. And do you know where this zero came from? From India. It went to West Asia first, then to Europe and from there to the whole world. See what I mean? Do you know how the system worked before?'

Badan Babu shook his head. How very limited his own knowledge was!

'They used the Roman system,' said the newcomer, 'there were no digits. All they had were letters. One was I, two was II, three was III, but four became a combination of two letters, IV. Five was again just one letter, V. There was no logic in that system. How would you write 1962? It would simply mean writing four different digits, right? Do you know how many letters you'd need in Roman?'

'How many?'

'Seven. MCMLXII. Does that make any sense at all? If you had to write eight hundred and eighty-eight, you would normally need only three digits. To write that in the Roman style, you'd need a dozen. DCCCLXXXVIII. Can you imagine how long it would have taken scientists to write their huge formulae? They would have all gone prematurely grey, or—worse—totally bald! And the whole business of going to the moon would have been delayed by at least a thousand years. Just think—some unknown, anonymous man from our own country changed the whole concept of mathematics!'

He stopped for breath.

The church clock in the distance struck six.

Why did it suddenly seem brighter?

Badan Babu looked at the eastern sky and saw that the moon had risen behind the roof of the Grand Hotel.

'Things haven't changed,' the man continued, 'there are still plenty of people in our country who are quite unknown and will probably always stay that way. But their knowledge of science is no less than that of the scientists of the west. They do not often work in laboratories or need papers and books or any other paraphernalia. All they do is think and work out solutions to problems—all in their mind.'

'Are you one of those people?' asked Badan Babu softly.

'No. But I was lucky enough to meet such a man. Not here, of course. I used to travel a lot on foot when I was younger. Went often to the mountains. That is where I met this man. A remarkable character. His name was Ganitananda. But he didn't just think. He wrote things down. All his mathematical calculations were done on the stones strewn about within a radius of thirty miles from where he lived. Every stone and boulder was scribbled on with a piece of chalk. He had learnt the art of travelling in time from his guru. It was from Ganitananda that I learnt that there had once been a peak higher than the Everest by about five thousand feet. Forty-seven thousand years ago, a devastating earthquake had made half of it go deeper into the ground. The same earthquake caused a crack in a mountain, from which appeared a waterfall. The river that is now flowing before us began its course from this waterfall.'

Strange! Oh, how strange it all was!

Badan Babu wiped his forehead with a corner of his *chadar* and said, 'Did you get that machine from him?'

'Yes. Well, no, he didn't actually give it to me. But he did tell me of the ingredients that went into making it. I collected it all and made the machine myself. These tubes here are not really made of rubber. It's the bark of a tree that's found only in the hills. I didn't have to go to a shop or an artisan to get even a single part made. The whole thing is made of natural stuff. I made the markings on the dial myself. But, possibly because it's hand-made, it goes out of order sometimes. The switch meant for the future hasn't been working for sometime.'

'Have you travelled to the future?'

'Yes, once I did. But not too far. Only up to the thirtieth century.'

'What did you see?'

'There wasn't much to see. I was the only person walking along a huge road. A weird looking vehicle appeared from somewhere and nearly ran me over. I did not try going into the future again.'

'And how far into the past have you travelled?'

'That's another catch. This machine cannot take me to the very beginning of creation.'

'Indeed?'

'Yes. I tried very hard, but the farthest back I could go was when the reptiles had already arrived.'

Badan Babu's throat felt a little dry.

'What reptiles?' he asked, 'snakes?'

'Oh no, no. Snakes are pretty recent.'

'Then?'

'Well, you know. . .things like the brontosaurus, tyrannosaurus and dinosaurus.'

'You mean you've been to other countries as well?'

'Ah, you're making the same mistake. Why should I have had to go to other countries? Do you think our own did not have these things?'

'Did it?'

'Of course it did! Right here. By the side of this bench.'

A cold shiver ran down Badan Babu's spine.

'The Ganga did not exist then,' said the man, 'this place was full of uneven, stony mounds and a lot of wild plants and creepers. There was a dirty pond where you can now see that jetty. I saw a will-o'-the-wisp rise over it and burn brightly, swaying from side to side. In its light, suddenly, I could see a pair of brilliant red eyes. You've seen pictures of a Chinese dragon, haven't you? This was a bit like that. I had seen its picture in a book. So I knew this was what was called a stegosaurus. It was crossing the pond, chewing on some leaves. I knew it would not attack me for it was a herbivorous animal. But, even so, I nearly froze with fear and was about to press the switch to return to the present, when I heard the flutter of wings right over my head. I looked up and saw a pterodactyl—a cross between a bird, an animal and a bat—swoop upon the stegosaurus. My eyes then fell on a large stone lying nearby and the reason for such aggression became clear. Inside a big crack in the stone lay a shiny, round, white egg. The pterodactyl's egg. Even though I was scared stiff, I couldn't resist the temptation. The two animals began fighting and I pocketed the egg. . . ha, ha, ha, ha!'

Badan Babu did not join in the laughter. Could this kind of thing really happen outside the realms of fiction?

'I would have allowed you to test my machine, but. . . .'

A nerve in Badan Babu's forehead began to throb. He swallowed hard. 'But what?'

'The chances of getting a satisfactory result are very remote.'

'Wh—why?'

'But you can try your luck. At least you don't stand to lose anything.'

Badan Babu bent forward. Dear God in heaven—please don't let me be disappointed!

The man tucked the tubes into Badan Babu's ears, pressed a switch and grabbed his right wrist.

'I need to watch your pulse.'

Badan Babu whispered nervously, 'Past? Or the future?'

'The past. Six thousand BC. Shut your eyes as tight as you can.'

Badan Babu obeyed and sat in eager anticipation for nearly a whole minute with his eyes closed. Then he said, 'Why, nothing seems to be. . . happening!'

The man switched the machine off and took it back.

'The chances were one in a million.'

'Why?'

'It would have worked only if the number of your hair was exactly the same as mine.'

Badan Babu felt like a deflated balloon. How sad. How very sad he was to lose such an opportunity!

The newcomer put his hand inside his bag again and brought out something else.

Everything was now quite clearly visible in the moonlight.

'May I hold it in my hand?' asked Badan Babu, unable to stop himself. The other man offered him the shiny, round object.

It was quite heavy, and its surface remarkably smooth.

'All right. Time to go now. It's getting late.'

Badan Babu returned the egg. Heaven knows what else this man had seen. 'Hope you're coming here again tomorrow,' said Badan Babu.

'Let's see. There's such an awful lot to be done. I am yet to test the validity of all that the history books talk about. First of all, I must examine how Calcutta came into being. What a hue and cry has been raised over Job Charnock. . . ! Allow me to take my leave today. Goodbye!'

Badan Babu reached the tram stop and boarded a tram. Then he slipped his hand into his pocket.

His heart stood still.

The wallet had gone.

There was nothing he could do except make an excuse and get down from the tram immediately.

As he began walking towards his house he felt like kicking himself. 'Now I know what happened,' he thought. 'When I closed my eyes and he held my hand. . . what a fool I made of myself!'

It was past 8 p.m. by the time he reached home.

Biltu's face lit up at the sight of his father.

By then, Badan Babu had started to feel more relaxed.

'I'll tell you a good story today,' he said, unbuttoning his shirt.

'Really? You mean it? It won't be a flop like all those others. . .?'

'No, no. I really mean it.'

'What kind of story, Baba?'

'The Pterodactyl's Egg. And many more. It won't finish in a day.'

If one considered carefully, the material he had collected today to make up stories for Biltu to bring a few moments of joy in his life, was surely worth at least fifty-five rupees and thirty- two paise?

Barin Bhowmik's Ailment

Mr Barin Bhowmik got into compartment D as instructed by the conductor and placed his suitcase under his seat. He would not need to open it during his journey. But he must keep the other smaller bag somewhere within easy reach. It contained such essentials as a comb, a hair brush, a toothbrush, his shaving kit, a book by James Hadley Chase to read on the way and several other knick-knacks, including throat pills. If the long train journey in a cold, air-conditioned compartment resulted in a sore throat, he would not be able to sing tomorrow. He quickly popped a pill into his mouth and put his bag on the small table before the window.

It was a Delhi-bound vestibule train. There were only about seven minutes left before its departure, and yet there was no sign of the other passengers. Would he be able to travel all the way to Delhi all alone? Could he indeed be so lucky? That would really be the height of luxury. The very idea brought a song to his lips.

He looked out of the window at the crowd on the platform. Two young men were glancing at him occasionally. Clearly, he had been recognized. This was not a new experience. People often recognized him for many were now familiar not just with his voice but also with his appearance. He had to give live performances at least half a dozen times every month. Listen to Barin Bhowmik tonight—he will sing songs written by Nazrul as well as *aadhunik*. Money and fame—both had come to Barin Bhowmik in full measure.

However, this had happened only over the last five years. Before that he had had to struggle a lot. It was not enough to be a talented singer. He needed a suitable break and proper backing. This came in 1963 when Bhola-da—Bhola Banerjee—invited him to sing in the Puja *pandal* in Unish Palli. Barin Bhowmik had not looked back since then.

In fact, he was now going to Delhi at the invitation of the Bengal Association to sing at their jubilee celebrations. They were paying for his travel by first class and had promised to make all arrangements for his stay in Delhi. He intended spending a couple of days in Delhi. Then he would go to Agra and Fatehpur Sikri and return to Calcutta a week later. After that it would be time for Puja again and life would become madly hectic.

'Your order for lunch, sir. . .?'

The conductor-guard appeared in the doorway.

'What is available?'

'You are a non-vegetarian, aren't you? You could choose between Indian and western food. If you want Indian, we've got. . . .'

Barin placed his order for lunch and had just lit a Three Castles cigarette when another passenger came into his compartment; the same instant, the train began pulling out of the station.

Barin looked at the newcomer. Didn't he seem vaguely familiar? Barin tried to smile, but his smile vanished quickly as there was no response from the other. Had he made a mistake? Oh, God—how embarrassing! Why did he have to smile like an idiot? A similar thing had happened to him once before. He had thumped a man very hard on the back with a boisterous, 'Hel-lo, Tridib-da! How *are* you?' only to discover he was not Tridib-da at all. The memory of this incident had caused him much discomfort for days afterward. God laid such a lot of traps to embarrass one!

Barin Bhowmik looked at the other man once more. He had kicked off his sandals and was sitting with his legs outstretched, leafing through the pages of the latest *Illustrated Weekly*. Again, Barin got the feeling that he had seen him somewhere, and not just for a few minutes. He had spent a long time in this man's company. But when was it? And where? The man had bushy eyebrows, a thin moustache, shiny hair and a little mole in the middle of his forehead. Yes, this face was certainly familiar. Could he have seen this man when he used to work for Central Telegraph? But surely the whole thing could not have been one-sided? His companion was definitely not showing any sign of recognition.

'Your order for lunch, sir?'

The conductor-guard had reappeared. He was a portly, rather amiable, gentleman.

'Well,' said the newcomer, 'we'll worry about lunch later. Could I have a cup of tea first?'

'Of course.'

'All I need is a cup and the beverage. I prefer drinking black tea.'

That did it. Barin Bhowmik suddenly began to feel rather unwell. There was a sinking feeling in the pit of his stomach. Then it seemed as though his heart had grown wings and flown straight into his lungs. It was not just the man's voice but also the words he uttered with a special emphasis: black tea. That was enough to remove the uncertainties from Barin's mind. Every memory came flooding back.

Barin had indeed seen this man before and that too—strangely enough—in a similar air-conditioned compartment of a train going to Delhi. He himself was going to Patna to attend the wedding of his cousin, Shipra. Three days before he left, he had won a little more than seven thousand rupees at the races. He could, therefore, afford the luxury of travelling by first class. This happened nine years ago, in 1964, long before he had become a well-known singer. He could vaguely recall the other man's surname. It began with a 'C'. Chowdhury? Chakravarty? Chatterjee?

The conductor-guard left. Barin realized he could no longer sit facing the other man. He went and stood in the corridor outside, well away from his fellow passenger. Yes, coincidences did occur in life. But this one was unbelievable.

But had 'C' recognized him? If he had not, there might be two reasons for it. Perhaps he had a weak memory. Or perhaps Barin's appearance had undergone significant changes in these nine years. He stared out of the window and tried to recall what these changes might possibly be.

He had gained a lot of weight, so presumably his face now looked fuller than it had before. He did not wear glasses in those days. Now he did. And his moustaches had gone. When did he shave them off? Ah yes. Not very long ago. He had gone to a salon on Hajra Road. The barber was both young and inexperienced. He failed to get the symmetry right while trimming the moustaches. Barin himself did not notice it at first; but when everyone in his office from the chatty old liftman, Sukdeo, to the sixty-two- year-old cashier, Keshav Babu, began commenting on it, he shaved his precious moustaches off totally. This had happened about four years ago.

So he had lost the moustaches, but gained a bit of flesh on his cheeks and acquired a pair of glasses. Feeling a little reassured, he returned to his carriage.

A bearer came in with a pot of tea and placed it in front of 'C'. Barin, too, felt the need for a drink, but did not dare speak to the bearer. What if 'C' recognized his voice?

Barin did not want even to think about what 'C' might do to him if he did get recognized. But, of course, everything depended on the kind of man 'C' was. If he was anything like Animesh-da, Barin had nothing to fear. Once, in a bus, Animesh-da realized someone was trying to pick his pocket. But he was too shy to raise a hue-and-cry, so he practically gave away his wallet to the pick-pocket, together with four crisp ten-rupee notes. He told his family afterwards, 'A big scene in a crowded bus with me playing a prominent role in it—no, I could not allow that to happen.'

Was this man a bit like that? Probably not. People like Animesh-da were hard to come by. Besides, his looks were not very reassuring. Everything about him—those bushy eyebrows, the blunt nose and that chin that jutted out—seemed to suggest that he would not hesitate at all to plant his hairy hands on Barin's throat and say, 'Are you not the same man who stole my clock in 1964? Scoundrel! I have spent these nine years looking for you! Today, I shall. . . .'

Barin dared not think any more. Even in this air-conditioned compartment there were beads of perspiration on his forehead. He stretched himself out on his berth and covered his eyes with his left arm. It was one's eyes that gave one away. In fact, 'C' had seemed familiar only because Barin recognized the look in his eyes.

He could now recall every incident vividly. It was not just the matter of stealing 'C' 's clock. He could remember every little thing he had stolen in his life ever since his boyhood. Some were totally insignificant things like a ballpoint pen (Mukul Mama's), or a cheap magnifying glass (his classmate, Akshay's), or a pair of bone cuff-links that belonged to Chheni-da and which Barin did not need at all. He never wore them even once. The only reason he stole these—and, for that matter, all those other things—was that they were near at hand and they belonged to someone else.

Between the ages of twelve and twenty-five, Barin Bhowmik had removed at least fifty different things from various people and made a collection in his house. What could one call it but stealing? The only difference between him and a regular thief was that a thief stole to survive in life; Barin did it out of habit. Nobody ever suspected him. He had, therefore, never been caught. Barin knew that this habit, this strange compulsion to steal things, was a kind of illness. Once he had even learnt the medical term for it from one of his friends who was a doctor, but now he could not remember what it was.

But 'C''s clock was the last thing he had stolen. In the last nine years, he had never experienced that sudden, strong urge. He knew he had got over his illness and was now totally cured.

The difference between stealing 'C' 's clock and all the other petty thefts he had indulged in was that he had really wanted that clock. It was a beautiful travelling clock, made in Switzerland. It lay in a blue square box and stood upright the moment the lid was lifted. It was an alarm clock and the sound of the alarm was so sweet that it was a pleasure to wake up to it.

Barin had used that clock consistently over these nine years. He took it with him wherever he went. Even today, the clock was resting within the depths of the bag kept on the table before the window.

'How far are you going?'

Barin gave a violent start. The other man was actually speaking to him!

'Delhi.'

'Pardon?'

'Delhi.'

The first time, in an effort to disguise his voice, Barin had spoken so softly that the man had clearly not heard him.

'Do you find it a bit too cold in here? Is that what's affecting your voice?'

'N-n-no.'

'It can happen, of course. Actually, I would have preferred going by ordinary first class if it wasn't for the dust.'

Barin did not utter a word. He did not want to look at 'C', but his own curiosity forced him to cast frequent glances in 'C' 's direction. Was 'C' showing signs of recognition? No. He appeared quite relaxed. Could he be pretending? But there was no way of being sure. After all, Barin did not know him well. All he had learnt the last time about his fellow passenger was that he liked having black tea and that he was wont to get down at every station to buy snacks. Thanks to this habit, Barin had had the chance to eat a lot of tasty stuff.

Apart from this, Barin had seen one other side to 'C''s character, just as they were about to reach Patna. This was directly related to the incident involving the clock.

They had been travelling by the Amritsar Mail. It was supposed to reach Patna at 5 a.m. The conductor came and woke Barin at 4.30. 'C', too, was half awake, although he was going up to Delhi.

Just about three minutes before the train was to reach Patna, it suddenly screeched to a halt. What could be the reason? There were a few people with torches running about on the tracks. Was it anything serious? In the end, the guard turned up and said that an old man had been run over by the engine while crossing the track. The train would start as soon as his body was removed.

'C' got very excited at this news and clambered down quickly in the dark, still clad in his sleeping suit. Then he went out to see for himself what had happened.

It was during this brief absence that Barin had removed the clock from 'C''s bag. He had seen 'C' wind it the night before, and had felt tempted immediately. But since the chances of finding a suitable opportunity were dim, he had told himself to forget the whole thing. But, when an opportunity presented itself so unexpectedly, Barin simply could not stop himself. Even at the risk of being seen by the other passenger lying on the upper berth, he had slipped his hand into 'C''s bag and had taken the clock out. Then he had dropped it into his own case. It took him between fifteen and twenty seconds to do this. 'C' had returned about five minutes later.

'A horrible business! A beggar, you see. The head's been totally severed from the body. I fail to see how an engine can possibly hit somebody despite a cow-catcher. Isn't it supposed to push aside all obstacles on the track?'

Barin got off safely at Patna and was met by his uncle. The faint uneasiness in the pit of his stomach vanished the instant he got into his uncle's car and drove off. His heart told him that that was the end of the story. No one could catch him now. The chances of running into 'C' were one in a million; or perhaps even less than that.

But who knew that one day, years later, by such an incredible coincidence, they would meet again? 'A thing like this is enough to make one turn superstitious,' thought Barin to himself.

'Do you live in Delhi? Or Calcutta?' asked 'C'.

He had asked him a lot of questions the last time as well, Barin recalled. He hated people who tried to act friendly.

'Calcutta,' said Barin. Oh no! He had spoken in his normal voice. He really must be more careful.

Good God—why was the man staring so hard at him? What could be the reason for such interest? Barin's pulse began beating faster again.

'Did your photograph come out in the papers recently?'

Barin realized it would be foolish not to tell the truth. There were other Bengali passengers on the train who might recognize him. There was no harm in telling this man who he was. In fact, if he could be told that Barin was a famous singer, he might find it difficult to relate him to the thief who had once stolen his clock.

'Where did you see this photograph?' Barin threw a counter question.

'Do you sing?' came another one!

'Yes, a little.'

'Your name. . .?'

'Barindranath Bhowmik.'

'Ah, I see. Barin Bhowmik. That's why you seemed familiar. You sing on the radio, don't you?'

'Yes.'

'My wife is an admirer of yours. Are you going to Delhi to sing at some function?'

'Yes.'

Barin was not going to tell him much. If a simple 'yes' or 'no' could suffice, there was no need to say anything else.

'I know a Bhowmik in Delhi. He's in the Finance Ministry. Nitish Bhowmik. Is he a relative or something?'

Indeed. Nitish was Barin's first cousin. A man well known for his rigid discipline. A close relative, but not one close to Barin personally.

'No, I'm afraid I don't know him.'

Barin decided to tell this one lie. He wished the man would stop talking. Why did he want to know so many things?

Oh good. Lunch had arrived. Hopefully, the volley of questions would cease, at least for a little while.

And so it did. 'C' was obviously one who enjoyed eating. He began to concentrate on his food and fell silent. Barin no longer felt all that nervous, but still he could not relax completely. They would have to spend at least another twenty hours in each other's company. Memory was such a strange phenomenon. Who could tell what little thing—a gesture, a look, a word—might make some old and forgotten memory come to life?

Black tea, for instance. Barin believed that if those two words had not been uttered, he would never have recognized 'C'. What if something he said or something he did made 'C' recognize *him*?

The best thing, of course, would be not to say or do anything at all. Barin lay down on his berth, hiding his face behind his paperback. When he finished the first chapter, he turned his head cautiously and stole a glance at 'C'. He seemed to be asleep. The *Illustrated Weekly* had dropped from his hand on to the floor. An arm was flung across his eyes, but from the way his chest rose and fell it seemed as though he had fallen into a deep sleep. Barin looked out of the window. Open fields, trees, little huts—the barren landscape of Bihar flashed past. The noise of the wheels came very faintly through the double glass of the windows, sounding as though, in the far distance, a number of drums were being beaten in the same steady rhythm: *dha-dhinak, na-dhinak, dha-dhinak, na-dhinak. . . .*

Another sound from within was soon added to this: the sound of 'C''s snoring.

Barin felt a lot more reassured. He began humming a Nazrul song. His voice did not sound too bad. He cleared his throat once and began to sing a bit more loudly. But he had to stop almost immediately.

Something else was making a noise in the compartment. It shocked Barin into silence.

It was the sound of an alarm clock. The alarm on the Swiss clock kept in his bag had somehow been set off. And it continued to ring, non-stop.

Barin discovered he could not move his limbs. They were paralysed with fear. His eyes fixed themselves on 'C'.

'C' moved his arm. Barin stiffened.

'C' was now awake. He removed his arm from his eyes.

'Is it that glass? Could you please remove it? It's vibrating against the wall.'

The noise stopped the instant Barin took the glass out of the iron ring attached to the wall. Before placing it on the table, he drank the water that was in it. This helped his throat, but he was still in no mood to start singing again.

Tea was served a little before they reached Hazaribagh Road. Two cups of hot tea and the absence of any further curious questions from 'C' helped him relax more. He looked out once again and began humming softly. Soon, he was able to forget totally the danger he was in.

At Gaya, not unexpectedly, 'C' got down on the platform and returned with two packets of peanuts. He gave one of them to Barin. Barin consumed the whole packet with considerable relish.

The sun had set by the time they left the station. 'C' switched the lights on and said, 'Are we running late? What's the time on your watch?'

Barin realized for the first time that 'C' was not wearing a watch.

This surprised him and he could not help but show it. Then he remembered that 'C''s question had not been answered. He glanced at his wristwatch. 'It's 7.35,' he said.

'Then we're running more or less on time.'

'Yes.'

'My watch broke this morning. It was an HMT. . .gave excellent time. . .but this morning someone pulled my bedsheet so hard that the watch fell on the ground and. . . .'

Barin did not comment. Any mention of watches and clocks was reprehensible.

'What make is your watch?' asked 'C'.

'HMT.'

'Does it keep good time?'

'Yes.'

'Actually, I have always been unlucky in the matter of clocks.'

Barin tried to yawn, simply to assume an unconcerned air, but failed in his attempt. Even the muscles in his jaw appeared to be paralysed. He could not open his mouth. But his ears continued to function. He was forced to hear all that 'C' had to say.

'I once had a Swiss travelling clock, you see. Made of gold. A friend of mine had brought it from Geneva. I had used it for barely a month and was carrying it with me on a train to Delhi—exactly like this, you know, in an air-conditioned compartment like this. There were only two of us—another Bengali chap. Do you know what he did? Just think of his daring! In my absence—while I may have gone to the bathroom or something—he nicked that clock from me! He looked such a complete gentleman. But I suppose I'm lucky he didn't murder me in my sleep. I stopped travelling by train after that. This time, too, I would have gone by air, but the pilots' strike upset my plans. . . .'

Barin Bhowmik's throat was dry, his hands felt numb. But he knew if he said absolutely nothing after a tale like that, it would seem odd. In fact, it would seem distinctly suspicious. With a tremendous effort, he forced himself to speak.

'Did. . .did you not look for it?'

'Ha! Can any stolen object be found simply by looking for it? But, for a long time, I could not forget what the man looked like. Even now I have a vague recollection. He was neither fair nor dark, had a moustache and must have been about the same height as you, but was slimmer. If I could meet him again, I would teach him a lesson he'd remember all his life. I was a boxer once, you know. A light heavyweight champion. That man is lucky our paths never crossed again. . . .'

Barin could now remember the full name of his companion. Chakravarty. Pulak Chakravarty. Strange! The minute he mentioned boxing, his name flashed in Barin's mind like a title on a television screen. Pulak Chakravarty had talked a lot about boxing the last time.

But even if his name had come back to him, what good did it do? After all, it was Barin who was the culprit. And now it had become impossible to carry his load of guilt. What if he went and confessed everything? And then returned the clock? There it was in that bag. . .so near at hand. . . !

No! Was he going mad? How could he entertain such thoughts? He was a famous vocalist. How could he admit to having stooped so low? Would his reputation not suffer? Would anyone ever invite him to sing at their function? What would his fans think? Where was the guarantee that this other man was not a journalist or someone connected with the media? No, there was no question of making a confession.

Perhaps there was no need for it, either. Perhaps he would be recognized, anyway. Pulak Chakravarty was giving him rather odd looks. Delhi was still sixteen hours away. There was every chance of being caught. In Barin's mind flashed a sudden image— his moustaches had grown back, the flesh on his face had worn away, his glasses had vanished. Pulak Charavarty was staring hard at the face he had seen nine years ago. The look of amazement in his slightly hazel eyes was slowly turning into a look filled with anger. His lips were parting in a slow, cruel smile. 'Ah ha!' he seemed to be saying, 'you *are* the same man, are you not? Good. I have waited all these years to lay my hands on you. Now I shall have my little revenge. . . .'

By 10 p.m., Barin had acquired a fairly high temperature, accompanied by intense shivering. He called the guard and asked for an extra blanket. Then he covered himself from head to foot with both blankets and lay flat on his back. Pulak Chakravarty closed the door of their compartment and bolted it. Before switching off the lights, he turned towards Barin and said, 'You appear unwell. I have some very effective pills with me—here, take these two. You're not used to travelling in an air-conditioned coach, are you?'

Barin swallowed the tablets. Well, given his present condition, Chakravarty might spare him a ruthless punishment. But Barin had made up his mind about one thing. He must transfer that clock to the suitcase of its rightful owner. He must try to get this done tonight, if possible. But he could not move until his temperature went down. His body was still shivering occasionally.

Pulak has switched on the reading lamp over his head. He had a paperback open in his hand. But was he reading it, or was he only staring at a page and thinking of something else? Why did he not turn the page? How long could it take to read a couple of pages?

Suddenly Barin noticed Pulak's eyes were no longer fixed on the book. He had turned his head slightly and was looking at Barin. Barin closed his eyes. After a long time, he opened one of them cautiously and glanced at Chakravarty. Yes, he was still staring hard at Barin. Barin promptly shut his eye again. His heart was jumping like a frog, matching the rhythm of the wheels—*lub dup*, *lub dup*, *lub dup*.

A faint click told him that the reading light had been switched off. Slightly reassured, he opened both his eyes this time. The light in the corridor outside was coming in through a crack in the door. Barin saw Pulak Charkravarty put his book down on the table beside Barin's bag. Then he pulled his blanket up to his chin, turned on his side, facing Barin, and yawned noisily.

Barin's heart beats gradually returned to normal. Tomorrow— yes, tomorrow morning he must return the clock. He had noticed Pulak's suitcase was unlocked. He had gone and changed into a sleeping suit only a little while ago.

Barin had stopped shivering. Perhaps those tablets had started to work. What *were* they? He had swallowed them simply so that he would recover in time to be able to sing at that function in Delhi. Applause from an audience was something he had no wish to miss. But had he done a wise thing? What if those pills. . .?

No, he must not think about such things. The incident of the glass vibrating against the wall was bad enough. Obviously, all these strange ideas were simply a result of a sick and guilt-ridden mind. Tomorrow, he must find a remedy for this. Without a clear conscience, he could not have a clear voice and his performance would be a total failure. Bengal Association. . . .

The tinkle of tea cups woke Barin in the morning. A waiter had come in with his breakfast: bread, butter, an omelette and tea. Should he be eating all this? Did he still have a slight fever? No, he did not. In fact, he felt just fine. What wonderful tablets those were! He began to feel quite grateful towards Pulak Chakravarty.

But where was he? In the bathroom, perhaps. Or was he in the corridor? Barin went out to take a look as soon as the waiter had gone. There was no one in the corridor outside. How long ago had Pulak left? Should he take a chance?

Barin took a chance, but did not quite succeed in his effort. He had taken the clock out of his own bag and had just bent down to pull out Pulak's suitcase from under his berth, when his fellow passenger walked in with a towel and a shaving kit in his hands. Barin's right hand closed around the clock. He straightened himself.

'How are you? All right?'

'Yes, thank you. Er. . .can you recognize this?'

Barin opened his palm. The clock lay on it. A strange determination had risen in Barin's mind. He had got over the old compulsive urge to steal a long time ago. But this business of playing hide-and-seek, was this not a form of deception? All that tension, those uncertainties, the anxiety over should-I-do-it-or- shouldn't-I, this funny, empty feeling in his stomach, the parched throat, the jumping heart—all these were signs of a malady, were they not? This, too, had to be overcome. There could never be any peace of mind otherwise.

Pulak Chakravarty had only just started to rub his ears with his towel. The sight of the clock turned him into a statue. His hand holding the towel remained stuck to his ear.

Barin said, 'Yes, I am that same man. I've put on a bit of weight, shaved my moustaches and have started wearing glasses. I was then going to Patna and you to Delhi. In 1964. Remember that man who got run over by our train? And you went out to investigate? Well, I took your clock in your absence.'

Pulak's eyes were now looking straight into Barin's. Barin saw him frowning deeply, the whites of his eyes had become rather prominent, his lips had parted as though he wanted to say something but could not find speech.

Barin continued, 'Actually, it was an illness I used to suffer from. I mean, I am not really a thief. There is a medical term for it which escapes me for the moment. Anyway, I am cured now and am quite normal. I used your clock all these years and was taking it with me to Delhi. Since I happened to meet you—it's really a miracle, isn't it?—I thought I'd return it to you. I hope you will not hold any. . . er . . . against me.'

Pulak Chakravarty could do no more than say 'thanks' very

faintly. He was still staring at the clock, now transferred to his own hand, totally dumbfounded.

Barin collected his toothbrush, toothpaste, and shaving kit. Then he took the towel off its rack and went into the bathroom. He broke into song as soon as he had closed the door, and was pleased to note that the old, natural melody in his voice was fully restored.

It took him about three minutes to get N. C. Bhowmik in the Finance Ministry in Delhi. Then, a deep, familiar voice boomed into his ear.

'Hello.'

'Nitish-da? This is Barin.'

'Oh, so you've arrived, have you? I'm coming this evening to hear you sing. Even *you* have turned into a celebrity, haven't you? My, my, who would have thought it possible? But anyway, what made you ring me?'

'Well—do you happen to know someone called Pulak Chakravarty? He is supposed to have been your batch-mate in college. He knew boxing.'

'Who? Old Pincho?'

'Pincho?'

'Yes, he used to pinch practically everything he saw. Fountain pens, books from the library, tennis racquets from our common room. It was he who stole my first Ronson. It was funny, because it wasn't as though he lacked anything in life. His father was a rich man. It was actually a kind of ailment.'

'Ailment?'

'Yes, haven't you ever heard of it? It's called kleptomania. K-l-e-p. . . .'

Barin put the receiver down and stared at his open suitcase. He had only just checked into his hotel and started to unpack. No, there was no mistake. A few items were certainly missing from it. A whole carton of Three Castles cigarettes, a pair of Japanese binoculars and a wallet containing five hundred-rupee notes.

Kleptomania. Barin had forgotten the word. Now it would stay etched in his mind—forever.

The Admirer

Arup Babu—Arup Ratan Sarkar—was visiting Puri again after eleven years. He noticed some changes in the city—a few new houses, new roads, and some new hotels, both large and small. But as he stepped on to the beach, he realized that that was something that would always stay unchanged.

The sea was not visible from Hotel Sagarika where he was staying. But, at night, when all its occupants had gone to bed, it was quite easy to hear the lashing waves. Last night the sound of the sea had actually made Arup Babu leave his hotel and come down to the beach. He had arrived in Puri the same day, but had to go out to do some shopping. There had been no time during the day to visit the beach. Now he could see the frothy, white waves clearly even in the darkness of a moonless night. He recalled having read somewhere that the water in the sea contained phosphorus, which was why the waves were visible even at night. How lovely the mysterious, luminous waves looked! Nobody in Calcutta would say he was imaginative. Never mind. Arup Babu knew that, deep inside, he had sensitivities that made him different from the average man. He took special care to ensure that the tensions and strife of daily living did not kill those feelings. He took himself occasionally to the riverside in Calcutta, or to the Eden Gardens. The sight of a rippling river, greenery and flowers could still give him joy. The song of a bird made him wonder which bird it might be: a koel or a cuckoo?

Several minutes of gazing at the waves took away some of the weariness sixteen years of being in a job had given him.

This evening, Arup Babu had returned to the beach. After walking along the waves for a few minutes, he stopped. There was a saffron-clad figure walking in the distance at great speed. His followers were running after him, unable to keep pace with the holy man. Arup Babu watched this spectacle, an amused smile on his lips. Suddenly, he heard a childish voice behind him.

'Was it you who wrote *The Little Boy's Dream*?' asked the voice.

Arup Babu turned around and found a boy of about seven, wearing a white shirt and blue shorts. His arms had a thick layer of sand up to the elbows. He was looking up at him, wide-eyed in wonder. Before Arup Babu could say anything, the boy continued,

'I have read *The Little Boy's Dream*. Daddy gave it to me on my birthday. I. . .I. . . .'

'Go on, say it. Don't be shy!'

This time it was the voice of a woman. It seemed to encourage the boy, who said quickly, 'I liked your book very much!'

Arup Babu glanced at the lady. A pleasant looking woman of about thirty, she was looking straight at him, smiling, and walking slowly in his direction.

Arup Babu addressed the boy, 'No, son. I haven't written any book. I think you've made a mistake.'

The lady was undoubtedly the boy's mother. There was a marked resemblance in their appearances, especially in the cleft on their chins.

Arup Babu's words did not take away the smile from her lips. In fact, it deepened as she came closer and said, 'We have heard of your reluctance to meet people. My brother-in-law had once written to you, asking you to preside over one of their functions. You had replied saying you were not in the least interested in that kind of thing. But you're not going to escape this time. We love your stories. Even we adults enjoy reading what you write for children.'

Arup Babu had no idea who had written *The Little Boy's Dream*, but it was evident that both the boy and his mother admired the writer equally. Who knew he would land in such a tricky situation? Obviously, these people would have to be told they had made a mistake, but he must not sound rude or say anything that might hurt their feelings.

Arup Babu's problem was that he was too soft. Once his dhobi, Gangacharan, had burnt a hole in one of his brand new kurtas. Anyone else would have given the dhobi a tight slap. But just one look at poor Ganga's apologetic face was enough to melt Arup Babu's heart. All he could bring himself to say was, 'Look, you really must be more careful in future.'

It was his kind heart that now made him say mildly, 'Well, how can you be so sure that it was I who wrote *The Little Boy's Dream*?'

The lady raised her eyebrows in surprise and said, 'Didn't your photo come out in the newspaper only recently? We heard on the radio one evening that you had won the Academy Award for your contribution to children's fiction, and the very next day we saw your photograph. So now a lot of other people know the name of Amalesh Moulik. It's not just us.'

Amalesh Moulik! He had heard the name, but Arup Babu had

not seen the photo. Did he look exactly like the man? But, of course, photographs printed in newspapers were usually hazy and unclear.

'The news of your arrival in Puri has spread already,' the lady continued. ' We went to Hotel Sea View the other day. One of my husband's friends was staying there until yesterday. The manager of the hotel himself told him that you'd be coming on Thursday. Today's Thursday, isn't it? Are you staying at the Sea View?'

'Uh. . . well, no. I had. . er. . . heard that the food there was not very good.'

'Yes, that's quite true. In fact, we were wondering why you had chosen that particular hotel. There are so many better ones. Where did you finally decide to go?'

'I am. . . staying at the Sagarika.'

'I see. That's a new hotel, isn't it? Is it good?'

'Just about OK, I'd say. After all, one hasn't come here to stay for a long time.'

'How long *will* you be staying here?'

'About five days.'

'Then you must come and visit us. We are at the Puri Hotel. You have no idea how many people are waiting to meet you, especially among the children. Look out—your feet are getting wet!'

Arup Babu had not noticed the large wave rushing towards his feet. But, it was not just his feet that were wet; his whole body, he discovered, had started to perspire, despite the strong wind. How did he manage to miss the chance to make a protest, to tell this lady she had indeed made a mistake? It was too late now. But he must remove himself from here and find a quiet corner to consider the possible consequences of his inaction.

'May I. . . now take my leave . . . .?'

'You must be writing something new.'

'N-n-no. I am now . . .taking a break.'

'Well, see you soon. I'll tell my husband about you. Will you be coming this way tomorrow?'

Arup Babu beat a quick retreat.

The manager of Sea View, Vivek Roy, had just finished stuffing a large paan into his mouth when Arup Babu arrived at the reception.

'Is Amalesh Moulik expected here?'

'Um.'

'When. . . do you think. . .?'

'Tuezhday. Wai?' Today was Thursday. Arup Babu was in town until the following Tuesday. If Mr Moulik had sent a telegram, it could only mean that he had had to postpone his arrival at the last minute. The manager confirmed he was originally scheduled to arrive the same morning.

In reply to Vivek Roy's 'Wai?' Arup Babu said that he had some business with Mr Moulik but would come back on Tuesday.

From the Sea View he went straight to the market and found a book shop. Here he managed to find four other books by Amalesh Moulik, although *The Little Boy's Dream* was not available. Two were novels and the other two collections of short stories.

By the time he returned to his own hotel, it was about 6.30 p.m. There was a hall just as one entered the hotel. The manager sat on its left and on the right were a bench and a couple of chairs. On these were sitting two gentlemen; the bench was occupied by two boys and a girl, none more than ten years old. Upon Arup Babu's arrival, the two men smiled and rose to their feet with their hands folded in a *namaskar*. They then nodded at the children, who came forward shyly and touched Arup Babu's feet before he could stop them.

'We are coming from the Puri Hotel,' said one of the men, 'I am Suhrid Sen and this is Mr Ganguly. Mrs Ghosh told us she had met you and this was where you were staying, so. . . .'

Thank goodness the man at the book shop had wrapped the books in brown paper. Otherwise God knows what these people might have thought at finding an author buying his own books!

Arup Babu nodded at everything his visitors said, although he knew it was not too late to correct the mistake they were obviously making. All he needed to say was, 'Look, something rather strange is happening. I have not seen Amalesh Moulik's photograph, but I assume he looks a bit like me. Perhaps he, too, has thin moustaches and curly hair and wears glasses just like me. It is also true that he is supposed to be visiting Puri. But, please, for God's sake, I am not that man. I do not write stories for children. In fact, I do not write at all. I work in an insurance company. I have come here simply to have a quiet holiday. Could you please leave me alone? The real Amalesh Moulik is going to arrive here next Tuesday. You can go and check at the Sea View, if you like.'

But would such a speech really help? These people were totally convinced he was Amalesh Moulik and since his initial protests had not worked, how could a telegram lying in the room of the manager of Sea View help? They would assume it was a trick to avoid people. They might even think he was staying at Sagarika under a false name and had sent the telegram to Sea View just to fool everyone.

Besides, there were all these children. One look at them made Arup Babu stop before uttering more protests. All three were staring at him in open admiration. One word of denial would wipe out all their enthusiasm.

'Babun, you can now ask Amalesh Babu what you wanted to know,' said Suhrid Sen, nodding at the older boy.

There was now absolutely no way of backing out. The boy called Babun was looking up at him, his head to one side, his fingers interlinked, ready to ask his question.

'That old man who put the little boy to sleep... did he know magic?'

At this crucial moment, Arup Babu discovered that his brain had started to function better than before. He stooped a little and whispered into Babun's ear, 'Well, what do *you* think?'

'I think he did.'

The other two children said simultaneously, 'Yes, yes, he did know magic. We all think he did!'

'Exactly,' Arup Babu straightened, 'whatever you think is correct. I wrote what I had to write. Now you must figure out what it means. And what *you* think it means is right. Nothing else matters.'

All the three children seemed very pleased at this answer. Before they left, Suhrid Sen invited him to dinner. There were eight Bengali families staying at Puri Hotel. The group included quite a few children who were regular fans of Amalesh Moulik. Arup Babu did not object for he had realized that he would simply have to play the role of Amalesh Moulik, at least temporarily. There was no point now in worrying about the possible consequences. But there was one thing Arup Babu felt he had to insist upon.

'Look,' he said to Mr Sen, 'I really am not fond of a lot of fuss. I am not used to mixing with people at all. So please may I request you not to spread the news that I am staying here?'

Suhrid Sen promised him that after the dinner the following evening, none of them would disturb the peace and quiet Arup Babu was hoping to enjoy. Mr Sen also offered to warn the others to leave him alone as far as possible.

Arup Babu had an early dinner and retired to bed with one of

Moulik's books called *Habu's Tricks*. The other three were *Tutul's Adventure*, *Checkmate* and *Sparklers*. The last two were collections of short stories.

It was true that Arup Babu was no authority on literature. However, he had read, in his school days, a number of children's stories written both by Indian and foreign writers. Thirty-nine years later, he realized to his surprise that he still remembered most of what he had read so many years ago. Not only that, he could even find similarities in ideas and plots between Amalesh Moulik's stories and those that he had read as a schoolboy.

All four books, published in large print, amounted to about 125 pages. When Arup Babu put the last one down and switched his light off, the hotel had fallen totally silent. The sea was rumbling in the distance. What time was it? Arup Babu's watch was lying by his pillow. He picked it up. It had once belonged to his father and had a radium dial. It gleamed in the darkness like the foam of the sea. The time was a quarter to one in the morning.

Amalesh Moulik was a well-known author, a popular writer of children's fiction. One had to admit that his language was very lucid and his style unusual. It was difficult to put his books down. But even so, there was not much originality of thought. One heard so many different tales from one's friends; people had such varied experiences. Strange and interesting things could happen even to oneself. Surely all one needed to do was draw on those experiences and mix them with a bit of imagination? Where was the need to borrow ideas from other authors?

Arup Babu lost a little of his respect for Moulik. At the same time, he felt more relaxed. He was now going to find it easier to pretend to be the famous author.

The admiration of the fans of Amalesh Moulik was considerably enhanced after the dinner at Puri Hotel. Arup Babu had, in the meantime, managed to find a copy of *The Little Boy's Dream* from another shop. It was, therefore, not difficult to answer the thousand questions thirteen small children showered upon him.

By the time the party ended, the children had started calling him 'Honeylick Babu', since he told them that the word *mou* in Bengali meant 'honey' and everyone knew what 'lick' meant in English.

When he heard this, Dr Dasgupta, a guest at the party,

remarked, 'You created all the honey; and all these children are licking it.' At this, Surangama Devi, his wife, said, 'It's not just the children. Don't forget the adults!'

Two things happened after dinner. The first was that the children asked him to tell them a story. Arup Babu said in reply that he could not make up a story on the spot, but would relate an incident that had occurred in his childhood.

Arup Babu's family used to live in Banchharam Akrur Datta Lane in those days. When he was about five, an expensive clock in his house was found missing. His father called a local pandit, who claimed to have special magical powers. 'I shall find the thief in no time!' he had said.

He then brought out a large pair of scissors and, holding them like a pair of tongs, picked up a small cane basket. After chanting a few mantras and throwing handfuls of rice over the basket, he declared the thief was none other than the new servant, Natabar. Arup Babu's uncle caught Natabar by his hair and was about to hit him very hard when the clock slipped out from under a bedsheet.

Everyone clapped when his story ended. Arup Babu rose to take his leave, but was stopped by a chorus of childish voices saying, 'No, no, please wait. Don't go!'

About half a dozen children rushed out of the room and returned with seven books by Amalesh Moulik that they had just bought. 'Please sign these books for us!' they said.

Arup Babu said, 'Well, I don't put my signature on books—ever. Tell you what, I'll take these away and draw a picture in each. Come to my hotel at 4.30 in the evening the day after tomorrow and take your books back.'

The children clapped again.

'Yes, yes, a picture is better than a signature!'

Arup Babu had once won a prize for drawing in school. He had not drawn since then, but surely it would not be impossible to draw some little things in these books if he tried?

The next day was Saturday. Arup Babu left in the morning with the books and his ball point pen. Near the colony of the Nulias, he discovered, there were plenty of things he could sketch. It took him just about an hour to finish his task. In the first book he drew a crab; in the second, three sea shells lying side by side on the sand; and then a couple of crows, a fishing boat, a Nulia's hut, a Nulia child and, finally, a Nulia wearing a hat with a pointed peak, making a fishing net.

Seven little children turned up at his hotel exactly at 4.30 p.m. on Sunday and went away jumping in joy and excitement at the drawings.

That night, when he had retired to his room after dinner, Arup Babu discovered that the feeling of pleasure had given way in his mind to one of anxiety. It was true that not once had he actually said to anyone, 'I am Amalesh Moulik.' But he knew whatever he had done over the last three days could not be seen as anything other than large scale fraud. The day after tomorrow, on Tuesday, the real Amalesh Moulik was going to arrive. The affection and admiration Arup Babu had received from all those children and their parents was actually meant for this other man. It did not matter whether Mr Moulik wrote well or not. He was obviously a hero to all these people. What on earth would happen when he turned up in person and the manager of Sea View went about telling everyone of his arrival? The thought made Arup Babu feel decidedly uncomfortable.

Should he then try to leave a day earlier? Or else what was he going to do all day on Tuesday? Where would he hide? Would people not thrash him black and blue when they learnt the truth? What about Mr Moulik himself? He, too, might raise his hand. After all, who could say for sure that all writers were peace-loving and non-violent? And the police? What if the police came to know? Could one be jailed for the kind of thing he had done? Possibly. There was no doubt that what he had done was wrong indeed.

Arup Babu got up and swallowed a sleeping pill for fear of having to spend a sleepless night.

In the end, however, he decided to leave by the night train on Tuesday. The temptation to take a look at the real Amalesh Moulik was too great. He had managed to get a copy of the newspaper that had carried his photograph. Amalesh Moulik did indeed have thin moustaches, curly hair and glasses set in thick frames. But it was necessary to look at the real person to see how far the resemblance went. The picture in the paper was not clear enough.

Arup Babu decided to go to the station not only to look at the man but also to exchange a few words, if possible. It should seem natural enough if he said something like, 'You're Amalesh Moulik, aren't you? Saw your photograph the other day. I enjoy reading your stories. . . ' or words to that effect.

He would then leave his luggage at the station and leave for Konark, which he had not yet seen. He could spend the day at the

Sun temple in Konark and return in time to catch his train back to
Calcutta. There was no better way of hiding.

The Puri Express reached the station twenty minutes late on Tuesday. Arup Babu stood behind a pillar, keeping an eye on the
passengers getting down from the first class coaches. A foreigner,
clad in shorts, was the first to alight. He was followed by a large
Marwari. From the other door an old woman emerged, helped by
a young man in white trousers. Behind him came an old man, and
after that—yes, there could be no mistake, this was Mr Amalesh
Moulik. There were certainly a few basic resemblances in their
appearances, but if Arup Babu went and stood beside him, there
was positively no danger of being mistaken for his twin. Mr Moulik
was shorter by about a couple of inches and his complexion was
darker. He even appeared to be older for his side-burns had distinct
touches of grey, which was something Arup Babu had not yet
acquired.

The man lugged his suitcase off the train and yelled to a coolie.
The coolie and Arup Babu went forward together.

'Mr Moulik, I presume?'

The man looked surprised. Then he turned towards Arup Babu
and nodded. 'Yes,' he said briefly.

The coolie had picked up the suitcase and placed it on his head.
Arup Babu had a bag and a flask slung from his shoulder. The
three began walking towards the main exit.

'I have read your books,' said Arup Babu , 'I saw the news of
your winning the Academy Award and also saw your photograph.'

'Hm.'

'You're booked at the Sea View, aren't you?'

This time Amalesh Moulik looked at Arup Babu rather suspiciously. It was not difficult to guess what he was thinking.

'The manager of Sea View is an admirer of yours, you see,'
explained Arup Babu, 'it is he who has spread the news.'

'Ah.'

'A lot of children here are looking forward to your visit.'

'Hm.'

Why did the man say so little? He had now slackened his pace.
What could he be thinking of?

Amalesh Moulik came to a halt. Then he turned towards Arup

Babu again and asked, 'Have a lot of people learnt about my coming?'

'Yes, so I gathered. Why, does that put you to some inconvenience?'

'No, but I like to be al-al-al—'

'Alone?'

'Yes.'

The man clearly had a stammer. Arup Babu recalled that when Edward VIII of England had decided to step down from the throne, his brother, George, had got quite worried at the thought of becoming king since he had a stammer and being a king inevitably meant having to give speeches.

The coolie was waiting near the exit. Both men hurried their steps.

'This is the p-p-p-rice of f-f-f-ame!'

Arup Babu tried to imagine the reaction of all those children if they met their stammering hero. He did not like what he saw.

'You could do one thing,' he said to Amalesh as they came out of the station.

'What?'

'I don't like the idea of your holiday being spoilt by your fans.'

'Neither do I.'

'Then don't go to Sea View.'

'Wh-wh-at?'

'The food there is awful. I was in Sagarika. My room is now vacant. I suggest you go there.'

'Oh.'

'And don't use your real name. It really would be best if you could shave off your moustaches totally.'

'Mous-s-s—?'

'Immediately. You can go into the waiting room and do it. A matter of no more than ten minutes, I should say. If you do this, no one will recognize you and disturb the peaceful holiday you have no doubt planned for yourself. I can send a telegram from Calcutta tomorrow morning to Sea View and tell them you had to cancel your visit.'

The worried lines on Mr Moulik's forehead took about twenty seconds to disappear. Then a few new creases appeared near his eyes and mouth. Amalesh Moulik was smiling.

'I d-d-d-on't know how to th-th-th-ank. . . .'

'Never mind. But please will you sign these books for me? Let's stand behind that neem tree. No one can spot us there.'

Hidden by the tree, Amalesh Moulik took out his red Parker pen from his pocket and smiled benignly at his admirer. He had put in a lot of effort, right from the day the award was announced, in perfecting his signature. Five signatures on five books. He knew very well that even if his tongue stuttered, his pen could fly smoothly.

The Vicious Vampire

I have always harboured an intense dislike for bats. Whenever a flitter-mouse flits into my room in my house in Calcutta, I feel obliged to drop everything and rush out of the room. In the summer, particularly, I feel distinctly uneasy at the thought of one of those creatures knocking against the fan spinning at full speed and dropping to the ground, hurt and injured. So I run out of my room and yell at my cook, Vinod, to come and rescue me. Once, Vinod even managed to kill a flitter-mouse with my badminton racquet. To tell the truth, my dislike is often mixed with fear. The very sight of a bat puts me off. What peculiar creatures they are: neither birds nor animals, and their queer habit of hanging upside down from trees makes me think the world would have been a far better place to live in if bats did not exist.

My room in Calcutta had been invaded by flitter-mice so many times that I had begun to think they had a strange fondness for me. But I never thought I would find a bat hanging from the ceiling in my room in this house in Shiuri. This really was too much. I could not stay in the room unless it was removed.

My father's friend, Tinkori Kaka, had told me about this house. He was a doctor and had once practised in Shiuri. Now he had retired and moved to Calcutta, but, needless to say, he still knew a lot of people in Shiuri. So I went straight to him for advice when I discovered that I would have to spend about a week there.

'Shiuri? Why Shiuri? What do you want to do there?' he asked.

I told him I was working on a research project on old terracotta temples of Bengal. It was my ultimate aim to write a book. There were so many beautiful temples strewn about the country, but no one had ever written a really good book on them.

'Oh, of course! You're an artist, aren't you? So your interest lies in temples, does it? But why do you want to limit yourself just to Shiuri? There are temples everywhere—Shurul, Hetampur, Dubrajpur, Phoolbera, Beersinghpur. But, perhaps, those aren't good enough to be written about?'

Anyway, Tinkori Kaka told me about this house.

'You wouldn't mind staying in an old house, would you? A patient of mine used to live there. He's now shifted to Calcutta. But I believe there is a caretaker in Shiuri to look after the house. It's a fairly large place. I don't think you'll have any problem. And you wouldn't have to pay anything, either. I snatched this man back, so to speak, from the jaws of death as many as three times. He'd be only too pleased to have a guest of mine stay in his house for a week.'

Tinkori Kaka was right. There was no problem in getting to the house. But the minute I got off the cycle rickshaw that brought me from the station and entered my room, I saw the bat.

I called the old caretaker.

'What's your name?'

'Madhusudan.'

'I see. Well, then, Madhusudan—is Mr Bat a permanent resident of this room or has he come here today to give me a special welcome?'

Madhusudan looked at the ceiling, scratched his head and said, 'I hadn't noticed it, sir. This room usually stays locked. It was only opened today because you were coming .'

'But I cannot share a room with a bat.'

'Don't worry about it, sir. It will leave as soon as the sun goes down.'

'All right. But can't anything be done to make sure it doesn't return?'

'No, sir. It won't come back. Why should it? After all, it's not as though it's built a nest here. It must have slipped in last night somehow and couldn't get out for it can't see during the day!'

After a cup of tea, I went and occupied an old cane chair on the veranda outside. The house was at one end of the town. On the northern side was a large mango grove. Through the trees it was possible to catch glimpses of rice fields that stretched right up to the horizon. On the western side was a bamboo grove and, beyond it, the spire of a church stood out. This must be the famous ancient church of Shiuri.

I decided to walk round to the church in the evening. I should start working from tomorrow. Shiuri and about twenty-five miles around it had at least thirty terracotta temples. I had a camera with me and a large stock of film. Each carving on the walls of these temples should be photographed. The temples might not last for very long. Once these were destroyed, Bengal would lose an important part of its heritage.

It was now 5.30 p.m. The sun disappeared behind the church. I got up, stretched and had just taken a step towards the stairs when something flew past my left ear making a swishing noise, and vanished into the mango grove.

I went into the bedroom and looked at the ceiling. The bat had gone.

Thank goodness for that. At least I could work in the evening peacefully. Perhaps I should start writing about the temples I had already seen elsewhere in Burdwan, Bankura and the Twenty-four Parganas.

As soon as darkness fell, I took out my torch and began walking towards the church. The red earth of Beerbhum, the uneven terrain, the rows of palms —I loved them all. This was my first visit to Shiuri. I was not really here to look at nature and its beauty, yet the church and its surroundings struck me as beautiful. I passed the church and began walking further west. Then I saw what looked like a park. There was an open space surrounded by a railing. It had an iron gate.

As I came closer, I realized it was not a park but a graveyard. There were about thirty graves in it. A few had carved marble pillars. Others had marble slabs. All were undoubtedly quite ancient. The pillars were cracked. Little plants peeped out of some of these cracks.

The gate was open. I went in and began trying to read some of the hazy, indistinct epitaphs. All were graves of Britons, possibly those who had died in the very early stages of the Raj, as a result of some epidemic or the other.

One particular marble slab seemed to have a slightly more legible inscription. I was about to switch the torch on to read it, when I heard footsteps behind me. I turned around quickly. A short, middle-aged man was standing about ten feet away, smiling at me. He was wearing a black jacket and grey trousers. There was an old, patched up umbrella in his hand.

'You don't like bats, do you?'

I started. How did this stranger know that? The man laughed. 'You must be wondering how I learnt this. Very easy. When you were telling that caretaker to drive the bat away this morning, I happened to be there in the vicinity.'

'Oh, I see.'

Now the man raised his hands in a *namaskar*.

'I am Jagdish Percival Mukherjee. My family has lived in Shiuri for a long time. Four generations, you know. I like visiting the church and this graveyard in the evening. I am a Christian, you see.'

It was getting darker. I turned to return to the house. The man began walking with me. He seemed a bit strange, although he appeared to be harmless enough. But his voice was funny—thin and, at the same time, harsh. In any case, I could never take to people who made such an obvious attempt to get friendly.

I pressed the switch of the torch, but it did not work. Then I remembered I had meant to buy a couple of batteries at the station, and had quite forgotten to do so. How annoying! I could not see a thing. What if there were snakes?

The man said, 'Don't worry about your torch. I am used to moving in the dark. I can see quite well. Careful—there's a pot-hole here!' He pulled me to one side. Then he said, 'Do you know what a vampire is?'

'Yes,' I said briefly.

Who did not know about vampires? Blood-sucking bats were called vampires. They sucked the blood of animals like horses and cows. I did not know whether such bats could be found in India, but I had certainly read about them in books from abroad. And those did not just talk about bats. They even spoke of bodies of dead men that came out of graves in the middle of the night to drink the blood of people who were asleep. Such creatures were also called vampires. The story of Count Dracula was something I had read in school.

It annoyed me to think that the man had raised the subject of vampires in spite of being aware of my aversion to bats.

We both fell silent.

Then we came to the mango grove and the house could be seen quite clearly. Here he stopped abruptly and said, 'It's been a pleasure meeting you. You're going to stay here for some time, aren't you?'

'About a week.'

'Good. Then we shall certainly meet again. Usually, in the evening,' he said, pointing towards the graveyard, 'I can be found there. My forefathers were buried in the same place. I shall show you their graves tomorrow.'

I said silently to myself, 'The less I see of you the better.' Bats I could not bear to look at, anyway. A discussion on those stupid creatures was even worse. There were plenty of other things in life to think about.

As I went up the steps of the veranda, I turned back for a moment and saw the man disappear among the mango trees. By that time, the jackals had started their chorus beyond the rice fields.

It was the month of October; yet, it felt hot and oppressive inside the room. I tossed and turned in my bed after dinner, toying with the idea of opening the door of my room which I had closed for fear of the bat flying in again. In the end, I decided against it, not so much because of the bat, but because of something else. If the caretaker was a light sleeper, perhaps there was no danger of being burgled. But what if a stray dog came in through the open door and chewed my slippers? This could happen easily in a small mofussil town. In fact, I had already had that kind of experience more than once. So, instead of opening the door, I opened the window that faced the west. A lovely breeze came wafting in.

I soon fell asleep and began having a strange dream.

In my dream I saw the same man peering through the window of my room and smiling at me. His eyes were bright green and his teeth sharp and narrow. Then I saw the man take a step back, raise his arms and leap through the window. It seemed almost as though it was the sound of his arrival that woke me.

I opened my eyes and saw that dawn had broken. What an awful dream!

I rose and yelled for a cup of tea. I must finish breakfast and leave early, or I would never get all my work done.

Madhusudan seemed a little preoccupied as he placed my tea on the table outside on the veranda. I asked, 'What's the matter, Madhusudan? Are you unwell? Or didn't you sleep last night?'

Madhu said, 'No, Babu. I am quite all right. It's my calf.'

'What happened to your calf?'

'It died last night. Got bitten by a snake probably.'

'What!'

'Yes, sir. It was only a week old. Something bit its throat—God knows if it was a cobra.'

I began to feel uneasy. Bitten on the throat? Where did I. . .? Of course. A vampire bat! Wasn't it only yesterday that I was thinking of the same thing? Vampire bats did suck blood from the throats of animals. But, of course, the calf might indeed have been bitten by a snake. That was perfectly possible, especially if the calf happened to be sleeping. Why was I trying to link the death of a calf with vampire bats?

I uttered a few words of comfort to Madhusudan and returned to my room. My eyes went towards the ceiling involuntarily.

The bat was back.

It was my own mistake. I should not have left the window open. I decided to keep all the doors and windows closed tonight, no matter how stuffy it became.

I spent a rather enjoyable day among old terracotta temples. The workmanship of those who had done the carving on the walls was truly remarkable.

I took a bus from Hetampur and returned to Shiuri at about half-past-four in the evening.

I had to pass the graveyard in order to get home. The busy day had nearly made me forget all about the man I had met the day before. The sight of the man, standing under a tree just outside the graveyard, therefore, came as a surprise. Perhaps the best thing would be to pretend not to have seen him and walk on. But that was not to be. Just as I bent my head and increased the speed of my walking, he leapt towards me.

'Did you sleep well last night?'

I said 'Yes' without stopping. But it was clear that, like yesterday, he would walk with me. He began walking fast to keep pace with me. 'I have a funny habit, you see,' he said, 'I cannot sleep at night. So I sleep tight during the day and from evening to early morning, I roam around here and there. Oh, I cannot explain to you the joy of walking around at night. You have no idea how many different things are simply crying to be seen, to be heard in this very graveyard! Have you ever thought of these beings that have spent years and years, lying under the ground, stuffed in a wooden box? Have you wondered about their unfulfilled desires? No one wants to stay a prisoner. Each one of them wants to come out! But not many know the secret of getting out. So, in their sadness, some weep, some wail and other's sigh. In the middle of the night, when the jackals go to sleep and the crickets become quiet, those who have sensitive ears—like mine—can hear the soft moaning of these people, nailed into a box. But, as I told you, one would have to have very sharp ears. My eyes and ears work very well at night. Just like a bat's.'

I must ask Madhusudan about this man, I thought. There were a few questions I wanted answered, but I knew there would be no point in asking the man. How long had he really spent in Shiuri? What did he do for a living? Where did he live?

He continued to walk beside me and talk incessantly.

'I don't often make the effort to go and meet people,' he said, 'but I simply had to come and meet you. I do hope you won't deprive me of the pleasure of your company for the remainder of your stay.'

This time I could not control myself. I stopped, turned towards the man and said rather rudely, 'Look, mister, I have come only for a week. I do have a vast amount of work to do. I cannot see how I can possibly spend any time with you.'

The man, at first, seemed a little crestfallen at my words. Then he smiled and said in a tone that sounded mild yet oddly firm, 'You may not give *me* your company, but surely I can give you mine? Besides, I was not talking about the time when you'd be busy doing your work—during the day, that is.'

There was no need to waste any more time with him. I said *namaskar* abruptly and strode towards my house.

'Jagdish Mukherjee? I don't think. . . . Oh, wait a minute! Is he short? Wears a jacket and trousers? Is a little dark?'

'Yes, yes.'

'Oh, Babu, that man is crazy. Quite mad. In fact, he's only recently been discharged from the asylum. They say he's now cured. How did *you* come across him? I haven't seen him for ages. His father was a priest called Nilmani Mukherjee. A nice man, but I believe he, too, went quite cuckoo before his death.'

I did not pursue the matter. All I said was, 'That bat had come in again. But it was entirely my own fault. I had kept the window open. I hadn't realized some of its grills were broken.'

Madhu said, 'Tomorrow morning I shall have those gaps filled. Perhaps during the night you should keep the window closed.'

After dinner, I finished writing my notes on the temples I had seen that day. Then I loaded my camera with a new roll. Glancing out of the window, I saw that the clouds of last night had cleared, leaving everything awash in the moonlight.

I went and sat outside on the veranda for a while and returned to my room at around 11 p.m. Then I drank a glass of water and finally went to bed. Jagdish Mukherjee's words were still ringing in my ears. No doubt, in this scientific age, his words were no more than the ravings of a mad man. I must find out which asylum he had gone to and which doctor had treated him.

The clouds having dispersed, the oppressive feeling of the night before had gone. Keeping the window closed was not difficult. In fact, that night I had to use the extra sheet I had brought. I fell asleep soon after closing my eyes. But I woke a little while later, though I could not tell the time nor what it was that had disturbed my sleep. Then I saw a square patch of moonlight on the wall and my heart lurched.

God knows when the window had opened. Light was coming in through the open window. In that patch of light, I saw the shadow of something flying in a circle, again and again.

Holding my breath carefully, I turned my head and looked up. This time I could see the bat.

It kept flying in a circle right over my bed, and slowly began to come down.

I mustered all my courage. It would be disastrous if I lost my will power at a moment like this. Without taking my eyes off the bat, I stretched my right hand towards the bedside table and picked up my large, hardbound notebook. Just as the bat made a final swoop, ready to attack my throat, I struck its head with the notebook, using all my strength.

It went shooting out of the window, knocking once against the broken grills, and landed on the ground outside. The next instant, I thought I heard someone running across the ground.

I rushed to the window and peered out. Nothing could be seen. There was no sign of the bat.

I could not go back to sleep after that.

The first rays of the sun in the morning wiped out the horrors of the night. There was no reason to assume that the bat was a vampire. Yes, it had certainly come very close to me, but how could it be proved that it had done so with the intention of sucking my blood? If that weird character in the graveyard had not raised the subject of vampires, I would not even have dreamt of it. A bat in Shiuri would have struck me as no different from a bat in Calcutta.

I decided to forget the whole thing. There was some work to be done in Hetampur. I finished my cup of tea and left at around half-past-six.

As I approached the graveyard, I came upon a startling sight. A few local people were carrying Jagdish Mukherjee. He appeared to be unconscious and his forehead had a large, black bruise.

'What happened to him?' I asked.

One of the men laughed.

'Fell down from a tree, probably,' he said.

'What! Why should he fall from a tree? What could he have been doing on a tree top?'

'You don't know, Babu. This man is totally mad. He seemed to have made a slight recovery lately. Before that, every evening as soon as it got dark, he used to go and hang upside down from trees. Just like a bat!'

The Millionaire

Unable to contain his annoyance any longer, Tridib Chowdhury pressed the bell to call a bearer. For quite some time now, he had had the feeling that his compartment was not as cool as it ought to have been. And yet, the other three passengers were already snoring. Tridib Babu failed to figure out how this could possibly happen. The basic problem, of course, was that no one ever thought of protesting against injustice. No wonder the entire race was going to the dogs.

There was a knock at the door.

'Come in.'

The door slid to one side and a bearer appeared.

'What is the temperature inside this room?' said Tridib Babu, somewhat aggressively.

'I don't know, sir.'

'Why? Why don't you know? Why should one make a booking in an air-conditioned coach and still have to suffer in the heat? Do you not have a responsibility in this matter?'

What could the bearer say? He only looked on, smiling foolishly. Tridib Babu's words had woken the south Indian gentleman on the upper berth. Tridib Babu had to swallow his anger.

'All right, you may go. Don't forget to bring me a cup of tea exactly at six-thirty in the morning.'

'Very well, sir.'

The bearer left. Tridib Babu closed the door and lay down. He would not have had to suffer such inconveniences if he had gone by air. People like him would normally fly if they had to go to a place like Ranchi from Calcutta. But Tridib Babu happened to suffer from an abject fear of flying. About twelve years ago he had flown to Bombay. What a terrible experience that had been! The weather was awful that day, and the bumping that started as soon as the plane took off did not stop until it had actually landed. Tridib Babu had vowed that day never to climb into a plane again. When it became necessary to go to Ranchi on this occasion, he booked himself on the Ranchi Express straightaway. But now it was obvious that all thoughts of comfort in an air-conditioned coach would have to be abandoned. Tridib Babu closed his eyes in the darkened room and was left alone with his thoughts.

Thoughts of his childhood came back to him. He was born in Ranchi. His father, Adinath Chowdhury, was a well-known doctor. After finishing school, Tridib Babu went to Calcutta for further studies. He stayed in an uncle's house there and completed his graduation. Soon afterwards, a Marwari friend advised him to start his own business. A small beginning—dealing with scrap metal—showed him that Lady Luck was certainly going to smile on him. Money began pouring in. He stayed on in Calcutta, though his parents continued to live in Ranchi.

He took a flat on Sardar Shankar Road at first. Then, as his earnings grew, he shifted to a ground floor flat in a two-storey house on Harrington Street. But he stayed in touch with his parents. He went back to Ranchi once very year and spent at least a week with them. At his parents' request, he married when he was twenty-six. A couple of years later his son was born—now studying in America. Tridib Babu had no other children. His wife had died three years ago. He lost his mother in 1972 and his father in '74. The house in Ranchi was looked after by a servant and a gardener. Tridib Babu had been paying them regularly for the last ten years. The aim behind keeping the house was simply to have somewhere to go and rest for a few days. But his busy life very seldom gave him the opportunity to do so. Besides, being away even for three days meant a loss of at least five thousand rupees. There was no question of taking a break for a man whose sole mission in life was to make money. Tridib Babu was a millionaire today, a living contradiction to the general belief that Bengalis could not flourish in private enterprise.

His visit to Ranchi this time was also connected with his business. There were great possibilities in the business of lac. Tridib Babu was going to examine these. He would stay in his own house, and thought he'd be able to finish his work in two days. He had written to Prasant Sarkar. Prasant would tell his servant and make all arrangements. He was a friend from Tridib Babu's childhood. He now taught in a missionary school in Ranchi. It was not as if the two of them were still in regular contact, but Tridib Babu knew that, if requested, Prasant would readily agree to do this for an old friend.

Tridib Babu's mind jumped from one thought to another. He could not tell when he finally fell asleep. Nor did he realize that, in his sleep, he joined the chorus of the other three passengers, snoring in harmony.

The Ranchi Express was scheduled to arrive at a quarter-past-seven in the morning. Prasant Sarkar reached the station ten minutes before its arrival to greet his friend. He had been quite close to Tridib, alias Montu, when they were in school. They wrote to each other regularly even after Tridib Babu went to Calcutta. But, soon after he left college, their intimacy began to wane. Tridib Babu, of course, was largely to blame. On the few occasions he came to Ranchi to see his parents, he would arrive without telling Prasant. As a result, most of the time, the two could not even meet for a chat. Prasant could not at first understand the reason behind the change in his friend's behaviour. Then he read in the papers that Tridib had become an important businessman, which meant that he was now beyond Prasant's reach, belonging to a different class. This was made obvious by the dry and matter-of-fact tone of the brief letter Tridib had sent him.

Prasant Babu felt sad at this change in his friend. The millionaire T. Chowdhury of today was different indeed from the simple, fun-loving Montu he had once known. Did people really change so much over a period of time? It was true that Tridib Chowdhury's financial status had changed dramatically. But Prasant Sarkar was not a man who judged people by their possessions. This aspect of his character was something he had inherited from his father. Pramatha Sarkar, Prasant's father, had been a believer in Gandhian principles. There had been no major upheaval in Prasant's own life. After all, a schoolmaster's life did not have much scope of being filled with new excitements. It was, therefore, not difficult to place him as the Panu one had known as a child. But could the same be said about Tridib Chowdhury? Prasant waited eagerly to find out. If Tridib had indeed turned into a snob, Prasant would find that difficult to put up with.

The train was late by ten minutes. Since the visit was going to be a short one, Tridib Babu had brought nothing except a small suitcase and a flask. Prasant Babu took the suitcase from his hand, despite his protests. Then they both began to walk towards the taxi-stand.

'Did you have to wait for a long time?' Tridib Chowdhury asked.

'Just about twenty minutes.'

'I did not expect you to come to the station. There was no need. After all, this is not my first visit to Ranchi.'

Prasant Babu smiled but did not comment. He had not failed to note the slightly formal tone his friend was using.

'Are things all right here?' asked Tridib Babu.

'Yes, everything's arranged. Your gardener and Chintamani are both very excited at the thought of their Babu returning to the house.'

Chintamani was the cook-cum-*chowkidar*.

'Is the house still liveable? Or has it turned into a haunted house?'

Prasant Babu smiled again. Then, after a few moments of silence, said, 'I don't know about the house being haunted, but there's something I ought to tell you. I saw a little boy playing in your garden the other night as I was passing by.'

'At night?'

'Yes, it was pretty late. About eleven-thirty. I was startled. It seemed as though the ten-year-old Montu had come back!'

'Anyway, obviously it wasn't a ghost. My father had this house built, so I know all about those who lived and died here. What I'm more concerned about is whether they've kept it clean.'

'It's spotless. I saw that for myself yesterday. Well—what do you have to do now? Where do you have to go?'

'I need to go to Namkan today after lunch. There's a man called Maheshwar Jain there dealing with lac. My appointment is for two-thirty.'

'All right. You can keep the same taxi that we're going to take now. It can come back after lunch and take you to Namkan. Shouldn't take you more than ten minutes to get there.'

Both men got into the taxi. Prasant Sarkar came to the point a little later.

'Er. . .how long are you here for?'

'If I don't finish talking business with Jain today, I'll have to go back tomorrow. Then I'll return to Calcutta the day after.'

'You seem so different. . .one feels hesitant to talk to you.'

'Tell me what you must. Don't beat about the bush. I get suspicious when people do that.'

'It's nothing much, really. Just a request. If you agree, this childhood friend of yours would feel most grateful.'

'What is it?'

'Do you remember Father William?'

'William? Willie. . .the red beard?'

'Yes, the red beard. About five years ago, he opened a school for poor children. All kinds of children go there regardless of what families they come from—Hindus, Muslims, Christians. Father William's worked really hard to get it going. He's very keen that you go and visit the school. It shouldn't take you more than half an hour. He'd feel very encouraged if you went.'

'Going there means being offered a begging bowl.'

'Meaning?'

'Do you not know the real reason behind such an invitation? A new institution, need for funds, a wealthy client and a begging bowl. If I must give my money away in the name of charity, I shall do so in my old age, when it's time to think of the other world. But now is not the time for this. This is the time to save. If it gets known that I am the loving and giving kind, there shall be no end to appeals for help. So don't try to make a request like this. I shall pay no attention. I'm sure if you explained things to Father, he'll understand. All I want to do here, apart from making a business deal, is to rest. I don't get much relaxation in Calcutta.'

'All right.'

Prasant had not expected such a violent reaction. But perhaps it was natural enough. This man was not the Montu he had once known. He was a stranger.

But the sight of the place he was born in made Tridib Babu grow a little less pompous and more cheerful. Prasant Babu took this opportunity to make the second request.

'You rejected one of my proposals, dear friend, but you've got to accept this one. My wife gave me strict instructions to bring you over to our house for dinner tonight. We are not very wealthy ourselves, but I can say with full confidence that no one in my house shall greet you with a begging bowl.'

Tridib Babu accepted his invitation readily enough. Was it simply out of pity? Prasant Babu chose not to brood on the issue. He had a lot of work to do now—finish all the shopping, go back home, have a bath, then a meal and then go to his school.

'I will come myself to fetch you at around eight,' he told Tridib Babu as they parted, 'and I promise to drop you back by ten o'clock.'

It was proved once more that day that it was the personality of Tridib Chowdhury and his sharp communications skills that were responsible for his success. His visit to Ranchi resulted in the addition of a new side to his business—the development of trade dealing with lac. No doubt this also meant additional complications, but they seemed insignificant when one considered the extra income that would be generated.

Tridib Babu returned home at about five in the evening, just in time for a cup of tea. Then he moved about in the house, looking carefully at everything. This was where he was born. The ground floor had the living and the dining-rooms, a guest-room and the kitchen. There were two bedrooms on the first floor, a bathroom and a covered veranda facing the west. The smaller of the two bedrooms had been his own.

The room seemed much smaller than he remembered possibly because he had grown in size. He stared for a few minutes at the bed and decided to sleep in the same room. Chintamani had already asked him once, but he had then been undecided. He called the servant before setting out with his friend and told him to make his bed in the small bedroom.

Prasant Sarkar's wife, Bela, was not only an efficient housewife but also an excellent cook. The dinner, therefore, was a success. Prasant Babu had spared no expense to feed his friend well—there were meat and fish dishes of more than one kind, pulao, puris and sweets. Tridib Babu ate everything with relish but did not stay for more than ten minutes after dinner. Prasant Babu did not get a single opportunity to ask him about his present position in society and how he had got there. Tridib Babu returned to his own house at a quarter-to-ten.

The house was in a relatively quiet locality. All was silent when he reached home. As Tridib Babu began to go up the stairs, the sound of his footsteps, even to his own ears, seemed unnaturally loud.

His bed had been made in the same room where he had spent his childhood. It was too soon after dinner to go to sleep. Tridib Babu decided to rest for a while in an easy chair on the veranda.

In less than half an hour he realized all his fatigue had vanished. He began to feel fresh and totally relaxed. There was a pale moon in the sky and, in its light, he could see the dark branches of a bare shirish tree. He could even hear himself breathe. It seemed as though that was the only sound on earth.

But was it?

No, the sound of something else was added to it. A faint voice. Difficult to say where it was coming from.

Tridib Babu listened carefully. A little boy was reciting a poem. A well-known nursery rhyme that Tridib Babu recognized at once.

The voice still came only faintly, but the words were clear.

> *Baa   Baa   black sheep*
> *Have you any wool?*

It was as though these few lines had been hiding in a corner of his mind. The voice made them leap out of memory.

The voice grew fainter. Tridib Babu rose. It was no use looking back. What mattered in life was the future, not the past. He knew he had to make a lot more money in the future, climb higher on the social ladder, become a billionaire. The past made a man weak. Thoughts of the future, on the other hand, would give him new strength.

He went into the room and frowned. There was a power cut. A candle flickered on a table by the bed. Even in its dim light, he could see clearly that the bed had not been properly made. The bed-sheet and the pillow case were both wrinkled. He straightened them and took off his kurta. Then he lay down. Should he let the candle burn? No, there was no need. He snuffed it out. The pungent smell of burnt wax hung in the air for a few minutes before fading away gradually. The window was open. Through it, he could see the sky. The moonlight seemed brighter. From where he lay, he faced the door. That too, was open. A portion of the veranda and the staircase could be seen. There was really no reason for him to look at the stairs, but something made him do so—it was the strange sound of bare feet coming up the stairs.

But no one actually arrived. The sound stopped in the middle of the staircase.

Tridib Babu suddenly felt he was being very foolish. The whole thing was no more than his imagination. He removed all fanciful thoughts from his mind and closed his eyes determinedly. The Japanese clock in the dining-room downstairs struck eleven. It had stopped working but, this morning, Tridib Babu had got it going again.

The silence seemed to deepen as the last chime of the clock faded away.

Even with his eyes closed, Tridib Babu began to see things—broken little pictures, disjointed pieces of a dream. He knew he would soon fall asleep. Just as a singer hummed a tune first quietly to himself before starting a song, these broken dreams were a prelude to slumber.

But he was not quite asleep yet. In spite of his closed eyes, his sixth sense told him someone had entered his room. No, it was not just his sixth sense. His ears, too, said the same thing. He could actually hear someone breathe. It sounded as though someone had come running up the stairs and was now panting in the room.

Tridib Babu opened his eyes, convinced he would actually be able to see this person. He was not mistaken.

A boy was standing at the door, his right hand resting lightly on the doorknob, his left foot slightly raised, as though the sight of another person in the room had startled him into halting in his tracks.

Tridib Babu realized a cold shiver was working its way up his legs, past his spine and on to his head! Prasant had said he had seen a boy in the garden...a little boy...the Montu of his childhood. . . .

His limbs froze, a nerve throbbed at his temple. He thought he would faint, his mounting terror choked him.

The boy took a step forward. He was wearing a purple shirt. . . .why, this was the same shirt. . . .

Just before passing into oblivion, he heard a question, spoken in a sweet, boyish voice:

'Who is sleeping in my bed?'

Tridib Babu woke as usual at half-past-six in the morning. He could not recall when he had regained consciousness at night and when he had dropped off to sleep again.

Prasant had said he could come and have breakfast with him at seven-thirty. Tridib Babu could not focus on any of his routine activities. What happened last night had left him feeling totally shaken. Never before in his life had such a thing happened.

That nursery rhyme he had heard last night was one that he had recited in class when he was small and even won a prize for. And the second prize? That had gone to Prasant Sarkar. Montu had been displeased at this.

'What fun we would have had if we'd both won the first prize!' he had said to his dearest friend, Panu.

He had not looked at the face of the boy who had come into his room last night, but he had definitely noticed the shirt the boy was wearing. It was the same purple shirt his aunt had given him. It was his favourite shirt. The first time he wore it to school, Panu had said, 'Good heavens—you look like a European today!'

The meaning of the incident last night was clear enough. The Tridib Chowdhury of today was definitely not the Montu he had once been. The child Montu was no more. It was his ghost that had come the night before and told him that the new Tridib Chowdhury—the great millionaire—was an obnoxious idiot. He could not be tolerated.

Tridib Babu did not say anything to Prasant about his experience. But he knew that he was still tense and nervous and quite unable to relax. It was possibly because of this reason that Prasant Babu, after a while, happened to remark, 'What is the matter with you? Didn't you sleep well last night?'

'No. . .uh. . .I mean, since I've finished all my work already, couldn't we go and visit Father William's school today?'

'Excellent idea,' said Prasant Sarkar cheerfully.

But he had to hide a smile. His plan had worked beautifully. He must drop in at his neighbour's house on his way back and tell his son, Babu, that his recitation and acting the night before had been just perfect. And, of course, Chintamani would have to be given a fat tip for his contribution!

Load Shedding

Phoni Babu realized shortly before reaching his bus stop that the entire area was plunged in darkness. Another power cut. More load shedding. By the time he had left his office this evening, having worked over-time, it was already a quarter-past-eight. It had taken him about thirty-five minutes to get to his area from Dalhousie Square. There was no way of telling how long ago the power cut had started, but he knew that it normally took about four hours for the supply to be resumed.

Phoni Babu got off his bus and made his way to the lane where he lived. Not a glimmer of light anywhere. Ironically, things had appeared to have improved lately. Why, wasn't it only yesterday that his servant, Nabeen, had asked, 'Should I buy a dozen candles today?' And Phoni Babu had replied, 'No, no. I bet the power cuts will start again the minute you get the candles. Don't buy any now.'

This meant that there were no candles in the house. It was sometimes possible to move about in his room on the second floor, aided by the streetlight. But even the streetlights were out today. Phoni Babu did not smoke, and so did not bother to keep a matchbox in his pocket. He had been toying with the idea of buying a torch for some time, but had not got round to doing so.

A three minute walk down the lane took him to the house where he lived, at number 17/2. Carefully stepping over the three pups that lay near the front door, Phoni Babu went through.

He and Nabeen had moved into this block of apartments only a month ago. Each floor of the house had two flats. Phoni Babu noticed while moving towards the staircase that the flickering yellow light of a candle was falling across the veranda from the window of one of the ground floor flats where Gyan Datta lived. The other flat was in total darkness. No one seemed to be about. It was only two days before Puja. Perhaps the occupant, Ramanath Babu, had already left for Madhupur—or was it Ghatshila?—to spend his holidays.

'Nabeen!' yelled Phoni Babu as he reached the bottom of the stairs. There was no reply. Clearly, Nabeen was not at home. He often left the house as soon as a power cut began.

Phoni Babu began climbing the stairs without waiting for Nabeen. It was possible to see the first few steps in the candlelight, but beyond that it was pitch dark. Not that it bothered him. He knew there were exactly seventy-two steps to be climbed. He had counted them one day for just such an eventuality.

It was strange how easy it was to go up a flight of stairs if the lights were on. In the darkness, Phoni Babu shivered as his hand fell on something soft, something very different from the wooden banister. Then he forced himself to put his hand back on the railing and realized it was only a towel someone had carelessly hung on it.

The first floor, too, was completely dark, which meant both flats were empty. In one of them lived Bijan Babu with his wife and two boys. The younger one of these was very naughty and a remarkable chatterbox. The other flat was occupied by Mahadev Mandal, who owned a shoe shop in College Street. He might have gone to play cards with his friends. And Bijan Babu must have taken his family to a Hindi film, as he occasionally did.

Phoni Babu continued going up the stairs. As he turned right after the sixtieth step, his foot suddenly knocked against what must have been a metal container. The racket it made caused him to halt in his tracks and wait until his heartbeat returned to normal. The remaining twelve steps had to be negotiated with extreme caution.

Now he had to turn left. An empty cage hung where the stairs ended. It had once contained a mynah. Phoni Babu had often asked his next door neighbour, Naresh Biswas, to have the cage removed. There seemed little point in hanging on to the cage when the mynah had died, but Mr Biswas had paid not the slightest attention to him.

Phoni Babu bent his body like a hunchback in order to avoid banging into the cage and groped his way to the door of his own flat.

From somewhere, not very far away, came the strains of a Tagore song.

Perhaps someone in the house next door was playing a transistor. At a moment like this, in this somewhat spooky and all-engulfing darkness, the sound of music helped bring a little courage to his mind, though Phoni Babu was certainly not afraid of ghosts.

As his fingers fell on his door, he stopped and took the keys out of his pocket. There were two sets of keys. He kept one and Nabeen had the other. It was easy enough to reach for the padlock but, to Phoni Babu's surprise, he discovered there was no padlock at all. This was distinctly peculiar since he could remember quite clearly having locked the house as usual, placing the key in his pocket. Was Nabeen responsible for this? Could he have bolted the door from inside and gone to sleep?

Phoni Babu tried knocking on the door and then stood foolishly as it opened at his touch.

'Nabeen!'

Still no answer. Surely he was not sleeping in the dark?

Phoni Babu crossed the threshold and entered his living-room. But perhaps it would be wrong to put it like that for what lay beyond the door was impossible to see. Phoni Babu shut his eyes and opened them again. He could feel no difference. Now, if he so wished, he could do what he liked with his eyes closed. The darkness seemed as though it were a solid obstruction that must be physically pushed aside.

The wall to the left had a switchboard. The door to the next room was behind this, and a clothes rack stood near the door. Phoni Babu was carrying an umbrella. This would have to be hung from the rack. And he was feeling hot. So he would need to take his shirt off and place it on the rack as well. But, before he did that, he had better take out his wallet from his pocket and put it in the drawer of the table that stood to the left of the rack.

Phoni Babu reached for the switchboard. Although there was no point now in pressing the switches on, he did not want to miss the joy of seeing the whole house light up silently when the power came back.

One of the two switches on the board had a loose head. Nabeen had been groping in the dark recently and had felt an electric shock even during a power cut. Phoni Babu's finger nimbly skipped this particular switch and pressed the second one. It was quite pleasant to hear the switch faintly click into place.

Then he passed the switchboard and slipped through the open door to the next room. The rack was fixed on the wall at about the same height as his own. . . .

But no.

His groping hand could find no rack. What it did fall upon was something quite different. Not only that, a miscalculated jab made it slip from the wall and crash to the ground.

A picture? Or was it a mirror? Shards lay all around his feet. He was not worried about his feet for they were protected by the slippers he wore, but where had the rack gone? He stood still, trying to think. There was, of course, a picture of Paramahansa in his room but it should have been hanging on the opposite wall. His mirror usually stood on the table.

Nabeen must have moved the furniture around, as was his habit. Phoni Babu had had to tell him off a number of times for moving his slippers from under the table, where he liked to keep them, and putting them elsewhere.

Still puzzled, Phoni Babu placed his old and worn out umbrella on the floor, carefully balancing it against the wall. Then he took the wallet out of his pocket and began walking towards the invisible table. Pieces of broken glass crunched beneath his feet.

Now all he had to do was find a corner of the table, and then finding the drawer would not be difficult.

But he could not find the table. He took another step forward. It was still impossibly dark. Perhaps if he opened the window that faced the street, it might help.

This time his hand struck against something solid.

Furniture of some kind. Yes, it was wooden. But no, not a table. Was it a cupboard?

Yes, here was the handle. A long, vertical one, made of cut glass. Many old cupboards had handles like that. Phoni Babu did have an old cupboard, but what was its handle made of? He failed to remember.

But—why, this cupboard wasn't locked!

He released the handle. The cupboard gently swung open.

It just didn't make any sense. He never left his cupboard unlocked. God knows he possessed no valuables, but his cupboard did contain all his clothes, some old documents and whatever little cash he had.

Had he forgotten to lock the cupboard this morning?

But where was the table? Could it be—?

Yes, that must be it. Phoni Babu suddenly hit upon an explanation.

The day before had been a Sunday. It had rained heavily in the afternoon and a small portion of the ceiling had started to leak. Water had dripped on to his table, which was why Nabeen had spread a few newspapers on it. The building was quite old. He would have to tell the landlord to have the roof repaired. Judging by the puddles he had found on the way, it had rained again during the day. If Nabeen had moved the table near the window and shifted the rack to the opposite wall, one must say he had acted with considerable thoughtfulness.

Phoni Babu returned the wallet to his pocket and moved towards the window. Again he collided with an object.

A chair. Nabeen had obviously moved the chair as well.

Phoni Babu gave up. There was no point in trying to find his way in the dark. He might as well sit in the chair and wait until the lights came back.

He sat down. The chair had arms and the seat was made of cane. Wasn't the chair in his room an armless one? No, he must be mistaken. He had learnt today how little one noticed or remembered details of one's own furniture.

He sat facing the door and could see a small square piece of the sky just over the terrace on the other side. It was reflecting faintly the light from the neighbouring areas as yet unaffected by a power cut.

There were no stars for it was still cloudy but at least it gave him something to look at.

Something was ticking in the room. An alarm clock? There was definitely no alarm clock in his room. So how come—? But before he could think any further, an ear-splitting noise made him nearly fall off his chair.

A telephone.

Just behind his head was a table, and on it a telephone, ringing insistently. It pierced through the silent darkness and stopped finally, after a whole minute of complete cacophony.

One thing had now become clear to Phoni Babu. This was not his room at all. He had walked into someone else's. And with this realization, everything fell into place.

17/2 and 17/3 were two similar blocks of apartments. Both had three storeys, and both were owned by the same man. Phoni Babu had never been inside 17/3, but obviously its design and plan were identical to that of his own house. He was now sitting in a room in one of the two flats on the second floor of 17/3. There was no electricity, the front door was open, the cupboard unlocked.

What could it mean? But whatever the implication of these things, Phoni Babu was not going to let that worry him. He had realized his mistake and must leave at once. He started to rise, but another noise made him fall back into the chair.

It had come from the left, quite close to where he was sitting. It sounded like a box—a tin suitcase, perhaps?—being dragged across the floor.

Phoni Babu's throat began to feel dry and his heart thudded faster.

A thief!

There was possibly a bed right next to the chair and, under it, a thief. In his haste to get out, he had clearly banged into a tin suitcase kept under the bed.

It was now easy enough to guess why the door and the cupboard were open.

If the thief was armed, Phoni Babu might be in some danger. His only weapon, his umbrella, was now lying beyond his reach. And, in any case, it was so old that if he hit the thief with it, the umbrella was likely to sustain more injuries.

But the thief was now quiet, possibly as a result of having unwittingly revealed his presence.

Phoni Babu felt like kicking himself. What a stupid mistake to have made and what an impossible situation to be in!

A petty thief was unlikely to carry a revolver, but could well have a knife. But, of course, not all thieves were armed. If it was a question of unarmed combat Phoni Babu was not afraid for he had once been a sportsman. But the biggest problem was this power cut. Even the strongest might feel helpless in such utter darkness.

What on earth was he to do? Should he simply get up and walk away? But what if the lights came back just as he reached the stairs? And what if, in that instant, the thief tried to get away from one side and the real owner of the flat turned up from the other? If the owner saw he had been burgled, wouldn't he—

Phoni Babu's thoughts came to an abrupt halt.

There were footsteps coming up the stairs. Slow, measured steps.

Almost unconsciously, Phoni Babu began counting. When the other man reached the forty-ninth step, Phoni Babu began to feel convinced that it was indeed the owner of this flat who was coming up the stairs. And, in a flash, he remembered something else: he knew the owner!

Why hadn't he thought of it before? He had once shared the same taxi with him right up to Dalhousie Square. The man had introduced himself as Adinath Sanyal. About fifty years of age, a stern demeanour, a fair complexion, clad in a fine cotton kurta. Greenish eyes below thick, bushy eyebrows.

Sixty-two, sixty-three, sixty-four. . .the footsteps were getting louder.

There were fresh noises inside the room. Someone scurried across the floor and then came a faint 'ouch'! Perhaps a piece of broken glass had cut into the thief's foot? Serve him right! The faint patch of light visible in the sky was covered for an instant and then it reappeared. The thief had turned to the right. He had no choice but to jump out of the window and go down the pipe.

The footsteps were now outside on the veranda. Phoni Babu rose, and walked towards the door, taking great care not to step on the shards of glass. Then he picked up his umbrella and went into the living-room.

The footsteps stopped just outside the front door. Then, after a few moments of silence, came an explosion, 'What! Why is the door. . .?'

The unmistakable raucous voice of Adinath Sanyal. He had talked quite a lot in the taxi.

There were other things about him that Phoni Babu could now recollect. His own next door neighbour, Naresh Biswas, had once told him that Adinath Sanyal had pots of money stacked away somewhere. Apparently, he owned three houses in Calcutta. All were let and he himself lived in these two rooms. The way he earned his living was reportedly not a straightforward one. The drawers of his table and the shelves of his cupboard were supposed to be filled with black money. . . .

Mr Sanyal had now gone into the bedroom, breathing heavily and walking all over the broken glass, in the hope of catching the thief red-handed.

Phoni Babu had nothing to fear now. He slipped out of the front door that was still open, and silently went down the seventy-two steps that he had climbed only a few minutes ago. Then he made his way to number 17/2.

As he climbed up the steps of his own house and came to the spot where the empty cage hung, the lights came back. Much relieved, Phoni Babu looked down and found himself clutching a brand-new, fashionable, Japanese umbrella.

Spotlight

We often came to this small town in Chhota Nagpur to spend our Puja holidays like many other Bengali families. Some stayed in houses of their own, some rented a bungalow or went to the local hotels. Ten days in a place like this was enough to add at least six months to an average lifetime. My father often said, 'The cost of living may have gone up a little, but the water you drink and the air you breathe are still free. And no one can say their quality has suffered in any way.'

We usually arrived in a large group, so ten days went by very quickly, despite the absence of cinemas, theatres, markets and other attractions. If one were to ask whether what we did in these ten days varied from one year to the next, it would be difficult to find an answer, for we inevitably ate the same stuff every day: chicken, eggs, *arhar daal*, fresh milk, guavas and other fruits from our own garden; followed the same routine—to bed at 10 p.m., rise at six, spend the afternoon playing cards and Monopoly, walk to Raja Pahar after tea in the evening; have a picnic at least once during our stay, by the side of Kalijhora; everything we saw was always just the same:bright sunshine and fluffy white clouds; the birds, the animals, the insects, the trees, the plants and the flowers.

But not this time.

On this occasion, things took a different turn.

Personally, I had never liked Anshuman Chatterjee. But, of course, that did not stop him from being the most popular film-star in West Bengal. My twelve-year-old sister, Sharmi, had filled a whole scrapbook with pictures of Anshuman from film magazines. There were boys in my own class who were his admirers, and had already started copying his hair-style, his speech, his mannerisms and style of dressing.

The famous Anshuman Chatterjee was in the same town this time, staying in the house the Kundus owned. He had brought three of his sycophants with him in a yellow air-conditioned Mercedes with tinted glass windows.

Once, on our way to the Andamans, I had noticed how the smaller boats rocked and swayed in the huge waves our own ship kept throwing up. Here, Anshuman became a ship like that. When he came out on the street, the other visitors simply drowned in the ripples he left behind.

There had never been such excitement in this small town. Chhoto Mama was not interested in films. But palmistry intrigued him.

'I must,' he declared, 'take a look at his fate line. I'd never get the chance back in Calcutta.'

Mother wanted to invite him to dinner. 'Sharmi,' she asked, 'do your film magazines ever mention what kind of food he prefers?' Sharmi promptly rattled off a long list that ended with '. . .but what he likes best is Chinese.' Mother sighed. Father said, 'I see no problem in asking him to dinner one evening. He might even accept. But I don't like those hangers-on. . . .'

Chheni-da was a cousin of mine. He worked for a newspaper as a journalist and almost never got any leave. This time he had come with us only to write a feature on a festival of the local Santhals. He felt he had to corner Anshuman for an interview. 'That man has shooting three hundred and sixty-seven days a year. How on earth did he manage to come away on holiday? God, that itself would make a story!'

Chhoto-da was the only one who displayed no emotion. A student of the Presidency College, he was a rather grave young man. He also happened to be a member of a film society and, having seen all kinds of German, Swedish, French, Cuban and Brazilian films, was now working on a critical thesis on the films of Bengal. He had spent three minutes watching Anshuman's *Sleepless Nights* on television, before saying 'Disgusting!' and leaving the room. It was his view that the film-star's arrival had spoilt the entire atmosphere of this beautiful place.

There were a few Bengalis who lived in the town permanently. Gopen Babu was one of them. He had lived here in a tiny house for twenty-two years and had a small farm. Slightly older than Father, he was a jovial old fellow. We all liked him.

He turned up a couple of days after our arrival clad in a *khaddar* kurta and a dhoti, a stout walking-stick in his hand, brown tennis shoes on his feet.

'Mr Chowdhury!' he yelled from outside, 'are you home?'

We were having breakfast. Father went out and escorted him in.

'Good heavens!' he exclaimed, 'what a spread! All I want is a cup of tea.' The last time we had seen him, he had had a cataract in one eye. He had had it removed last March, he said. 'Now I can see things quite clearly.'

'Well, there's certainly a lot going on here,' said Father.

'Why?' Gopen Babu frowned.

'Haven't you heard? The stars from heaven have descended on earth!'

'Your vision cannot be clear enough,' said Chhoto Mama, 'if you haven't noticed the great hullabaloo over the arrival of the film-star.'

'Film-star?' Gopen Babu was still frowning, 'why make a fuss over a film-star? They're all shooting stars, aren't they? They spend their lives shooting. You know what a shooting star is, don't you, Sumohan?' he said, turning towards me, 'Here today, gone tomorrow. Liable to slip from the sky any minute and burn to ashes. There wouldn't be anything left of it after that. Nothing at all.'

Chhoto-da coughed gently. Clearly, Gopen Babu's words had pleased him.

'This can only mean you haven't heard of the real star,' Gopen Babu added, sipping his tea.

'Real star?' asked Father. All of us stared at Gopen Babu.

'You must have seen the bungalow behind the church,' he said, 'you know, the one with a garden? That is where the gentleman is staying. His name, I think, is Kalidas. . . or is it Kaliprasad. . .? something like that. The surname's Ghoshal.'

'Why do you call him a star?'

'Because he is one. Absolutely the Pole Star. Steady. Eternal. More than a hundred years old, but doesn't look it at all!'

'What! A centurion!' Chhoto Mama gaped, a half-eaten piece of toast stuck in his open mouth.

'Century plus twenty-six. He is a hundred and twenty-six years old. Born in 1856. Just a year before the revolt. A few years before Tagore. Tagore was born in 1861.'

We fell silent. Gopen Babu continued sipping his tea.

After about a whole minute of silence, Chhoto-da asked, 'How do you know his age? Did he tell you himself?'

'Yes, but not deliberately. He's a most unassuming man. I learnt of it by accident. We were sitting in the front veranda of his house. Through the curtain, I happened to catch a glimpse of a woman— grey hair, glasses in a golden frame, a sari with a red border. So I said, "I hope this climate here suits your wife?" Mr Ghoshal smiled at this and replied, "Not my wife. My grandson's." I was amazed!

After a while I said, "Please forgive my asking, but how old are you?" Again he smiled and said, "How old do you think?" "About eighty?" I said. "Add another forty-six," he told me. Now you know. It's a simple calculation.'

None of us could eat our breakfast after this. A piece of news like this was enough to kill one's appetite. The very thought that the oldest man in the country—no, possibly in the whole world—was actually staying in the same town as us made my head reel.

'You must meet him,'said Gopen Babu, 'I couldn't keep this news to myself, so I told a few people before you came—Sudheer Babu, Mr Sen, Mr Neotia of Ballygunj Park. They've all visited him. Now it's just a matter of time before you get to see the attraction of a real star.'

'Is his health. . .?' asked Mama.

'A couple of miles. Twice a day.'

'You mean he walks?'

'Yes, he walks. He does take a walking-stick. But then, so do I. Just think—he's twice my age.'

'I must look at his life line. . . .' muttered Mama, his mind running on the same old track.

'Yes, I'm sure he wouldn't mind you looking at his palm!'

Chheni-da was sitting quietly in a corner. Now he sprang to his feet.

'Story! I couldn't get a better story. This could be a scoop!'

'Are you going to meet him right away?' asked Father.

'Yes, If he's a hundred and twenty-six years old, I'm taking no chances. Anything can happen to a man of that age, any time. He may not even have a period of illness before he dies. So, if I must interview him, I'd better hurry before the word spreads.'

'Sit down,' Father ordered, 'we shall all go together. You're not the only one who'd like to meet him. You may bring your notebook and jot things down.'

'Bogus!' said Chhoto-da softly. Then he added with a little more force, 'Bogus! Fraud! Liar!'

'What do you mean?' Gopen Babu sounded annoyed, 'Look, Suranjan, you've read Shakespeare, haven't you? "There are more things in heaven and earth. . . ." You do know the line, don't you? So you mustn't dismiss everything as bogus.'

Chhoto-da cleared his throat.

'Let me tell you something, Gopen Babu. It has been proved that those who claim to be more than a hundred are either liars or barbarians. Once there were reports of a group of people who lived in a village in Russia at a high altitude. A majority of them were supposed to have completed a hundred years and were still fit enough to ride. So there was an investigation and it showed that these people were all totally primitive. There was no record of their birth. When asked about things that had happened in the past, their replies were all mixed up. It's not easy to cross the nineties. There is a limit to man's longevity. That is how nature has created man. Bernard Shaw, Bertrand Russell, P.G. Wodehouse—none of them lived to a hundred. Jadunath Sarkar in our own country couldn't. And here's your man saying he's a hundred and twenty-six. Ha!'

'Have you heard of Zoro Agha?' snapped Mama.

'No. Who's he?'

'Man from Turkey. Or maybe from Iran. Can't remember now. He died sometime between 1930 and 1935 at the age of a hundred and sixty-four. Every newspaper in the entire world covered the event.'

'Bogus!' said Chhoto-da adamantly.

However, when we left for Kali Ghoshal's house, he joined us, possibly only to have his scepticism reinforced. Gopen Babu led the group.

'It would be nice,' said Father, 'if you could introduce us. After all, we're just strangers, and we cannot drop in casually simply because we've heard about his age.'

Chheni-da did not forget to take a notebook and a ball point.

'You go first,' said Mother, 'I'll go and visit some other time.'

The front veranda of Kali Ghoshal's house was full of cane and wooden chairs and stools. Obviously, he had started to receive a large number of visitors. We had gone within an hour of breakfast as Gopen Babu said that was the best time to get him. He came out in answer to Gopen Babu's greeting spoken from the veranda, 'Are you home, Mr Ghoshal?'

A hundred and twenty-six? No, he really didn't look more than eighty. A clear complexion, a mole on his right cheek, a sharp nose, a bright look in his eyes and a bald dome, except for a few strands of grey hair over his ears. Of medium height, he must once have been good looking. He was today wearing a white silk kurta and pyjamas and had white slippers on his feet. If his skin had wrinkles at all, it was only around the eyes and below the chin.

Introductions over, he asked us to sit down. Chhoto-da was probably planning to stand behind a pillar, but when Father said, 'Do sit down, Ranju,' he pulled up a stool and sat down. He was still looking grave.

'We are sorry to barge in like this,' Father said, 'but you see, none of us has been lucky enough to have met a man like you. . . .'

Mr Ghoshal smiled and raised a hand in protest, 'Please do not apologize. I do realize my age is my only distinction and the only thing that makes me special. Once people learnt the truth about my age, I knew they would wish to come and take a look at me. It's only natural, isn't it? Besides, isn't it a privilege for me to have met all of you?'

'Well, then,' said Father, 'perhaps I should tell you something frankly. This nephew of mine, Srikanta Chowdhury, is a journalist. He is very keen to have our discussions published. If you have no objection, that is.'

'No, not at all. Why should I object?' said Mr Ghoshal, still smiling. 'If a certain amount of fame comes my way at this late age, I should consider myself lucky. I've spent most of my life living in a village. Have you heard of a place called Tulsia? You haven't? It's in Murshidabad. There is no connection by rail. One has to get off at Beldanga and travel further south for another seventeen kilometres. We used to be landowners in Tulsia. There is, of course, nothing left of our old glory, except the ancestral house. That is where I live. People there call me "Reject". Rejected even by death. And they're right. My wife died fifty-two years ago. I have no living children or other brothers or sisters. All I have is a grandson, who was supposed to come with me. But he's a doctor, you see, and he had a patient lying in a rather critical condition. So he couldn't leave him and come away. I was prepared to come alone with a servant, but my granddaughter wouldn't let me. She came with me herself and has already settled down here so well.'

A ball point pen writes noiselessly. But I could see Chheni-da scribble furiously in his notebook. His tape recorder had no batteries, which was something he had discovered the day before we left. Everything, therefore, depended on how fast he could write. He had borrowed a Pentax camera from somewhere. No doubt it was going to be used at some stage. No article of this kind could be complete without a picture.

'Er. . .I happen to be interested in palmistry,' said Mama, 'could I look at your hand, just once?'

'Of course.'

Kali Ghoshal offered his right palm. Mama bent over it eagerly and, after a minute's silence, nodded vigorously and said, 'Naturally. Naturally. Your life line could not have been longer than usual. It would have had to come right down to your wrist if it were to reflect your age. I don't suppose the human hand has any provision for those who live to be more than a hundred. Thank you, sir!'

Father took over again.

'Is your memory still. . . I mean. . . .'

'Yes. I can remember most things.'

'Didn't you ever visit Calcutta?' asked Chheni-da.

'Oh yes. Certainly. I went to the Hare School and Sanskrit College. I used to stay in a hostel on Cornwallis Street.'

'Horse driven trams—?'

'Yes, I often rode in them. The fare was just two paise from Lal Deeghi to Bhabanipore. There were no rickshaws. But there was a big *palki* stand just off the main crossing at Shyam Bazar. The *palki* bearers once went on strike—I remember that. And there were the scavenger birds. As common as crows and sparrows nowadays. Quite large in size, high enough to reach my shoulders. But perfectly harmless.'

'Do you remember any famous personalities of the time?' Chheni-da continued.

'I saw Tagore a few times, much later. I didn't know him personally, of course. Who was I, anyway, to get to know him? But I saw the young Tagore once, an occasion I remember very well. He was reading poetry at the Hindu Mela.'

'That's a very well known event,' said Father.

'I never saw Bankimchandra, which I might have done, had I stayed on in Calcutta. But I went back to my village soon after college. I did see Vidyasagar, though. That was a memorable incident. I was walking along the road with two other friends and Vidyasagar was coming from the opposite side, carrying an umbrella, a cotton *chadar* on his shoulder, slippers on his feet. His height must have been even less than mine. Someone had left a banana peel on the footpath. He slipped on it and fell. We ran and helped him to his feet. His umbrella rolled away. One of us collected it and returned it to him. Do you know what he did as soon as he was back on his feet? Only he could have done such a thing.

He picked up the banana peel, threw it into a dustbin and calmly walked away, without showing the slightest sign of annoyance.'

We spent another half an hour with Mr Ghoshal. Tea was served and, with it, came home-made sweets—no doubt a contribution from the grandson's wife. When we rose to take our leave, Chheni-da had filled more than half of a brand new notebook with his scribbles. He had also taken at least ten photographs.

He posted a parcel to his office in Calcutta the same day. Five days later, a copy of his newspaper reached us, carrying the article he had written, together with a photo of Mr Ghoshal. The headline said, 'I had helped Vidyasagar.'

It was undoubtedly a scoop, and Chheni-da's office duly recognized his efforts. But soon after that, as many as seven different magazines and dailies from Calcutta sent their representatives to interview Kali Ghoshal.

Something else had happened in the meantime. Anshuman Chatterjee, the film-star, cut short his holiday and returned to Calcutta with his entourage. He was apparently called away for shooting. Sharmi did not seem to mind since she had already taken his autograph. To tell the truth, she had lost at least a quarter of her admiration for her hero the minute he had said to her, 'What's your name, little girl?' Besides, she was quite overwhelmed to have met the world's oldest man.

'I suppose,' said Father, 'the star felt offended at so much attention being paid to an old man.'

Kali Ghoshal and his grandson's wife dined with us the day before we returned. He ate very little, but with relish. 'I have never smoked in my life,' he told us, 'and I've always eaten moderately and walked as much as possible. Perhaps that is why death hasn't dared to approach me.'

'Were there others in your family who lived long?' asked Father.

'Oh yes. Both my grandfather and great-grandfather lived to be more than a hundred. The latter used to practise *tantra*. At the age of a hundred and thirteen, he called my grandfather one day and said,"It is now time for me to go. Please make all the arrangements." There was no sign of illness. His skin had no wrinkles, his teeth were intact, his hair only mildly touched with grey. But the arrangements for his funeral were made on the bank of the Ganga. Half immersed in water, Haranath Ghoshal closed his eyes, chanting hymns and breathed his last. I was standing by his side. I was then forty-two. I can never forget that scene!'

'Remarkable!' sighed Mama.

A week after our return to Calcutta, Chhoto-da arrived one evening with a large, fat book under his arm. But no, it was not really a book, but a few issues of a magazine called *Bioscope* bound together. The editor of *Navarang* magazine, Sitesh Bagchi, had taken a deposit of fifty rupees from Chhoto-da before letting him borrow the book for a day. A bus ticket flagged one of the pages. Chhoto-da opened the book at that page and threw it before me.

There was a still from an old mythological film, printed on glossy art paper. The film was called *Shabari*. The caption below the picture read, 'The newcomer Kalikinkar Ghoshal and Kiran-shashi as Sree Ram Chandra and Shabari in Pratima Movietone's film *Shabari* still under production.'

'Check the resemblances, stupid,' said Chhoto-da.

I did. The man was of medium height, had a clear complexion, a sharp nose and a mole on his right cheek. He appeared to be a man in his mid-twenties.

The pit of my stomach suddenly felt empty. 'When,' I gasped, 'was this picture taken?'

'Sixty-eight years after the revolt. In 1924. It was a silent film. And Kalikinkar Ghoshal was its hero. That was the first and the last film he ever made. A review was published about three months later in the same magazine. Do you know what it said? "No difference would have been made if this newcomer had never made an appearance. He has absolutely no future as an actor in films."'

'Then . . . that means his age. . . .'

'Yes, he is what he appears to be. About eighty. If he was twenty-five in 1924, then that lady who was with him must have been his own wife, not his grandson's wife. Gopen Babu was right.'

'Then the man must be. . . .'

'Bogus. A cheat. A crook. But you know what? I shall do nothing to have him exposed. After all, he's got quite a sharp brain. One must appreciate that. In his youth he may have failed. But now, in his old age, just look at how, with a nice white lie, he snatched the spotlight from the top star and trained it on himself! Bravo!'

Anath Babu's Terror

I met Anath Babu on a train to Raghunathpur, where I was going on holiday. I worked for one of the dailies in Calcutta. The pressure of work over the last few months had nearly killed me. I definitely needed a break. Besides, writing being my hobby, I had ideas for a couple of short stories that needed further thought. And I needed peace and quiet to think. So I applied for ten days' leave and left with a packet of writing paper in my suitcase.

There was a reason for choosing Raghunathpur. An old college mate of mine, Biren Biswas, had his ancestral home there. We were chatting in the Coffee House one evening, talking of possible places where one might spend one's holiday. Upon being told that I had applied for leave, Biren promptly offered me free accommodation in Raghunathpur. 'I would have gone with you,' he said, 'but you know how tied up I am at the moment. You won't have any problem, though. Bharadwaj will look after you. He's worked for our family for fifty years.'

Our coach was packed. Anathbandhu Mitra happened to be sitting right next to me. About fifty years of age, not very tall, hair parted in the middle, a sharp look in his eyes and an amused smile playing on his lips. But his clothes! He appeared to have dressed for a part in a play set fifty years ago. Nobody these days wore a jacket like that, or such collars, or glasses, or boots.

We began to chat. It turned out that he, too, was going to Raghunathpur. 'Are you also going on holiday?' I asked him. But he did not answer and seemed to grow a little pensive. Or it may be that he had failed to hear my question in the racket the train was making.

The sight of Biren's house pleased me very much. It was a nice house, with a strip of land in front that had both vegetables and flowers growing in it. There were no other houses nearby, so the possibility of being disturbed by the neighbours was non-existent.

Despite protests from Bharadwaj, I chose the room in the attic for myself. It was an airy little room, very comfortable and totally private. I moved my things upstairs and began to unpack. It was then that I realized I had left my razor blades behind. 'Never mind,' said Bharadwaj, 'Kundu Babu's shop is only a five minute walk from here. You'll get your "*bilades*" there.'

I left for the shop soon after tea, at around 4 p.m. It appeared that the place was used more or less like a club. About seven middle-aged men were seated inside on wooden benches, chatting away merrily. One of them was saying rather agitatedly, 'Well, it's not something I have only heard about. I saw the whole thing with my own eyes. All right, so it happened thirty years ago. But that kind of thing cannot get wiped out from one's memory, can it? I shall never forget what happened, especially since Haladhar Datta was a close friend of mine. In fact, even now I can't help feeling partly responsible for his death.'

I bought a packet of 7 O' Clock blades. Then I began to loiter, looking at things I didn't really need. The gentleman continued, 'Just imagine, my own friend laid a bet with me for just ten rupees and went to spend a night in that west room. I waited for a long time the next morning for him to turn up; but when he didn't, I went with Jiten Bakshi, Haricharan Saha and a few others to look for him in the Haldar mansion. And we found him in the same room—lying dead on the floor, stone cold, eyes open and staring at the ceiling. The naked fear I saw in those eyes could only mean one thing, I tell you: ghosts. There was no injury on his person, no sign of snake-bite or anything like that. So what else could have killed him but a ghost? *You* tell me?'

Another five minutes in the shop gave me a rough idea of what they were talking about. There was, apparently, a two-hundred-year-old mansion in the southern corner of Raghunathpur, which had once been owned by the Haldars, the local *zamindars*. It had lain abandoned for years. A particular room in this mansion that faced the west was supposed to be haunted. Although in the last thirty years no one had dared to spend a night in it after the death of Haladhar Datta, the residents of Raghunathpur still felt a certain thrill thinking of the unhappy spirit that haunted the room. The reason behind this belief was both the mysterious death of Haladhar Datta, and the many instances of murders and suicides in the history of the Haldar family.

Intrigued by this conversation, I came out of the shop to find Anathbandhu Mitra, the gentleman I had met on the train, standing outside, a smile on his lips.

'Did you hear what they were saying?' he asked.

'Yes, I couldn't help it.'

'Do you believe in it?'

'In what? Ghosts?'

'Yes.'

'Well, you see, I have heard of haunted houses often enough. But never have I met anyone who has actually stayed in one and seen anything. So I don't quite. . . .'

Anath Babu's smile deepened.

'Would you like to see it?' he said.

'What?'

'That house.'

'See? How do you mean?'

'Only from the outside. It's not very far from here. A mile, at the most. If you go straight down this road, past the twin temples and then turn right, it's only a quarter of a mile from there.'

The man seemed interesting. Besides, there was no need to get back home quite so soon. So I left with him.

The Haldar mansion was not easily visible. Most of it was covered by a thick growth of wild plants and creepers. It was only the top of the gate that towered above everything else and could be seen a good ten minutes before one reached the house. The gate was really huge. The *nahabatkhana* over it was a shambles. A long drive led to the front veranda. A couple of statues and the remains of a fountain told us that there used to be a garden in the space between the house and the gate. The house was strangely structured. There was absolutely nothing in it that could have met even the lowest of aesthetic standards. The whole thing seemed only a shapeless heap. The last rays of the setting sun fell on its mossy walls.

Anath Babu stared at it for a minute. Then he said, 'As far as I know, ghosts and spirits don't come out in daylight. Why don't we,' he added, winking, 'go and take a look at that room?'

'That west room? The one. . .?'

'Yes. The one in which Haladhar Datta died.'

The man's interest in the matter seemed a bit exaggerated.

Anath Babu read my mind.

'I can see you're surprised. Well, I don't mind telling you the truth. The only reason behind my arrival in Raghunathpur is this house.'

'Really?'

'Yes. I had learnt in Calcutta that the house was haunted. I came all the way to see if I could catch a glimpse of the ghost. You asked me on the train why I was coming here. I didn't reply, which must have appeared rude. But I had decided to wait until I got to know you a little better before telling you.'

'But why did you have to come all the way from Calcutta to chase a ghost?'

'I'll explain that in a minute. I haven't yet told you about my profession, have I? The fact is that I am an authority on ghosts and all things supernatural. I have spent the last twenty-five years doing research in this area. I have read everything that's ever been published on life after death, spirits that haunt the earth, vampires, werewolves, black magic, voodoo—the lot. I had to learn seven different languages to do this. There is a Professor Norton in London who has a similar interest. I have been in correspondence with him over the last three years. My articles have been published in well-known magazines in Britain. I don't wish to sound boastful, but I think it would be fair to say that no one in this country has as much knowledge about these things as I do.'

He spoke very sincerely. The thought that he might be telling lies or exaggerating things did not cross my mind at all. On the contrary, I found it quite easy to believe what he told me and my respect for the man grew.

After a few moments of silence, he said, 'I have stayed in at least three hundred haunted houses all over the country.'

'Goodness!'

'Yes. In places like Jabalpur, Cherrapunji, Kanthi, Katoa, Jodhpur, Azimganj, Hazaribagh, Shiuri, Barasat. . .and so many others. I've stayed in fifty-six dak bungalows, and at least thirty *neel kuthis*. Besides these, there are about fifty haunted houses in Calcutta and its suburbs where I've spent my nights. But . . . .'

Anath Babu stopped. Then he shook his head and said, 'The ghosts have eluded me. Perhaps they like to visit only those who don't want to have anything to do with them. I have been disappointed time and again. Only once did I feel the presence of something strange in an old building in Tiruchirapalli near Madras. It used to be a club during British times. Do you know what happened? The room was dark and there was no breeze at all. Yet, each time I tried to light a candle, someone—or something—kept snuffing it out. I had to waste twelve matchsticks. However, with the thirteenth I did manage to light the candle; but, as soon as it was lit, the spirit vanished. Once, in a house in Calcutta, too, I had a rather interesting experience. I was sitting in a dark room as usual, waiting for something to happen, when I suddenly felt a mosquito bite my scalp! Quite taken aback, I felt my head and discovered that every single strand of my hair had disappeared. I was totally bald! Was it really my own head? Or had I felt someone else's? But no, the mosquito bite was real enough. I switched on my torch quickly and peered into the mirror. All my hair was intact. There was no sign of baldness.

'These were the only two slightly queer experiences I've had in all these years. I had given up all hope of finding anything anywhere. But, recently, I happened to read in an old magazine about this house in Raghunathpur. So I thought I'd come and try my luck for the last time.'

We had reached the front door. Anath Babu looked at his watch and said, 'The sun sets today at 5.31 p.m. It's now 5.15. Let's go and take a quick look before it gets dark.'

Perhaps his interest in the supernatural was infectious. I readily accepted his proposal. Like him, I felt eager to see the inside of the house and that room in particular.

We walked in through the front door. There was a huge court-yard and what looked like a stage. It must have been used for pujas and other festivals. There was no sign now of the joy and laughter it must once have witnessed.

There were verandas around the courtyard. To our right, lay a broken palanquin, and beyond it was a staircase going up.

It was so dark on the staircase that Anath Babu had to take a torch out of his pocket and switch it on. We had to demolish an invisible wall of cobwebs to make our way. When we finally reached the first floor, I thought to myself, 'It wouldn't be surprising at all if this house did turn out to be haunted.'

We stood in the passage and made some rough calculations. The room on our left must be the famous west room, we decided. Anath Babu said, 'Let's not waste any time. Come with me.'

There was only one thing in the passage: a grandfather clock. Its glass was broken, one of its hands was missing and the pendulum lay to one side.

The door to the west room was closed. Anath Babu pushed it gently with his forefinger. A nameless fear gave me goose-pimples. The door swung open.

But the room revealed nothing unusual. It may have been a living-room once. There was a big table in the middle with a missing top. Only the four legs stood upright. An easy chair stood near the window, although sitting in it now would not be very easy as it had lost one of its arms and a portion of its seat.

I glanced up and saw that bits and pieces of an old-fashioned, hand-pulled fan still hung from the ceiling. It didn't have a rope, the wooden bar was broken and its main body torn.

Apart from these objects, the room had a shelf that must once have held rifles, a pipeless hookah, and two ordinary chairs, also with broken arms.

Anath Babu appeared to be deep in thought. After a while, he said, 'Can you smell something?'

'Smell what?'

'Incense, oil and burning flesh. . .all mixed together. . . .' I inhaled deeply, but could smell nothing beyond the usual musty smell that comes from a room that has been kept shut for a long time.

So I said, 'Why, no, I don't think I can . . . .'

Anath Babu did not say anything. Then, suddenly, he struck his left hand with his right and exclaimed, 'God! I know this smell well! There is bound to be a spirit lurking about in this house, though whether or not he'll make an appearance remains to be seen. Let's go!'

Anath Babu decided to spend the following night in the Haldar mansion. On our way back, he said, 'I won't go tonight because tomorrow is a moonless night, the best possible time for ghosts and spirits to come out. Besides, I need a few things which I haven't got with me today. I'll bring those tomorrow. Today I came only to make a survey.'

Before we parted company near Biren's house, he lowered his voice and said, 'Please don't tell anyone else about my plan. From what I heard today, people here are so superstitious and easily frightened that they might actually try to stop me from going in if they came to know of my intention. And,' he added, 'please don't mind that I didn't ask you to join me. One has to be alone, you see, for something like this. . . .'

I sat down the next day to write, but could not concentrate. My mind kept going back to the west room in that mansion. God knows what kind of experience awaited Anath Babu. I could not help feeling a little restless and anxious.

I accompanied Anath Babu in the evening, right up to the gate of the Haldar mansion. He was wearing a black high-necked jacket today. From his shoulder hung a flask and, in his hand, he carried the same torch he had used the day before. He took out a couple of small bottles from his pocket before going into the house. 'Look,' he said, 'this one has a special oil, made with my own formula. It is an excellent mosquito repellent. And this one here has carbolic acid in it. If I spread it in and around the room, I'll be safe from snakes.'

He put the bottles back in his pocket, raised the torch and touched his head with it. Then he waved me a final salute and walked in, his heavy boots clicking on the gravel.

I could not sleep well that night.

As soon as dawn broke, I told Bharadwaj to fill a thermos flask with enough tea for two. When the flask arrived, I left once more for the Haldar mansion.

No one was about. Should I call out to Anath Babu, or should I go straight up to the west room? As I stood debating, a voice said, 'Here—this way!'

Anath Babu was coming out of the little jungle of wild plants from the eastern side of the house, a neem twig in his hand. He certainly did not look like a man who might have had an unnatural or horrific experience the night before.

He grinned broadly as he came closer.

'I had to search for about half an hour before I could find a neem tree. I prefer this to a toothbrush, you see.'

I felt hesitant to ask him about the previous night.

'I brought some tea,' I said instead, 'would you like some here, or would you rather go home?'

'Oh, come along. Let's sit by that fountain.'

Anath Babu took a long sip of his tea and said, 'Aaah!' with great relish. Then he turned to me and said with a twinkle in his eye, 'You're dying to know what happened, aren't you?'

'Yes, I mean. . .yes, a little. . . .'

'All right. I promise to tell all. But let me tell you one thing right away—the whole expedition was highly successful!'

He poured himself a second mug of tea and began his tale:

'It was 5 p.m. when you left me here. I looked around for a bit before going into the house. One has to be careful, you know. There are times when animals and other living beings can cause more harm than ghosts. But I didn't find anything dangerous.

'Then I went in and looked into the rooms in the ground floor that were open. None had any furniture left. All I could find was some old rubbish in one and a few bats hanging from the ceiling in another. They didn't budge as I went in, so I came out again without disturbing them.

'I went upstairs at around 6.30 p.m. and began making preparations for the night. I had taken a duster with me. The first thing I did was to dust that easy chair. Heaven knows how long it had lain there.

'The room felt stuffy, so I opened the window. The door to the passage was also left open, just in case Mr Ghost wished to make his entry through it. Then I placed the flask and the torch on the floor and lay down on the easy chair. It was quite uncomfortable but, having spent many a night before under far more weird circumstances, I did not mind.

'The sun had set at 5.30. It grew dark quite soon. And that smell grew stronger. I don't usually get worked up, but I must admit last night I felt a strange excitement.

'I couldn't tell you the exact time, but I guess it must have been around 9 p.m. when a firefly flew in through the window and buzzed around the room for a minute before flying out.

'Gradually, the jackals in the distance stopped their chorus, and the crickets fell silent. I cannot tell when I fell asleep.

'I was awoken by a noise. It was the noise of a clock striking midnight. A deep, yet melodious chime came from the passage.

'Now fully awake, I noticed two other things—first, I was lying quite comfortably in the easy chair. The torn portion wasn't torn any more, and someone had tucked in a cushion behind my back. Secondly, a brand new fan hung over my head; a long rope from it went out to the passage and an unseen hand was pulling it gently.

'I was staring at these things and enjoying them thoroughly, when I realized that from somewhere in the moonless night a full moon had appeared. The room was flooded with bright moonlight. Then the aroma of something totally unexpected hit my nostrils. I turned and found a hookah by my side, the rich smell of the best quality tobacco filling the room.'

Anath Babu stopped. Then he smiled and said, 'Quite a pleasant situation, wouldn't you agree?'

I said, 'Yes, indeed. So you spent the rest of the night pretty comfortably, did you?'

At this, Anath Babu suddenly grew grave and sunk into a deep silence. I waited for him to resume speaking, but when he didn't, I turned impatient. 'Do you mean to say,' I asked, 'that you really didn't have any reason to feel frightened? You didn't see a ghost, after all?'

Anath Babu looked at me. But there was not even the slightest trace of a smile on his lips. His voice sounded hoarse as he asked, 'When you went into the room the day before yesterday, did you happen to look carefully at the ceiling?'

'No, I don't think I did. Why?'

'There is something rather special about it. I cannot tell you the rest of my story without showing it to you. Come, let's go in.'

We began climbing the dark staircase again. On our way to the first floor, Anath Babu said only one thing: 'I will not have to chase ghosts again, Sitesh Babu. Never. I have finished with them.'

I looked at the grandfather clock in the passage. It stood just as it had done two days ago.

We stopped in front of the west room. 'Go in,' said Anath Babu.

The door was closed. I pushed it open and went in. Then my eyes fell on the floor, and a wave of horror swept over me.

Who was lying on the floor, heavy boots on his feet? And whose laughter was that, loud and raucous, coming from the passage outside, echoing through every corner of the Haldar mansion? Drowning me in it, paralysing my senses, my mind. . .? Could it be . . . ?

I could think no more.

When I opened my eyes, I found Bharadwaj standing at the foot of my bed, and Bhabatosh Majumdar fanning me furiously. 'Oh, thank goodness you've come round!' he exclaimed, 'if Sidhucharan hadn't seen you go into that house, heaven knows what might have happened. Why on earth did you go there, anyway?'

I could only mutter faintly, 'Last night, Anath Babu. . . .'

Bhabatosh Babu cut me short, 'Anath Babu! It's too late now to do anything about him. Obviously, he didn't believe a word of what I'd said the other day. Thank God you didn't go with him to spend the night in that room. You saw what happened to him, don't you? Exactly the same thing had happened to Haladhar Datta all those years ago. Lying on the floor, cold and stiff, the same look of horror in his open eyes, staring at the ceiling.'

I thought quietly to myself, 'No, he's not lying there cold and stiff. *I* know what's become of Anath Babu after his death. I might find him, even tomorrow morning, perhaps, if I bothered to go back. There he would be—wearing a black jacket and heavy boots, coming out of the jungle in the Haldar mansion, a neem twig in his hand, grinning from ear to ear.'

Glossary

Aadhunik: modern or contemporary (in this case, contemporary music)

Aamra: a kind of fruit

Arahar daal: lentil soup

Baba: Father

Baisakh: the first month on the Bengali calendar (begins mid-April)

Boro, Mejo, Shejo, Shona, Chotto: These are kinship terms in Bengal to distinguish one sibling from another. 'Boro' is the first (or the oldest), 'Mejo' the second, 'Shejo' the third, 'Shona' the fourth and 'Chhoto' is the youngest

Chadar: a sheet or drape, usually made of cotton

Da: Shortened from 'dada', meaning elder brother; often used after the name of a man older than one

Jamrool: a variety of greenish-white juicy fruit

Kaka: father's younger brother

Mama: mother's brother

Nahabatkhana: a music room, usually built over the main entrance of a palace or mansion

Neel kuthi: indigo factory, built during British times

Nulia: a community that lives near the sea, well known for their ability to dive into and swim even in a turbulent sea

Pataal: underground. The metro railway in Calcutta is often referred to as 'pataal rail'.

Shehnai: a wind instrument, played chiefly at weddings

Shimul: cotton tree

Tantrik: one who practices 'tantra', a particular form of religious worship meant for the goddess Kali who symbolizes power. Tantriks are often reputed to possess extraordinary supernatural powers.

MORE ABOUT PENGUINS

For further information about books available from Penguins in India write to Penguin Books (India) Ltd, B4/246, Safdarjung Enclave, New Delhi 110 029.

In the UK: For a complete list of books available from Penguins in the United Kingdom write to Dept. EP, Penguin Books Ltd, Harmondsworth, Middlesex UB7 0DA.

In the U.S.A.: For a complete list of books available from Penguins in the United States write to Dept. DG, Penguin Books, 299 Murray Hill Parkway, East Rutherford, New Jersey 07073.

In Canada: For a complete list of books available from Penguins in Canada write to Penguin Books Canada Ltd, 2801 John Street, Markham, Ontario L3R 1B4.

In Australia: For a complete list of books available from Penguins in Australia write to the Marketing Department, Penguin Books Australia Ltd, P.O. Box 257, Ringwood, Victoria 3134.

In New Zealand: For a complete list of books available from Penguins in New Zealand write to the Marketing Department, Penguin Books (N.Z.) Ltd, Private Bag, Takapuna, Auckland 9.

FOR THE BEST IN PAPERBACKS, LOOK FOR THE 🐧

THE ADVENTURES OF FELUDA
Satyajit Ray

In this collection of four novellas—*The Golden Fortress, The Buccaneer of Bombay, Mystery at Golok Lodge* and *Trouble in the Graveyard,* Satyajit Ray, the noted film-maker, introduces readers to his incomparable Bengali detective Feluda (a.k.a Prodosh Mitter). He sends his hero (along with two lieutenants—Tapesh, Feluda's eighteen-year-old cousin and Lalmohan Ganguly, a bumbling, timid writer of cheap thrillers) to locales as diverse as a sandstone castle in Rajasthan, the film studios of Bombay and a crumbling old cemetery in Calcutta to solve a series of particularly baffling mysteries. A detective in the immoral mould of Father Brown and Sherlock Holmes.

"Unputdownable detective stories"—*Sunday Chronicle*

"A *swadeshi* Sherlock Holmes.... (which) is by no means a shoddy *swadeshi* imitation. It is first class and can stand by itself."—*The Hindu*

FOR THE BEST IN PAPERBACKS, LOOK FOR THE Ⓟ

TIME STOPS AT SHAMLI

Ruskin Bond

Ruskin Bond's characters—who live for the most part in the country's small towns and villages—are not the sort who make the headlines but are, nonetheless, remarkable for their quiet heroism, their grace under pressure and the manner in which they continue to cleave to the old values: honesty, fidelity, a deep-rooted faith in God, family and their neighbour. They do have problems, of course—the sudden death of a loved parent, unfulfilled dreams, natural calamities, ghostly visitations, a respected teacher gone crooked, strangers who make a nuisance of themselves in a town marooned in time—but these are solved with a minimum of fuss and tremendous dignity. Taken together these stories are a·magnificent evocation of the real India by one of the country's foremost writers.

'An educative, charming and often memorable onetime read....'

— *Sunday Observer*

'An enjoyable rustic trip back in time.'

— *Straits Times*